The Athenian Murders

V.J. Randle

BLOODHOUND
BOOKS

www.bloodhoundbooks.com

Print ISBN: 978-1-916978-79-9

The Broken Head

In the alley that winds around the Temple of Hephaestus, leading towards the Plaka, lay the body of a good-looking man of around thirty years old. Nobody had found him yet. His eyes were an unusual shade of light blue, though their glint had faded somewhat, even as they reflected the early yellow rays.

His mouth hung open; he looked as if he had been taken by surprise. He was arranged on his back with his head tilted to one side. It was his head that would come to cause the most alarm. This is because it was split almost into two parts. It was perfectly done. And not at all in the way one might expect. The wound began at his right temple and scored, widthways, across the top of his brow, ending at the other side. Symmetrical and beautiful, the coroners would say. His forehead took on the appearance of a giant lethal smile.

It was, of course, the cats that found him first. A small tabby slipped through the iron fence that separated the sanctuary from the path, and sniffed and trotted, in feline rhythm, until she spied the unusual sight. From where she stood, she could not quite see the wound in all its glory but must have known, in the way that cats always know, that something was terribly

1

amiss. She did not hiss; this was no threat. But she did bow and stretch and flex her ears. A strange sight for sure. Her colony followed. Pink, black, and white noses appeared in turn through the gates, pressing through the long grasses, stalking their way from their night-time sanctuary. Two black cats trotted around the other side of the man, eyes wide, pupils dilated. They could see the wound from here. There was no panic; cats are at ease with death. They minced towards the pooling blood and sniffed it, ever so carefully, cautious of dirtying their freshly licked coats.

And then, the scream. A woman. A cleaner opening the door to the café opposite. The sun rose from behind the columns of the temple, the effect of the light making it heavenly as though a halo shimmered above it, as her mouth dropped open. Usually, this was a comfort to her. She often told her daughters how the magnificent shrine spurred her on to clean.

But now this. Her temple spoiled by this poor boy laid out in the street, cursed to be sniffed by cats. She felt her hand tremble as it moved towards her mouth, still holding the café keys that rattled between her fingers. She shooed the cats away and made for the old landline behind the counter.

Despite the shock, she delivered the message in a clear, though low, voice.

'I have found a male, of about thirty years, lying on his back with his head severed. No. The head is not removed: let me rephrase, the head is cut into two pieces, along the horizontal axis. He is dead, yes, of that I am certain. As I said, Café Kuzina, Adrianou, by the temple, yes. I am the cleaner.'

The message was reiterated through the proper personnel and channels.

A head?

A severed head.

The head is gone?

It is attached, yet split.

A head, you say?

The operator, who was convinced this was a hoax, though a well-executed one, lazily put the call through to the Hellenic Police Department, rolling her eyes.

It was Police Sergeant Michail Mikras whom the message finally reached. He was sipping his first thick coffee of the day, sitting on a red plastic chair at a café on Iraklidon. He stirred his coffee three times to the right and then three times to the left, and to the right again. It would not be proper to finish the ritual on the left-hand side.

It was a superb morning. A jogger, sensibly avoiding the heat of the high sun, panted past him. Her running shoes looked like they had seen better days: she ought to think of her knees. Michail took a sip of coffee and was comforted as the grainy liquid coated his throat, bringing him wakefulness, signalling to his body, as the sun was drawn across the blue sky, that every day could bring success. He checked his phone. Katerina was running late. Three minutes and forty seconds late.

Michail sighed, louder than he had wanted, and gestured to the café owner to bring him another cup. Across the road, a group of old men sat in a small circle, around their *To Fos* newspapers, rolling their dice and making private sports bets about things unknowable and unimportant. They were drinking beer already. As his second coffee was brought to him, Michail's phone rang. He jumped, very slightly, causing one man on the opposite side of the street to raise him a cheer.

'Our health,' the old man said, with a gravitas that could only be reserved for morning alcohol.

'Our health,' Michail murmured, looking down busily at his

3

lap to answer his phone. No doubt Katerina, full of excuses and extraneous chatter.

'Yes?' Michail spoke impatiently, keen that the crowd of old men might recognise him as a serious and competent law enforcer. It was the station.

'Oh! I see... yes, yes, I am close, I will not need to take the car. Yes, yes, I will move as swiftly as possible.'

Michail placed his phone slowly onto the table, careful not to make a dramatic clunk against the ceramic top. Merit. With *recommendation*. There were a few points to be improved upon, of course; that would be the same for any newly qualified police sergeant. Interpersonal skills had come up (rather a lot), as if talent for conversation was important for maintaining law and order in the city. But with *recommendation*. Recommended for precisely this moment in time!

Michail forced himself to breathe slowly; there was no use in hyperventilating. He was a trusted professional. His eyes trailed along the green and brown slopes to that crown of a building. It towered above him every day. It was truly a monument of peace. A monument of order in the face of chaos. If only Katerina would take her duties as seriously as him. If only she would see that hard work and attention to detail were the making of a person. Charm and good looks were not sufficient. He took another hurried sip of his drink.

And there she finally was, running up the street, belt askew, shirt pressed moderately, though not expertly, sweating already, breathless and rushed. 'Michail! I am sorry!'

'Again,' Michail replied flatly as she reached his table.

Katerina smiled and slapped him on the shoulder. 'Again.'

She sat down on the chair beside him, chattering about her sisters and her mother and her aunty and some other irrelevant business. Michail held a hand up to her. 'Stop.'

She blinked at his hand and patiently lifted her own,

grasped his, and pushed it back to the table. Michail found himself looking at his lap again. He knew that communication through hand-signalling was frowned upon, no matter how obviously efficient. It made people uneasy, apparently. He must endeavour to improve on this.

'What is it then?' Katerina did not seem annoyed with him, thank goodness.

'We need to go.' Michail stood with the swift importance and urgency he had promised his superior on the telephone.

Katerina nodded, eyeing his coffee. 'Now?'

'Yes, now.' He grabbed her by the arm and lifted her off her seat. 'Coffee will have to wait.'

Katerina adjusted her belt and followed his gaze up the slopes. She nudged him. 'Always staring at it.'

Michail jumped away from her, shaking his head. 'Of course, the Parthenon is perfection. But now to Adrianou, there's a broken head.'

A small, circular crowd had already formed by the time Michail and Katerina jogged down the length of Iraklidon, turning a sharp right into Adrianou. Michail held himself tall, fighting the urge to rest his hands on his thighs and catch his breath. He pushed past the onlookers.

'Hellenic Police! Hellenic Police!' he shouted, clearing a path through the mix of eager, solemn and excited faces. 'And no filming! Put that phone *down*!'

The fact the body was already cordoned off with tape suggested that the Violent Crime Squad had already arrived. Michail sighed, he had been slowed down by Katerina; they would need to have further words. He would not allow this case – his first as a sergeant – to be usurped. He observed the area and spotted two senior officers, one male and one female, in deep conversation, backs turned to the crowd. Wasting no time, he displayed his badge to the guards and made straight for them. Tapping her on the shoulder, he held out his hand to a petite woman, who wore shoes unsuitable for most of the city, let alone a crime scene. 'Michail Mikras,' he announced, ignoring the woman's unexpectedly red lips.

She surveyed him for longer than Michail thought was the customary amount of time; her arms were folded, her weight resting on one of her legs so that her hips jutted to one side. The combination of those heels and bad posture risked serious spinal damage. Still waiting for a response, Michail wondered whether he ought to repeat himself. There might be a variety of unknown factors at play here: most obviously, she could be deaf. He resolved to introduce himself again, this time with heavily enunciated consonants, making sure that he maintained important eye contact. Thinking that he had rectified the situation, he held his hand out again. Surprisingly, the woman frowned at him and said, 'Constable–'

'Sergeant,' he corrected her swiftly. The hierarchy of rank was essential for the efficient working of the Hellenic Police Force.

The woman narrowed her eyes. There were tiny specks of black powder settled upon her cheekbones. She was not attractive in a conventional way but had a robust charm about her. Although this was, of course, irrelevant.

'Sergeant,' she said, in a tone that suggested to Michail he was exhibiting some sort of social misjudgement. He noted her English accent; could this be the infamous Sofia Sampson he had read about? From memory, she had transferred to Athens from London a few years previously, before securing a permanent position with the Special Violent Crime Squad. The woman stepped forwards, placed two hands on his shoulders and spun him around. Michail flushed as he realised the mistake he had made: the woman was not deaf, nor lacking in concentration. She had expected him to acknowledge the terrible (and obvious) corpse that lay in plain sight. He hoped she would understand his confusion. Introductions were always tricky. Unexpected incidents always impeded his otherwise well-honed method of prioritisation: the appropriate greeting gesture; then, an enquiry into the well-being of the person (depending on whether they were a stranger or not); otherwise, a casual comment about the weather or the daily news would suffice. Clearly, a dead body in the middle of the street surpassed all of these in precedence.

'The scene of crime,' she said, a bit slowly for Michail's liking. 'I appreciate the formality, but... well, best to see it first.'

Michail nodded, seeing that his partner Katerina was already circulating the dead man, who was a similar age to himself, lying on the ground, with a head cut into two pieces. Michail was both logically and factually unsurprised: the station had given him the details over the phone. However, seeing the wound in the flesh, it was what he would call an unearthly experience. Michail's feet felt light upon the pavement. He wiggled his toes, encouraging circulation, though this did not seem to take any effect. In fact, it only drew his attention to the dead man's own feet, which stuck up ludicrously and perpendicular, as if mocking his otherwise horrific state. Michail gulped, wishing this woman would let go of his shoulders, Special Violent Crime Squad or not.

'Yes,' the woman said, as though she were replying to something. 'Extraordinary, no?'

Michail found himself unable to speak, so settled for shaking his head. The worst was about to happen, he felt it, moments before the signs prevailed. The convulsions in his throat; the rising heat; the soft, dull ache at the back of the tongue. To cry in front of the Special Violent Crime Squad would be disastrous. He would be a laughing stock, a joke, Michail Mikras, the Weeping Sergeant. The morning breeze had already settled, and the stillness brought flies and the faint, though noticeable, smell of death.

Finally, the red-lipped woman let go of his shoulders and stood to the side, observing the body. 'Sofia Sampson,' she said, without offering her hand. 'It is good of you to come, *Sergeant*, but we can take it from here.'

Michail's eyes swam with the threat of tears. He raised his hands to his temples and rubbed them gently, closing his eyes, rocking backwards and forwards, drifting to a calmer, simpler place. He was grateful that Ms Sampson said nothing.

Eventually, Michail opened his eyes. But instead of focusing on the body, which he knew he would eventually have to do, he gazed up once again at the Parthenon. He liked how uncompromising this temple was, sitting calmly at the top of the Acropolis hill. Its cool and white rocks were built to last, an engineering feat based on the purest mathematical equation known to humanity: one that ran through the folds of nature herself. This equation never failed to relax him. He repeated the ratio under his breath, 'One point six one eight, one point six one eight, one point six one eight.' He could do anything, really, with these numbers running through him.

Filled with a new strength, he lowered his eyes and took in the corpse once again. There was, expectedly, blood pooling around the main point of impact. The current had slowed somewhere near the man's feet, so that only the cracks between the pavement tiles flowed with tiny, red, saturated canals. Michail's gaze finally rested on the man's face. The edges of his lips were blue, contrasting with the white, youngish teeth. The face was exceptionally well-preserved, considering the wound. Ah, the wound. Michail took a step closer and craned his neck to get a look at it. It was the most open wound he had ever seen. So wide and confident. Some trick of the light made it seem like the point of contact had come from within the head, from behind the forehead. An impossible, fanciful thought; but it looked like the direction of thrust propelled outwards, the blood congealing mostly in the crevice of the chest. The skin around the wound folded back, as if encouraged by some sharp force. Michail looked over his shoulder as Ms Sampson said, 'This is new.'

Michail nodded and took a step back. 'Terrorism perhaps?' He assumed this was why the special force had been called so quickly. 'Far-right wing?'

She sighed, shrugging. 'You know, it's the same here as it was in London. People are so quick to jump to conclusions. It's almost as if they *want* murders to be terrorist attacks. As I say, we can take it from here.'

Sofia Sampson from London: it was her. She had quite the reputation, being well-known for her... directness. Michail considered his options. It was likely that Ms Sampson expected him – the capable young officer – to collect his partner (less capable, albeit) and leave the scene. She was probably prepared to remind them about keeping what they had already seen strictly classified – although, Michail hoped that she would suspect that he, at least, would need no reminding. She would want to convey that there was no good in rumours arising, nor panic. If it was terrorism, then the police should not fuel the fire. The press was likely to do their absolute worst; the police needed to resist the gossiping. She would argue that her team would cover this efficiently and that there was no need for Sergeant Michail Mikras's services. This, of course, would be an entirely unsatisfactory outcome.

Michail puffed three times into the air in front of him. Ms Sampson did not react. He tapped the top of his leg three times with his right hand, then three times with his left, and then three times again with his right.

'Sergeant?' Ms Sampson said gently, though firmly enough that Michail was forced to break his ritual.

He steadied himself. It was unclear even to him whether it was the shock of the crime scene, the one and a half coffees he had drunk, or simply the frustration of being tardy, but he closed his eyes and thought of something that was clear – beautifully clear – those numbers, strong and timeless as the universe. Then he said, 'Ms Sampson, I would like to remain on this case.'

He spoke very loudly, for effect, because he wanted Ms Sampson to fully understand his determination and pledge to the cause. Order over chaos. This was all there was; he would not let chaos prevail. What lay before him was undoubtedly chaotic.

Katerina was now leaning against the fence, tickling the ears of the cats, who still regarded the body with a quiet indifference. When she heard her partner's loud request she looked up. Michail was standing far too close to such an important woman; his hands were clenched by his hips, his face was set like marble, chin jutted forwards, brow tense and creased.

She recognised the woman from a training lecture at the Academy. It was one of the few that stuck in her mind because she had been pleased to see a woman standing behind the lectern, especially one of seniority. She also remembered the way Sofia's red lips had moulded around such an assured chorus of words. Her English accent had a certain ring to it, cutting through the air like a tight whip.

'Intolerance is idleness and idleness rots, decaying the

structures and the organisation around it. Idleness is turning a blind eye, idleness is voting for self-serving ego-narcissists.' A good few of the younger men, Katerina had noticed, shuffled uncomfortably in their seats. 'Idleness is hiding your true colours beneath the honesty of uniform. Idleness wrecks and ruins our ability to serve. Idleness is a closed mind. It is a closed soul.'

Perhaps the bit about the soul was a tad dramatic. Women in these positions had to be careful not to present themselves as overly emotional. It would have been wise, Katerina had thought, to finish with a joke. It was what the men did. But the lecture theatre responded with a silence she could practically taste. No man had yet had that effect in a lecture. Katerina had looked up at this woman, who had seemed to hold the stare of every one of the two hundred spectators at once. She had thought that Sofia must be either mad or brilliant. Well known, as it was, that a great portion of the force voted for the type of fanatical party she had described, well known, as it was, that corruption bled to the top, to the very men to whom she must answer. Well known, though, of course, not known at all. There was, inevitably, a cathartic applause. Katerina had wanted to shout, to whoop, or at least cheer, but she did not. She was not that sort of person.

Sofia was smaller than Katerina remembered. Despite this, she still experienced the awe she had felt those few years before. This awe, however, was combined with a sinking feeling that she would be implicated by Michail's more unusual behaviour. He took some getting used to. Katerina saw no choice but to intervene. She stood, brushing fur from her uniform, and walked around the body, careful not to stare at it any longer: that would not do. She was not that sort of person either.

By the time Katerina joined him, Michail remained rigid and upright. He would probably maintain this stance until he received a response. Katerina looked to Sofia Sampson, who was unreadable. It was difficult to tell what she thought about Michail, although she looked as if she was contemplating something deeply. Both Michail's patience and Sofia's silence were unnerving. Katerina stood to one side of her partner, forming an awkward trio around the corpse, and considered the best way to break their silence. She coughed, once, and then twice, but gained no reaction. Nudging Michail gently, growing conscious of the camera phones being pointed directly at them, she said, 'Michail...'

'Fine.' Sofia spoke quietly and firmly.

Katerina's head jerked towards Sofia Sampson. 'Ms–'

Sofia interrupted her. 'Yes, fine. Your determination,' she took Michail's fist in her hand and held it up to the sky, 'is good. I can tell that much. I will inform your station.' Her eyes trailed along the ground and up the legs of Katerina, who was struggling not to cringe at the dramatic gesture.

'Can you vouch for your partner? The one playing with the cats?' Sofia addressed Michail.

Katerina felt herself grow very red. She looked at the ground, thinking it best to say nothing. She had already begun studying the body seriously; there was something about the way the man was arranged, the way his palms faced the sky, that made his death seem ritualistic. Something about the body reminded her of a story she had heard long ago. She was looking forward to discussing this with Michail: he would be impressed. Yet, Michail, she knew, for all her smiles and cheer, would not vouch for her as he had for himself. She tried to match up to his high expectations but always seemed to fall short. She never seemed to be quick or clever enough. Katerina steadied herself, ready to be dismissed.

'Katerina,' Michail replied, 'is my trusted partner.' Katerina jerked her head up, eyes widening at Michail. 'In my opinion, she should remain on the case.'

Sofia Sampson did not seem surprised. Her expression was expertly manicured. Katerina opened her mouth to offer thanks but stopped herself when Sofia slowly raised what could only be described as an imperial eyebrow. Pencilled and arched, it was silencing. Only after a few moments did Sofia speak. 'Very well. In that case, I must ask that you investigate the sanctuary. We are desperately in need of a weapon.'

A Fitting Weapon

Michail did not need telling twice. Katerina, however, did.

'The weapon, Ms Sampson?' she asked.

'Yes, the weapon.' Sofia gestured to the body, thinking that the girl ought to pay more attention. 'There will be a weapon, I imagine.'

Katerina nodded, apparently keen, and followed Michail, who was already attempting to haul himself up over the black iron fence. He seemed like a person who did not pay heed to obstructions. A good sign, if slightly undignified at this very moment in time. He wriggled about on top of the spokes unceremoniously, his legs jutting out all over the place. Eventually, he was forced to reach down for his partner to catch his balance. 'We could just go to the main entrance...' Katerina called up, steadying him.

Sofia Sampson observed her two young, new recruits. She smacked her lips, hoping someone would bring her a cup of tea soon. Michail still had one leg stuck in an awkward position, knee to his cheek, as Katerina tried to guide him down from the fence safely. Flustered, he batted his hands in frustration and hissed at the cats. Katerina – who, Sofia noted, dealt with her partner with a rare patience – ended up marching to the café opposite and borrowing a chair. Sofia suspected the pair would make an excellent team as she watched them eventually parade up the road that led to the agora.

Katerina walked silently beside Michail. There was no way to thank him properly without doing herself a disservice. Instead, she allowed him to enjoy his moment of triumph. He walked with his fists clenched to his sides, arms stiff and torso fixed. This was a big moment for him, for them both. Katerina did not know of anyone who had been assigned onto a case with a special branch, let alone the Special Violent Crime Squad. Michail's instincts had been bold, but they had paid off.

'It is obvious that we will need to ask the museum to close the site,' Michail said to the air in front of him. Tourists laden with backpacks and maps were already beginning to emerge from their hotels, applying sunscreen, checking their phones.

'That was Sofia Sampson,' Katerina replied.

'Correct.'

'*The* Sofia Sampson, Michail! She's basically famous in the police.'

Michail nodded, though he seemed irritated. 'I am aware of her status and triumphs, of course. She held a senior position in London, I believe, before coming here.'

'Her mother is Greek, her father English, I think,' Katerina began. 'The boys, Theo's friends at the station, talk about her sometimes. I think she's pretty impressive, but they hate her, they say that she's a right–'

'Irrelevant,' Michail cut in, nodding towards the ruins on

their right. 'The agora, Katerina. You must focus. Ms Sampson is counting on us.'

'I'll call ahead,' Katerina said, reaching for her phone as they quickened their pace. Struggling to keep up with him, she noticed his darkened expression. She bit her lip, annoyed with herself. How could she be so insensitive? Michail did not need to hear about the boys at the station; they gave him enough of a hard time. And why did her thoughts keep wandering to Theo? *That* was very much over, at least, for her.

A tall man, slightly rotund about the middle, wearing well-cut chinos, waved at them from outside the shaded Church of Agios Philippos. He had white hair and the sort of wrinkles that suggested he had lived a good and enjoyable life. 'No tourists?' Katerina confirmed, nodding at the man, noticing a band of disgruntled Germans sitting on the ground cross-legged, sipping bottles of water.

'No, we have refunded tickets and explained the... pressing situation. Some will wait here, just in case, it seems,' replied the man, scratching his chin. 'Apologies, I am Dr Laurence-Sinclair, Museum Manager and Curator for the Acropolis Museum – the agora comes under my jurisdiction too. We spoke on the phone.' He extended a hand to Katerina, who noticed his eyes lingering on the bottom tip of her silver crucifix necklace.

Katerina reciprocated the handshake, refusing to follow his gaze. Someone had once told her to never look down in such situations. An empowering rule, apparently, although she wasn't sure that ignoring the problem made it any better. She made sure that she held his hand with a firm grip. Niceties were exchanged.

Michail shouted abruptly, 'We must be off. We have very important business to attend, you understand.'

Dr Laurence-Sinclair nodded. 'Of course, of course.' He pushed his linen sleeves further up his tanned arms. Katerina noted he wore the type of signet ring that was quite popular with the British men who came to study the city's ancient ruins. The top end of the ring enveloped his finger with what looked like two entwined snakes. He waved towards the agora. 'You can see the sanctuary of Hephaestus from here, on your right. You will enter in through the ancient Panathenaic Way. Just stick to the designated paths, if you don't mind, follow the arrows, it's all clearly marked. Is there anything else I can help you with? It's not a serious matter, I hope?'

Katerina smiled encouragingly and shook her head.

Michail said, 'That is the business of the Hellenic Police, sir.'

'Right,' Dr Laurence-Sinclair agreed, now eyeing their badges carefully. 'How long will you need?'

'An impossible question,' piped Michail. 'You will be notified...'

'We shouldn't need more than half a day!' shouted Katerina, pulling Michail through the entrance gates. The cross-legged Germans chattered excitably.

'We cannot possibly know–' started Michail.

'Keep him happy,' Katerina interrupted. 'Sofia does not want hysteria. If we don't find anything by lunchtime, then we can ask for longer. If we do, then he will be none the wiser.'

Michail opened his mouth to protest but could not think of a counter-argument.

Katerina smiled. 'No need for thanks, trusted partner.'

The sun beamed down on the empty agora as Katerina and Michail made their way through what had once been the ancient heart of the city. They picked their way through the ruins along the Panathenaic Way. Katerina remembered studying the route at school; she had labelled an illustration of the procession route in her textbook with bright yellows and reds and greens. Horses, children, flower girls and musicians had once paraded along this road, up towards the Parthenon temple.

But the Parthenon was not their destination today. They reached the turning in the path, marked, as Dr Laurence-Sinclair had said, by a small metal arrow, which would lead them to the Temple of Hephaestus. Michail halted abruptly causing Katerina to stop dead in her tracks too. Looking at him, Katerina saw that his abdomen had sagged slightly, pulling his shoulders forwards, looser, relaxed. He hummed. Katerina had heard the sound before. She had found it odd at first, but had come to like, perhaps enjoy, this throaty meditation. It was where animal met cultivation, she thought. Katerina considered it the sound of Michail organising his soul. People dealt with their raw emotions, the stress of living, as best they could. If this was how Michail liked to cope, then she was happy for him. She had come to realise that he made the humming sound whilst thinking.

Katerina placed a gentle hand on his shoulder. As she expected, he flinched, though only slightly. His humming stopped. Michail looked at his shoes and spoke slowly. 'His face, it was beautiful, no? Proportioned mathematically, symmetrical, a golden face. To ruin it so horribly, to crown it with that... cut. It is monstrous.'

'Murder is monstrous,' Katerina whispered.

Michail looked her in the eye. It was her turn to flinch.

'Yes. Correct. Monstrous. We must restore the balance here, Katerina. This is very important.' Michail did not suffix his sentence with the words 'to me', but she understood. They turned and made to find a murder weapon with quiet determination.

A tent had been constructed around the body. Sofia Sampson checked her phone. An hour and a half since he had been discovered by the poor cleaner. The corpse urgently needed to be moved out of the heat of the day. She observed the forensic scientists, padding about in their white spacesuits, placing fragments of rock, debris from the wound, strands of hair, into clear plastic bags and sealing them. Her own partner was dealing with the press standing behind the barrier rope. He was adequate at his job; a man slightly younger than her, thorough, ruthless in some ways. She knew he had a wife, perhaps a litter of children, but she had never asked after them. Yiorgos. He held both of his hands up, gesticulating to the young – increasingly young – journalists. He explained that privacy in a case like this was of the utmost importance and, no, there was no planned police statement at present, though information would be shared when deemed appropriate. Some trick of the sun, perhaps the shade of the sky, slowed down his gestures, making them appear deliberate and staged. Yiorgos shook his head, stepping back, shaking his arms to indicate he had answered his last question. To Sofia, it looked as if he was moving through heavy air. Perhaps this was the way it went. A body too many and the world gradually slowed until it grinded to a halt. She needed her morning tea.

And what was that look, now? Yiorgos turned his back to the yapping journalists and as he headed towards the body tent, glanced at her. A glint in his eye, a vague raised eyebrow. Pity, was it? Concern? He often claimed he was concerned, just within earshot of her desk. Concern for her well-being, how she worked too hard, how she lived so far from home, isolated: did every woman not want – need – a lover? A companion in life was necessary. It was not natural, how she lived. And for whom, really, *really*, for whom, was that lipstick? Sofia set her face into a cold smile. She could spot when she was being challenged.

Yiorgos shot her a disapproving look and made for the body tent without a word. He would have noticed she was keeping a safe distance from the body. A senior staff member like her should not be too keen to get her hands dirty. It was better to have the overview. It was better to be the commander. It was better to breathe. But she would not give Yiorgos a reason to think of her as weak. She placed one hand upon her waist, revealing her belt, reminding Yiorgos that she, too, was bestowed with heavy weaponry, and stalked quickly ahead of him. She held open the tent entrance, ushering him inside purposefully.

'Thank you,' Yiorgos mumbled, following her into the strange makeshift room. Two forensics swabbed the area behind the man's neck. The action reminded Sofia of the bodies she had investigated in Exarcheia a couple of years previously; all male, all immigrants, all written-off as drug-related violent crimes, only months apart from one another. The closed-shop, thick-blooded attitude of the area's squats had proved it near impossible to profile the victims thoroughly. For many good reasons, the residents distrusted the police. They were people of the world, people of the feeling, the fight, the freedom. Their perception of police arose from riots and oppression – the only occasions when law enforcement would enter the unofficial threshold between Omonoia and the university. Of course, this social divide and the trendy decay of the area proved irresistible for Athens's fashionable young, who paraded their anti-establishment haircuts around the streets of the central square. It was unlikely that any of the dead were in Greece legally, which meant that they had not been identified. Which meant that somewhere in the world a family waited in vain. The science and the swabs had not helped those men.

It was not just this new body's age that made Sofia think of the Exarcheia victims. Toxicology would confirm it, but his otherwise angelic face bore the familiar marks of ravaging. His lips, by now, were blue, this was to be expected. But his cheekbones, beautiful really, protruded just that little bit too richly, giving way to a sharp slope under the eye, which was brownish-red, ochre around the edges.

'Another junkie?' suggested Yiorgos from behind her.

'He will have a name,' Sofia replied, steadily, holding her hand out for forensics to pass her a pair of gloves. She ignored Yiorgos's mumblings about illegal underliers wasting precious police time. It would be unusual for a gang to be operating in this area of the city, generally reserved for tourists and wealthy residents. People knew to stay within their boundaries.

Carefully, she placed a finger beneath his upper lip. It was firm and cold. Lifting it gently, she pulled it back, nervous that she might interfere with the wound on his head. She peered into his mouth. His gums were slightly white, although that could have something to do with the impact to the head. His back teeth showed some signs of damage. She turned to Yiorgos, annoyed to give him any sort of satisfaction. 'We shouldn't rule out drugs, I agree.'

'Shame, he's a good-looking man.'

It was a fatuous remark, but Sofia found herself agreeing. The young man was very handsome, deified in his death. Though his hair was caked in blood, the few miraculous strands that remained unstained were golden. His chin had that majestic line about it. The jeans he wore clung easily to his thighs, accentuating defined, soft musculature. And then, the wound. She had seen it from metres away, considered it from a distance, watched as it had been photographed. Up close, it projected grainy detail. There were spikes, tiny little juts, of bone fibre, some splintering in towards where his mess of a brain would be, some splaying outwards. Sofia stood, rather too abruptly. Yiorgos moved to catch her; she stepped away from him, breathing through the dizziness. The tents were so claustrophobic.

'That's it,' Sofia managed. 'Pack him away. We'll go through the particulars at the station, as far as I am aware, he has no identification, no documents.'

'Hardly surprising...'

'We've got officers sourcing security footage, it will be ready by this afternoon, I should imagine. That should clear some things up. So far, we have no witnesses, or no willing witnesses, and no weapon, yet.'

'The press will want a statement.' Sofia saw that Yiorgos was practically salivating at the prospect of a public appearance. Completely typical. A body on the floor and all he could think about was his next press outing. She opened her mouth to protest but he cut in, 'We're practically in the Plaka, Sofia. People expect this sort of thing in Exarcheia, nobody bothers about a few foreign junkies there. But here, this is news. Tourists have seen him! And this injury, it's like nothing I have seen – anyone has seen – before. We need to control the narrative. You know they will run wild. This is how we do things here.'

Sofia placed her hands on her hips, fighting an urge to raise her voice; almost six years and he still did not respect her as a bona fide Greek. But shouting had never got her anywhere, especially not with that accent of hers; a source of comedy for the likes of Yiorgos. Also, he was not entirely wrong. 'Tomorrow. Let us at least attempt to identify the body first. It is unwise to spread panic.'

'We have no weapon.'

'Yet. We have no weapon yet. Now, I need tea.' Sofia left the tent in a hurry, throwing an apprehensive prayer to the Temple of Hephaestus, willing her new recruits to do her proud. She knew she should hate superstition, but it was all she could do for the moment and that made her feel better.

'The Temple of Hephaestus is the best-preserved temple in all of Greece. Sitting in the shadow of its far greater, younger cousin, the Parthenon, it is underrated by most visitors to the city.' Michail spoke monotonously, circulating the overgrown gardens of the sanctuary. It seemed that Katerina was uninterested in his excellent and relevant information. She was on all fours behind a pile of stones, looking for uneven mounds in the dry ground. Michail continued because it was essential they understood the greater context of the site and it was doubtful that Katerina knew much about these things.

'Completed in 416BC, it is an interesting convergence of the Doric and Ionic styles, obviously, retaining both friezes and metopes. The surviving metopes depict the labours of the great hero Herakles, though in my opinion, they are not expertly rendered. The reason the temple is sometimes known as the Theseum is because of the frieze that wraps around the pronaos inside of the temple: here we see the battle between Theseus and the Pallantidai. If...'

'Michail.' Katerina was now on her feet, her dark-blue trousers spoiled with dust. She was breathless, Michail noticed. He wondered whether she ought to get more exercise: it was not a steep ascent to the sanctuary from the agora. He guessed that she had some sort of query about the metopes: they could be confusing. However, Katerina looked thunderous, rather than confused; he had not expected her to be quite so moved by architectural history.

He decided to elaborate. 'Yes, I agree that the lack of surviving metopes is troubling. I have often tried to attribute good reason to why the architect decided to paint, rather than sculpt, the majority. For instance, the sculpting tends to focus on the east side which–'

'Michail! Please. I do not care about the temple.'

Michail frowned. It was difficult to understand what was troubling her, especially as he was being so helpful. Katerina's face softened. Even more confusing – her emotions ebbed and flowed like the tide. She exhaled deeply and spoke in a new voice, one that Michail associated with nursery-school teachers.

'Thank you, Michail, for the information. You know so much.'

'Correct. I have read many books and enjoy–'

'*But* our task is to find a weapon. We have been here for almost an hour. Perhaps you could tell me about the temple later?'

Michail observed the thick green gardens. 'You don't think it would help...'

Katerina walked up to him, also staring into the dense shrubbery. 'No. Not right now.' Then she grinned – unbelievable, like the tide – and said, 'If only marble could talk!'

He nodded, vigorously. 'Yes, that would obviously be useful.'

Katerina stepped over the low wire wrapped around the temple and beckoned Michail to join her. Clearly, they were not supposed to transgress over the barrier. He was almost certain that Katerina was aware of this. However, this was police business of the highest importance. This took precedence over the wire. He carefully followed her, warning her to be careful where she stepped: the old floor slabs were uneven.

As soon as they stepped up beneath the colonnade, the oppressive heat radiated away, giving way to a thin, ancient air. Michail had always loved the cooling quality marble possessed. They stood beneath what had once been a doorway and was now a tall, marble threshold, leading to the inner sanctum of the building. Katerina leaned back, craning her head to look at the frieze above. So, she was interested, after all. Michail opened his mouth to explain the scene but Katerina spoke first. 'The Centaurs and the Lapiths.' She chuckled at the shock on his face. 'It's the easiest myth to spot. Where else do you find men with horses' bodies?'

Michail moved through the entrance into the centre of the temple. He grew very silent. Not because the temple was intended as a place of worship: the ancients had only built their temples to house their gods, not to pray. He was silent because of the affinity he felt with the building. If forced to describe it, he would have said it was the sensation of his flesh turning to marble. The cold did not bother him at all; instead, it embraced him. The changing colours of the outside world seemed distant in here. This temple was the closest to permanence one could get, Michail considered. It was perfectly isolated from the chatter surrounding it. Its marble heart was cold. The thought suddenly compelled Michail to spin around, flexing his fingers, moving his arms; he exercised his ability to move. See! He was flesh and blood: capable of much more than marble.

'Michail!' It seemed Katerina was concerned. 'Is everything okay?'

He froze, arms suspended in mid-air, unable to put what he was feeling into words. 'Yes, thank you, Katerina, I am merely trying to think. If you were a murderer, where would you hide a weapon?'

Katerina nodded, trailing her hand around the inner walls. She sucked her teeth, which made an unpleasant sound. 'That's assuming the weapon is here at all. Why do you think Sofia was so certain?'

'The proximity and the terrain – the coverage the foliage gives – makes it an ideal place to discard a weapon. The wound suggests it would have had to be large, so the perpetrator most likely would not have wanted to leave the scene of crime with it on their person.' Michail turned to her squarely. 'Of course, the murderer would not have cared about the hubris of such an action, of disposing of a heinous weapon in a place such as this.'

'A temple?'

He nodded and clarified, 'A culmination of human skill, effort, engineering, precision and, of course, because it matters to some, collective belief.'

Katerina sat on the floor, which was most unhygienic. She looked up to the darkness of the roof. 'A big weapon then, yes, I agree. Something that would take you by surprise, sharp, of course, uncompromising?'

'Agreed,' Michail said.

For some unknown reason (Michail hoped that she had finally realised the value of his historical knowledge, but suspected that she had merely run out of ideas), Katerina turned her face to him and said, 'Well now we're in here, it seems rude to ignore the temple's history...'

Michail nodded. 'Correct. It is important to understand the full context.' He told her of how the temple had once housed the statues of two gods, not only Hephaestus, for whom the temple was built, but also for the city's patron Athena. He told her that when he said 'housed', he meant it. The gods had resided here, so it was believed, if they were too far away from Mount Olympus to return. He explained that the temple's pediments had been decorated with sculptures too: the birth of Athena on this side (he pointed eastwards) and the return of Hephaestus to Olympus here (he pointed to the west).

'Return from where?' Katerina asked. Michail groaned, something he had been advised not to do when he was disappointed by people's lack of knowledge. But this was basic stuff and she lived in Athens, after all. Had her mother never read to her at night? Where had she attended school?

'From Athena's birth!' Michail took Katerina by the arm and led them both back outside, sunlight flashing hastily through the gaps of the columns as he spoke. He grew more animated with each step.

'Here!' He pointed to the triangular shape at the top end of the temple. 'This pediment would have shown Athena's birth, where she emerged from the head of her father, Zeus, after he swallowed her mother...'

'Metis!' Katerina laughed, clapping her hands. 'Took a while but...'

Michail, relieved and spurred, continued on a roll, ignoring what he had been told about getting overexcited. This was not one of those occasions. This was work. 'And here!' They ran down the long side of the temple to view the second pediment. '*This* would have been where Hephaestus, the blacksmith god, successful in his mission at cutting Athena out from Zeus's forehead, would have been shown returning home, brandishing his glorious, immortal axe!' He turned to Katerina, ready to hear the joyous ring of laughter again. He had taken her breath away, as the saying goes! He had swept her off her feet with intellect and cultural heritage!

But then he felt the rate of his heart regulate as his breathing became deeper. He noticed the tremor of his hands, which occurred when he forgot himself like this. Looking towards her expectantly, still hoping she might be impressed by his enthusiasm, he saw her face fall. The feeling was terrible, as usual. This was how it went. He had misjudged it again, said the wrong thing, seen light where others had seen dark. He was clammy. He was exhausted.

'Michail.'

He raised his head nervously, thinking of a way to explain his social ineptitude. Perhaps he should apologise.

'Y-yes,' he stuttered, peering at Katerina from beneath his eyebrows.

He heard footsteps. The sound of her boots making their short way over to him. Then, she placed a hand on either side of his face and forced him to look at her properly. She was not angry, nor horrified. In fact, she seemed quizzical. He began to speak but she shook her head.

'It's fine. Michail, it's fine. But what did you say, about the axe, the head, what did you say before, about the birth of Athena?'

He breathed slowly, knowing that he must remain calm.

'Michail, the weapon?' she pressed. 'What did Hephaestus use to cut Athena from the forehead of Zeus?'

He found the words. 'An axe.'

In a moment that can only be described as deeply portentous, the eyes of Michail and Katerina moved steadily up the sharp grooves of the temple columns, over the entablature, over the metopes and the triglyphs, and stopped, incredulous, at the object that hung from the highest point of the building. Quite how no soul had noticed it until this moment cannot be explained. It was as bright a day as the Athenians can have. Both Sofia and Yiorgos were thorough individuals, their team delegated expertly. One may conjecture that the human psyche will avoid the thing that it looks for the most. Hundreds of lost hours spent searching for car keys displayed provocatively on the kitchen counter can attest to that. Or it might be that things simply have to live out their course. Time cannot be rushed. And for a short amount of time, the mystery of the murder weapon was known only by Michail and Katerina, who stood, heads tilted to one side, gazing at the large, bloody axe.

'This makes no sense,' Katerina breathed.

'In many ways, it makes perfect sense,' replied Michail.

Before the cleaner made the call to the Hellenic Police, a woman in thick-rimmed glasses had made her way around the long street of Adrianou. She had a small, yet unignorable, hangover. She seemed apprehensive. No, she was not a drinker; not a drinker with a problem, that is. But she did enjoy the first, the second, the third, and the fourth glass of red throughout an evening. This did not deter her from early wakefulness, however.

She took a seat at a café that had not yet opened. The chairs were stacked, but she helped herself to one from the smallest pile and turned to face what lay before her. She sat back, causing the plastic back of the chair to moan. The woman herself then sighed, and carefully removed a newish-looking laptop from her square wicker bag. In the absence of a table, she laid it out on her knees and opened it. From afar, it looked as if she was reciting some spell at the screen, pushing buttons, and then reciting once again. After a few minutes, she was satisfied and began to type. She was talented. She tapped away speedily as she peered over the screen of her computer, concentrating on the body that lay before her.

If anyone had, at this point, seen what she was writing, they would have seen the following:

Athena is arisen! It has begun, friends! Rejoice in the awakening of Athena and this pure and good city.

The Olive Branch

S ofia Sampson had, thankfully, found a cup of tea, albeit accompanied by long-life milk. She sat on one of the police department's most uncomfortable chairs, watching the security footage for the sixty-seventh time. She had watched it twice without her glasses, and twice with her glasses; she had removed her glasses again and rushed to the bathroom to insert her contact lenses, before returning to the viewing room to watch it again. She had then replayed the scene and planned to do so indefinitely until she was able to apply some sort of logic to what she saw.

This would be difficult because what she saw did not exist in the world of logic. The tape began as expected. The Temple of Hephaestus loomed in an orange haze behind the couples, families, groups of friends returning home from dinner. Nothing out of the ordinary there. She had scrutinised the intervening time between the last people turning off Adrianou towards Ermou at 1.46am and her victim sauntering onto the scene at 3.15am. The only activity in this dead hour and a half was the flash of cats' eyes at luminous intervals, floating bodiless in the grainy darkness. The victim was alone when he entered the frame of the camera. Stills, of course, had been taken of him. He was undeniably handsome and had nothing on his person, no bag, hands in his pockets. He did not look entirely at ease. Sofia noted the number of times he checked behind his shoulder: five. He also stopped short of continuing down the long, shadowy stretch of Adrianou, as if he wanted to find somewhere safer, more public.

He waited – Sofia specified in her notes, *waited*, because there was some purpose to the way he stood – just short of nine minutes outside the Kuzina café. He was not still. He shifted from foot to foot: he was expectant of something. It was during this period of waiting that his head looked as if it began to droop, like he was falling asleep standing up. Then, he jolted back upright again, awake and alert. This was not inconsistent with the use of certain substances. At one point, he knelt to the ground. The video was soundless, but his mouth was open wide; he was screaming, yet his arms lifted to the sky as if in an ecstatic prayer. Sofia had paused the recording at this point many times already: both hands gripped the sides of his head. Zooming in, she could see that his eyes were clenched shut. He looked pained, terribly pained.

Then the victim scratched his head. Not like he had an itch. No, he seemed to claw at his scalp. He placed his forehead against the ground and writhed, fingers mauling his own flesh. The first time she watched it, Sofia had leant forwards, trying to make out the cause of such behaviour. By the sixty-seventh watch, she resigned to just shaking her own head slowly – this made no sense at all. The scratching occurred for two minutes and reached a climax when the victim, mouth open again, lay face up, palms up on the ground. In the first viewing, everyone had teetered on the edge of their seats, expecting a great reveal. Breaths were held and then, unfortunately, let go. The killer was not shown.

Instead, the recording began to glow. It was not obvious at first, as the light encroached from the four corners of the computer screen. It was a white light, with a subtle golden tinge. The four corners converged around the whole frame of the image, causing Sofia to blink repeatedly. Then, from the centre of the screen, another light shone. It was so bright that Sofia had looked away. It grew and burned, distorting the image of the victim behind it, until the entire screen glowed with iridescent light.

'What is that? Is someone shining a torch at the camera?' Sofia asked.

Yiorgos shrugged. 'Perhaps. Doesn't look like it, though.'

Sofia slammed her hand down on the table. The space-bar of the keyboard fell out of its springs. 'We cannot see who did it! It's obstructed!'

As soon as she had shouted, the light began to fade. The grainy dark ate away at the light from the top of the screen and gradually revealed the full picture. 'Pause it,' demanded Sofia. Yiorgos grunted but did what he was told. Sofia peered at the image, searching for a clue, a perpetrator, the back of someone fleeing the scene. There was nothing. Just the body of the victim as they had found it.

'Useless!' she shouted. 'Completely corrupted. Send this to the technicians, tell them to scour it for meddling – maybe they can trace it.'

'Of course.' Yiorgos stood to leave.

'Will you hold a press conference tomorrow?' Sofia added, raising an eyebrow. He would, of course. Yiorgos did not even give her the credit of looking embarrassed.

'Yes. Tomorrow morning. It's late, Sofia, we still have no name for the body. The axe...'

'Has already been removed for examination.'

'Yes, I know. But it was found in such a... sensational

position. There are already hundreds of photos of it on social media. The press will not let this go.'

Sofia pushed back in the wheeled chair, smacking her lips. She hated social media. It was not social at all, far from it. It was insensitive and aggressive, full of people who had too much time to judge and no time to think things through properly. She could not imagine who in their right mind would want a picture of a bloody murder weapon decorating their feed. 'Can we get them removed?' she asked, already knowing the answer.

'No. In any case, the papers will want to publish the photos. I've seen them; they are perfect fodder. Nothing too gruesome: the Acropolis in the background, the Temple of Hephaestus crowned with an axe. There is no use in telling them not to.'

Sofia did not reply and pressed play on the recording again. 'Tell the technicians to look at this tonight, as a priority.'

Katerina sat opposite Michail in the cafeteria of the headquarters. Neither she nor Michail had been told by their new boss they could leave, so they had been drinking cans of fizzy pop for hours, flicking through files of known drug criminals, looking for anything that might connect a past crime to the current investigation. The Hellenic Police Headquarters was an imposing oblong building. Katerina did not like the way the numerous windows stacked up next to each other, like a one-thousand-eyed monster. It was better being on the inside than on the outside, at least. She flipped the ring on the top of her drink can and it snapped off. Michail's eyes flicked towards her.

'Sorry,' said Katerina. Michail did not reply.

They had not spoken since they found the axe. As soon as they had notified Sofia, a swarm of men in white overalls had entered the sanctuary. Michail and Katerina had been required to question a cleaner about the body. She had been put out, having already been questioned by someone else. Katerina had handled it well. 'I know it's difficult,' she said, thinking of some television show she had once watched. 'But any details you can provide us with could be vital.'

Michail had then proceeded to shoot one question after another at her.

'At what precise time did you reach for the key? Do you know? Can you be sure? Clarity is best. For how long did you look at the body? Before making the call? Was the body within your line of sight whilst you were on the telephone? We need to be extremely meticulous about this.'

Katerina said nothing but saw that he was not taking any notes. Instead, his fists were clenched in that familiar way and he tapped the side of his legs methodically. She had grabbed her own notebook to make sure they did not miss anything. She was not sure whether Michail had noticed or not.

By the time they had made it to headquarters, Michail had reached a state of catatonia. She was worried he was suffering from shock; he had succumbed to one of his more manic episodes in the temple earlier. She conceded it was best to keep a close eye on him. The first corpse usually resulted in some minor trauma to the mind: flashbacks, nightmares, that sort of thing; she remembered learning this. Katerina, for one, was looking forward to returning home and offloading to her sisters, asking them to entertain her, to take her mind off the axe. And the body. And his head.

'Michail,' she tried again.

Nothing, as expected.

'Michail?' She did not shout but made sure to raise her voice. 'Michail, please let me know if you are all right. It is natural to feel some–'

'I am fine. Thank you. I am thinking,' he replied.

Katerina scrutinised him. It was true that he seemed thoughtful. His hands were clasped tightly upon the tabletop, his back was straight, his eyes half-closed in concentration.

She seized the opportunity to ask, 'What are you thinking about?' She hid a wry smile, aware of the inanity of the question. She hated it when her mother asked her the same thing, hoping she would reply, 'Theo, Mother. I am dreaming of Theo.' As if she had changed her mind about him. As if it was any of her mother's business.

Michail turned his head slowly towards her, his eyes slightly glazed. Katerina was used to his idiosyncrasies, but she had never seen him so... robotic. She softened her expression as best she could. 'Lots of change, today,' she offered. 'Difficult to stick to routine.'

Michail's eyes widened. 'Yes. Everything is different.'

'Tomorrow, I can fetch your *spanakopita* for lunch? I think we will probably be eating here. We can eat together.' They had forgone lunch today; neither of them had been particularly hungry.

'That would be useful,' replied Michail.

Katerina smiled. She pushed her phone towards him. Having sat in silence for hours, she had used the time to sift through some social media posts about the murder. A friend had messaged her a picture of the axe at the top of the temple with the caption: *Murder imitates ancient myth.* Scrolling through numerous groups, there had been a few threads claiming that the goddess Athena had arisen from the head of a young man, aided by Hephaestus. The bloody weapon – significantly hung from Hephaestus's temple – was proof. *It is time the world woke up!* one enthusiastic commentator claimed. *The gods are back and here to stay! Deniers beware.*

'You see what they are saying?' she asked, rolling her eyes. 'People are crazy.'

She hoped that the messages would cheer him up, or at least garner his interest. Michail detested uncorroborated theories and enjoyed dismantling them at every available opportunity. Instead, he grabbed her phone and began scrolling the screen rapidly.

'What are you doing?'

He ignored her. His face was set, eyes keen and frantic. Katerina, accustomed to being patient, rarely got angry. But it had been a long day and she had tried her best. 'Will you give it back!' she shouted. The fluorescent cafeteria strip lighting flickered on and off. Her anger appeared to have little effect. Michail continued to scroll without looking up. His shoulders became hunched. Katerina pressed her fingertips to her forehead. She felt clammy; her skin was tired of the day. Tired of him. She took in a breath, about to begin a careful apology for shouting when Michail held up a hand to her. The gesture was familiar, at least, even if it was irritating.

He spoke whilst searching through her phone. 'There have been a number of unforeseen events today and I have spent this afternoon and evening processing them by way of deep, considerate thought. Clearly, in order to achieve excellence as an officer of the Hellenic Police, I must acclimatise myself to the unexpected. The mental processes I have now put in place will render me a more efficient and robust officer of the law.' He raised his eyes to Katerina. 'Perhaps some coping mechanisms would benefit you, Katerina, you are sweating heavily and have been for some time. This is a symptom of shock.'

Katerina threw her head back and laughed. She did not temper the sound, allowing it to ring out through the grey cafeteria, past the doorway and into the corridor.

Sofia approached the cafeteria, frowning at the loud laughter. In truth, she had been walking to her car when she had looked back at the headquarters building to see silhouettes on the sixth floor. She had forgotten about her new recruits.

'Ms Sampson!' The girl stood quickly as Sofia entered. Her eyes were glassy with hysteria. Sofia knew all too well the strange and varied effects a dead body could have upon an officer, especially a body that had been a victim of a violent crime. She waited whilst Katerina hastily collected the criminal profile notes, squirming and jittering. The man stood in one, swift movement and turned to face her.

'Evening, Michail.'

'Greetings.'

'Evening,' Katerina mumbled, fluffing the papers in her hands.

Sofia stalked her way over to the table and took a seat. She pointed at an unopened Fanta can. 'Anyone's?'

Both Katerina and Michail shook their heads. The liquid was warm to the tongue; she had never got used to the syrupy consistency of the fizzy drinks here, but sugar was what she needed. 'Did you find anything of interest?' She motioned to the files. Katerina spoke first. She was feverish, almost like she was apologising.

'Nothing, well, not a lot. The closest we have found in terms of the manner of murder is a knife through the left eye in Vathi. The body was found...' She began to fluster through the pictures. Michail handed her what she was looking for. 'The body was found in a similar position, prone, palms up. Though, there are clear signs of struggle recorded and the murder weapon, as you see, was left behind at the site of the crime. The pattern is not the same.'

Indeed, the knife stood proudly pointing out of the deceased's eye. The girl was correct: this was probably nothing. But Sofia, wanting to encourage the young officers, went through the motions. 'When was this?'

'June 2017. The murderer was never found. No suspects either, apart from a consensus that this was gang-related, possibly immigrant hostilities.'

Sofia nodded. She took the files from Katerina and bowed her head. 'I remember it. It's been a tough day, for both of you. Well done. You need rest. We can pick up in the morning.'

'Ms Sampson,' said Michail. Sofia faced him. 'Katerina has brought something important to my attention, which she has, for reasons that I imagine are related to stress, left out in her report to you.'

Katerina began to protest but Michail persevered. He pointed at a phone on the table. 'There are some troubling theories about the case emerging online.' Sofia peered over to see that Michail was pointing at some social media website. She stood to leave.

'Don't trouble yourself with that, Michail, we have real–'

'It is no trouble, Ms Sampson. Let me explain: a group, calling themselves The Awakening, is posting on mainstream social media, as well as links to lesser-known parts of the internet, claiming that our victim has given birth to the goddess Athena from his head and that the axe-wielding perpetrator is the god Hephaestus. They are purporting that life is imitating myth. They are saying that today marked the birth of the goddess Athena.'

'Well, that's obviously ridiculous...'

'Correct. The interesting point is that their first status is posted at 2.40 this morning.'

Out of the corner of her eye, Sofia sensed a shift in Katerina's mood. Glancing to one side, she saw she had turned pale and that she had placed her head in her hands. There was no telling what was the matter with this girl. Sofia hoped she would be able to pull through. A robust disposition was crucial.

Sofia held her hand out towards Michail. 'Give it to me, please.'

She scrolled through the posts, casting an urgent rhythm with her index finger. Scan, move on, scan, move on, scan, move on. The messages all touched upon the same sort of themes, nothing unusual for this sort of fanaticism. *The end is nigh. The righteous will be rewarded. The hubristic punished. The signs are everywhere, people just didn't bother to look.* The message stung of right-wing extremism. The tone was similar to the strands of propaganda Sofia had investigated in the not-too-distant past. The pure would conquer and all the rest of it. How did anyone fall for this rubbish? But Michail was right: 2.40am that very day: *Tonight, as the moon shines high above our virgin's glorious city, our patron will be born again. She descends to earth, friends. They suffer no fools. Repentance is not an option. Only the favoured will survive. Supplicate! Athena rises!*

Unbelievably, a lightning bolt emoji followed the post. It had received forty-two likes and had been shared twice. 'This was written before the victim died,' Sofia said.

'Correct,' replied Michail. 'You emailed us the details of the footage.' Sofia noticed that he sat up higher in his chair.

'Good work.' She nodded towards him. Then she added, 'And you too, Katerina, for coping with your first murder inquiry.'

'I–'

'My instincts were right,' Sofia cut in before the girl embarrassed herself. 'You make a good team. However, my sentiments about resting will need to be ignored for the moment. We will need to get the cyber team on this immediately–'

A vibration in her bag: Yiorgos.

'Excuse me.'

She left Katerina and Michail alone. With the phone pressed against her ear, she watched the pair at the cafeteria table. Did either of them sense the impending doom as she did? Or did they just feel exhaustion, two inexperienced officers, faced with the most sensational murder the city had ever seen?

Finishing her phone call, Sofia took a deep breath and walked back over to Michail and Katerina. 'We're needed.'

'Where?' asked Katerina.

Sofia leaned on the table with both fists. 'The Acropolis. There's another body.'

'I... I need to go and splash my face first, please,' Katerina said, making for the bathroom, clutching her phone. Sofia narrowed her eyes. Murder was a part of the job: the girl would have to buck her ideas up soon.

At night, the Acropolis was illuminated, celebrated as an orange beacon of Hellenic accomplishment. Sofia's mother used to keep an old photograph of it on the fridge when she was growing up. That second-floor flat in Wood Green seemed a world away. 'These are your ancestors,' her mother used to say, pointing to the image. 'Put your mind to anything and you will be as great as them.'

'She'll be even greater,' her father would say, with his usual paternal pride, winking at her.

'How many times do I tell the man?' mumbled her mother, cigarette dangling between her fingers. 'Too much pride is a sin. *Paidi mou*, will he listen...'

Sofia drove alone, instructing Katerina and Michail to follow her. Two bodies in less than twenty-four hours, she mused, was highly unusual. She gripped the steering wheel, forcing herself to look both ways at the junction. The weather had taken a dramatic turn: thick pellets of rain hammered onto her windscreen.

Yiorgos had not given her many details; just that it was a teenage boy. She took a deep breath and checked her rear-view mirror. Good, they were behind her; their faces pale and tense as they followed. Sofia was glad that the man drove; the girl clearly needed some headspace. Puffing her cheeks out in disapproval, Sofia remembered how she had never needed a man to drive for her. But there was no good in being judgemental of the girl now: the only judgement to be made tonight was about the body.

The pedestrianised streets surrounding the Acropolis were wide and well-lit. A few tourists milled about, happily drunk and full. Sofia remembered a time when she had seen the city through a sightseer's gaze. How much her perspective had changed since taking this job.

Sofia rolled by slowly, avoiding the excited stares. Everyone loved flashing lights. It was human. She pulled over on the side of the road Apostolou Pavlou, spotting Yiorgos gathered with a small team at the foothill of the Acropolis, shielding themselves from the rain. He had arrived quickly. Before getting out of the car, Sofia checked her reflection. In this artificial light, she recognised a remnant of the woman she had once been. Defiant cheekbones, a heart-shaped dip at the top of her forehead. Her Mediterranean looks had got her somewhere in London, even as she aged. Here, she melted – no, disintegrated – into the crowd. Nobody had warned her about that. There was no escaping those dark circles beneath her eyes, that was for sure. She reached behind her seat for her portable make-up bag and applied a thin layer of red to her lips. It was important to keep up appearances, to be a constant. She wanted her new officers to see that.

Resigning herself to her hair getting drenched, she stepped out of the car. Through the rain, carried the soft whispering, almost prayer-like, from Yiorgos and his cronies at the bottom of the hill. Sofia recognised the tone: the hushed dismay at the death of a child. She was not of the opinion that all life was precious: that was a fantasy. However, children were special. Their pure bodies did not deserve the indignity of a murder investigation.

'Are you both prepared? This will be tough.' Sofia spoke quickly to Katerina and Michail as they approached, Michail holding his hands over his head to keep off the rain. They nodded in unison. 'Good. Follow me. Come on.'

The girl hesitated, looking in the opposite direction. 'Um, Ms Sampson.' She pointed to a narrow dirt track that wound up the other side of the slope, lined with low lying bushes and trees. 'Perhaps it is better if Michail and I widen the search? In training, we were always told to spread out?'

Ah, so she was trying to show initiative; she was finding her feet. Sofia nodded, pleased. 'Very well, off you go. Look for anything peculiar. Nothing is too insignificant.' She watched them disappear into the shrubbery.

'Sofia! Over here!' Yiorgos greeted her like they were at a family lunch. She narrowed her eyes.

'Where is the victim?'

As if in response to her question, a loud clap of thunder rolled through the black skies. The men gave a cheer. She wrapped her coat closely around her, forcing herself to stand tall as the water beat steadily from the sky. 'The body, Yiorgos?'

He took a hurried step towards her. 'Your minions are going to get wet. It's slippery up there.'

Sofia followed his gaze; two small beads of light obediently hovered on the dark slopes. Like courting fireflies. 'They will be fine,' she said. She did not feel the need to explain what they were doing. It was good to maintain a sense of control. 'The body?' she repeated.

Yiorgos shifted from one foot to another, craning his neck as the rain grew heavier. Another clap of thunder hollered through the sky, this time accompanied with a flicker of lightning. 'Up there.' He pointed to the cluster of temples on the top of the hill. The rain spattered in wet chunks against Sofia's ankles. She squinted through the darkness. Outlines of police cones and tape were scattered along the paths. Forensics were already working. How long had Yiorgos been here?

'Will you be all right getting up there?' Yiorgos eyed her heels.

Without replying, Sofia turned her back to him and proceeded to take what looked like the shortest route to the entrance of the Acropolis.

'Sofia!' Yiorgos called behind her. 'It is safer to take the long way around, by the canteen!'

Ignoring him and what she counted as a jeering tone, furious that he had kept her out of the loop, she willed herself up the hill, clutching at a handful of foliage to haul her weight onto more steady ground. Setting her sights ahead, to the great gateway, the Propylaia, she scrambled up the loose dirt, ignoring the mud splattering her legs.

'Sofia!'

As she steadied herself on the plain that stretched out before the steps to the Propylaia, Yiorgos caught up with her. 'What on earth are you doing?'

She spoke as she walked. 'Since you see no urgency to call me about the death of yet another person in our city, nor to oversee the preliminary examination yourself, you force me to take matters into my own hands, Yiorgos.'

He held his suit jacket over his head as a canopy. Sofia allowed the rain to hammer against her skin. It was invigorating. It also messed up her lipstick. Yiorgos, still cowering under his suit, replied, 'Sofia, forgive me, but, as you will see, there is no need for urgency here.'

She pressed on. The steps to the Propylaia were slippery, almost impossible to climb. Wishing that Yiorgos had not followed her, she was forced to double over and use her hands as stabilisers.

'We should wait for the rain to pass,' Yiorgos shouted up to her. 'It's dangerous.'

Sofia, breathless, leaned against one of the columns at the top of the steps. She wiped her eyes clean of rainwater, sure that her face was now a mess of smudged mascara. Glimpsing through the scaffolding into the enclosed sanctuary, Sofia looked for the body tent. The uplit temple buildings glistened in the moon's white gaze. It was reassuring to have a little light, at least. Unable to make out where the tent was from here, she took a step forward and her foot slipped on the marble. Catching on to a piece of metal scaffolding she let out a pathetic yelp as her ankle gave way.

'For God's sake!' Yiorgos shouted from behind.

'I'm fine, Yiorgos,' she said through clenched teeth; more out of embarrassment than anything else. 'Will you let me get on?'

She did not wait for him to catch her up. Pulling herself back to a standing position, she checked her ankle was stable, and walked through the tremendous open doorway that led into the Acropolis. She took a moment to gather herself under the shelter of the archway, shielded from the rain. Clenching her jaw tight, she sat down, taking shallow, ragged breaths, listening to the rain's orchestral feet pound away on the site's floor. She bit her lip, furious at herself for overreacting. It had been a long day indeed. She allowed herself a moment to take in the Parthenon.

Yiorgos eventually sat beside her. She assumed he knew better than to place a comforting arm around her shoulders and she was right. He wrung his jacket tightly, propelling a spring of water in front of them. He seemed to be taking in the temple too. Sofia opened her mouth to apologise for her overzealous behaviour but could not quite find a way. Finally, she spotted the body tent. It was erected to the left of the Parthenon. It was so small in comparison; no wonder it had been hard to find. It glowed green and moved with the shadows cast by the forensic scientists inside it.

The rain began to slow. Yiorgos said nothing.

Sofia pushed herself up from the stone floor, careful not to slip. 'I'm here now. I may as well see the victim.'

Yiorgos nodded, following her lead, speaking behind her as she walked precariously through the open air. As quickly as it had begun, the rain stopped, and heat began to bleed into the saturated night. She made straight for the tent. Tiny brushes of steam rose from its roof. As if it burned.

'They are about to bring his body down by stretcher, Sofia. Like I said, there is no urgency. Forensics say it's a straightforward penetrative trauma to his neck.'

Him. His body. A boy child.

'He was unlucky, I think. Kids on a school trip broke out of their hotel and came up here. Sounds like there was some sort of a dare to climb up the temple, the Erechtheum. He fell. Had he fallen at another angle... they will need to confirm it, but it looks like the branch pierced his windpipe and obstructed his airway. He would have suffocated before bleeding out.'

They reached the tent as the forensic team began to pack away their equipment. Snatched greetings were exchanged. Sofia placed her hands on her hips, unable to enter the tent just yet. The body, before forensics arrived, would have laid in the view of the Caryatids, the marble maidens who acted as support columns for the Erechtheum temple. They hovered above like stone witnesses. Were theirs the last faces the boy had seen before he died?

And then Yiorgos's words caught up with her.

'Fallen?' she asked.

'What?' Yiorgos stood next to her.

'Fallen – you said that the boy had fallen.'

'Yes, I said that,' replied Yiorgos, seeming nervous.

Sofia ran her fingers through her sopping hair, piecing together the information she had been given, trying to understand the events of the night. 'This was an accident?' she asked.

Yiorgos nodded. 'I tried to tell–'

'Then why are we here?' Sofia looked around for a dry place to sit, her legs ached. There was nowhere appropriate. She did not want to think about the dead boy. She did not want it to be her business. And this was not her business, by the sounds of it. She could have avoided being here altogether.

'What do you mean?' Yiorgos asked.

'Why are we here? We investigate violent crimes. If this is not a crime, why are you here wasting my department's time?'

Just as she finished speaking, and just as Yiorgos opened his mouth to explain, a blast of sirens sounded from the bottom of the hill. Sofia looked at Yiorgos, who shrugged. Then, through the darkness, up the slopes, around the columns of the Propylaia, across the muddy ground, towards those tall and watchful Caryatid women, arose a chanting. Its source was not a huge crowd, Sofia surmised it was about ten, perhaps fifteen people, but the words were clear to her, all the same.

'What are they saying?' Yiorgos asked.

'Athena is victorious,' Sofia replied. 'Athena is victorious.'

'Fanatics,' sneered Yiorgos. 'They will be taken away.'

The forensic team exited the tent and stopped to listen to the shouts. The phrase, scuttling through the air with alternating stresses, seemed to grow louder the more they listened. Sofia had an odd compulsion to stand in front of the boy, to protect him from the noise. Heat rose from her feet up through her legs.

'A branch,' she whispered.

Yiorgos either did not hear her or did not care. She spoke again, more loudly, 'A branch, Yiorgos. You said something about a branch.' She turned to the forensic team impatiently. 'What killed him? Yiorgos, you said it was a branch, he fell upon a branch, what type of branch, do you know?'

Yiorgos stuck out his bottom lip and shrugged. One of the forensics stepped forwards. 'We believe it was a loose branch from the tree – the olive tree – just over there. There is a small section missing, probably blown off by a wind.'

Sofia ran towards the tent, ripping open the fabric door. He lay in a foetal position, one hand clasped over his mouth. His eyes were open, panicked. He must have only been about fourteen years old. Sofia felt the unacceptable prickle of tears brim at the bottom of her eyes. She shut them for a second, breathing slowly, deeply. Opening them again, she saw the thing that had killed him. The branch splintered through his throat completely. How innocuous it would have seemed, hiding on the ground. An innocent branch. A dormant snake. She bent down and recognised the unmistakable thin green leaves. The unquestionable round, bitter olive fruit.

The heat now reached Sofia's chest. She coughed, uncomfortable, and pushed her way out of the tent. She could not look at the boy any longer. She could not stand it. The heat.

'The olive tree?' she asked. 'The sacred olive tree?' She turned to look at where the tree stood, to the right of the

Caryatids, by the west porch of the Erechtheum. Planted by Athena herself, as the myth went. Her mother had recounted the story, in its various versions, countless times. Its branches wafted softly in the hot breeze. Indeed, there was a noticeable gap in the otherwise evenly spread branches.

Athena is victorious. Athena is victorious. The chants wove and wove around Sofia's head, covering her nose, her mouth, infiltrating her ears. The buildings glowed.

'Sofia?' Yiorgos grabbed her arm.

She fell to the ground, as if mourning. Yiorgos pulled her up but she wanted to fall again. Because what she saw was no longer the Acropolis with the temples and her colleagues and the tent. She saw a memory. A recent one. It was so bright and painful that she could not ignore it. She was branded by it. Sat at the cafeteria table in the Hellenic Police Headquarters, she watched herself, poised, flanked by two new officers, bent over a mobile telephone, scrolling, scrolling, scan, move on, scan, move on, scan, move on. But she had missed a detail. Funny how the memory works. Funny how it twists and hides and reveals only when it is good and ready. Funny how significance only is significant when it is too late. But then, memory makes everything significant. Scan, move on, scan, move on. But there it was, laid bare and open, a warning unheeded:

Supplicate Athena the Pure and Wise! Be grateful for the gift she bestowed. The olive tree was her weapon once and shall become her weapon again. Athena is victorious. Athena is victorious.

The Signet Ring

Michail sat at his dining-room table in his Thissio apartment. He had arranged the kitchen-cum-dining room-cum-living room-cum-bedroom so that the focal point of the flat – the medium-sized window exhibiting the Acropolis – could be seen from all necessary angles. As he woke in his fold-out bed, it was the first thing he saw. His sofa was arranged so that it commanded an uninterrupted view, and he could spend whole evenings meditating upon it. And so, still wet from the downpour and shocked to be alone at last, Michail stared at it. Dawn was rising. The Parthenon was pinkish. The boy's body would have been removed by now. One point six one eight.

It had been Katerina's idea to scan the area on the far side of the slope, following the main tourist path up to the Acropolis. She had thought it was worth widening the span of the search and it was, at least, better lit than the gaps between the trees. Michail had agreed, pleased she was showing some intuition.

It had also been Katerina who spotted Dr Laurence-Sinclair struggling to hoist himself up the steep slope behind the remains of the Theatre of Dionysus. She had run ahead to help him up from the slippery ground as the rain fell heavily. He had seemed confused for a brief amount of time; however, Michail had suspected nothing untoward. He had seemed so vulnerable, skidding about the slopes. It was, of course, highly irregular for him to be cavorting about the site in the middle of the night: that was obvious now. But hindsight is a tantalising beast. Laurence-Sinclair had prepared a credible explanation. Michail re-enacted the exchange slowly from his dining-room table, moving his lips as he remembered the words, the pauses, the expressions.

'What are you doing here?' Michail had said, not too aggressively, but loud enough to be heard over the thunder.

'Pardon me, sorry?' Laurence-Sinclair had asked. Michail thought he remembered that Laurence-Sinclair's eyes had darted about – a suspicious sign. He should have pressed him more thoroughly.

Katerina had by now steadied Laurence-Sinclair, helping him to his feet. His legs appeared to be wobbling uncontrollably. 'Why are you here?' Michail had asked again.

A garbled story about hearing sirens and lights and a general panic had followed. He had been working from the Acropolis Museum, it seemed, which loomed shiny and modern behind them. Michail had been tired, and the rain irritated him, more than it did most others. Laurence-Sinclair had taken great pains to explain his movements: he had been walking home from a late night's work when Katerina and Michail had frightened him. So, he had tried to run up the slope to the Theatre of Dionysus. 'Stupid thing, I am. This must look awfully suspect! Nothing untoward here, I can assure you.' Michail noted that Laurence-Sinclair reserved a significant gaze for Katerina.

It was around this time that the chanting had begun.

On his table, Michail knocked three times with his right hand and then three times with his left. As he knocked with his right again, he began to feel nauseous. He had made a mistake.

Laurence-Sinclair had looked vulnerable and Michail had allowed himself to be taken in by this narrative. He had ignored the obvious, that it was *highly irregular* to be strolling about the Acropolis site at night. Irregularities were the stars that made up the constellations of investigations. They drew patterns. They pointed to timelines and stories. 'Catastrophic,' Michail said to his window. 'A catastrophic mistake.' The reflection of his face hovered translucent over the dawn-kissed Acropolis.

Of course, the catastrophe was only fully realised when Katerina had found the ring. Wishing Laurence-Sinclair goodnight and telling him to go home, *thank you for your concern, Doctor, we appreciate it*, they had continued along the path, examining the shrubbery growing between the ancient stones. As they ascended the slope, Michail had taken a moment to peer over the Odeon of Herodes Atticus. It was a beautiful piece of architecture, of that he was certain. But he had allowed himself to become distracted. Every particle in his body should have been focused on the search, not the Odeon.

The strange chanting had continued to pervade the darkness. Katerina, he noticed, kept an eye on him. He wondered whether she was frightened, as ridiculous as that would be. Police officers existed to protect. Fear made them less efficient.

Katerina had got lucky. Luck was a term Michail disliked intensely. It was meaningless and reserved for those who did not apply themselves properly. Planning and logic could not simply be replaced by 'luck'. Katerina had displayed neither planning nor logic as she searched the Acropolis hill, despite Michail's best efforts to explain the most efficient and tactical approach of combing a large surface area. Instead, she had swivelled her phone this way and that, kicked aside random rocks and shaken the low-growing twigs as if clues might be spurting from them. But it seemed that luck favoured the irrational. Because, as

Michail stepped backwards, calculating where best to begin his grid-based search, she called out, 'His ring!'

In her hand, she held a small silver signet ring. Michail had run towards her, opened the evidence bag, and demanded that she stop contaminating potential evidence immediately. She dropped the ring into the clear plastic, carelessly, he thought, and mumbled something beneath her breath he did not hear properly. Thinking he ought to show her some encouragement, Michail held the evidence bag up to the torchlight. 'Whose ring?' he had asked.

'Laurence-Sinclair's ring!' Katerina pointed down the slopes to the Theatre of Dionysus. 'He must have been here earlier and dropped–'

'It could be anyone's.'

'No. I recognise the snakes.' Katerina took the evidence bag from him. 'See?' She pointed at two twisted serpents melded onto the ring's edges. 'I noticed them this morning.'

Attention to detail! Meticulous analysis! These were his best qualities. His strengths. How had he missed something so glaringly obvious? He blamed Katerina, of course. If she had noticed the ring that morning then she should have noticed Laurence-Sinclair *not* wearing it that night; especially as she had been the one to help him up.

It was obvious that Laurence-Sinclair had lied to them. He had said he had been at the Acropolis Museum, at the bottom of the hill. Yet his ring was here, just up from the Odeon, close to the body that lay on the Acropolis above.

In a fit of rage, fired by impulse, Michail had galloped back down the hill in pursuit of Laurence-Sinclair. At his dining table, Michail panted as he had done hours before. Leaping breathlessly, sliding down the gravel, Michail propelled himself towards the Theatre of Dionysus. He was aware of Katerina shouting after him. He hoped she did not follow him and put herself at risk of falling. But there was no time to lose.

'There is no time to lose!' he shouted from his seat, unsure whether he had actually shouted it whilst chasing Laurence-Sinclair or not. He gripped the edges of the table, rocking backwards and forwards. What a disaster! He was not fit to be an officer of the Hellenic Police Force. He was a detriment, a risk. How would the public rest easy and calm tonight, tomorrow, this week with such a liability as him? Michail could not take his eyes off the sunrise. It brought tears to them, the way it graced the Parthenon marble with such considerate intimacy. It illuminated his failure. Those masterfully rendered columns, the impeccably measured metopes were too perfect for him to bear at this moment. He looked away, shielding his eyes, returning to the memory.

He had skidded across the worn stones of the Theatre of Dionysus. He had shouted his name, 'Laurence-Sinclair! Laurence-Sinclair!' But the words had played to an empty audience. He ran down the path, across the street, over the wide slabs that led to the Acropolis Museum. He had hammered on the glass doors. 'Laurence-Sinclair!'

The rain had stopped. But Laurence-Sinclair was gone.

'A potential suspect!' Ms Sampson's eyes had been black when they reported back to her. She had kicked the side of her car.

Michail had remained silent. Katerina had tried to explain. 'We had no reason to suspect...'

'You had every reason to suspect him!' shouted Ms Sampson. 'And will you stop that stupid noise!'

This is when Katerina had squeezed his shoulder. Michail raised his arm to the spot now. It still felt warm. *Stop the noise, the stupid noise, Michail. Stop making it worse. Stop it.* Michail pursed his lips together. His tongue ached. His head resonated uncomfortably.

Every reason to suspect Laurence-Sinclair. Every reason to detain him. An escaped suspect. A suspect let go without so much as a fight.

Michail groaned again and stood, unable to sit any longer. Katerina had assured him it was fine: they had not been removed from the case. It had been a troubling day: neither of their brains had been working at full capacity. It was an understandable error. Michail checked the lock on his front door, as he had done twelve times since dragging his wet, tired body into his apartment. Standing was also intolerable. He lowered himself onto the ceramic tile floor and lay on his back, palms facing upwards. Birds sang from the roofs outside. He closed his eyes and arrived at his first year of the Gymnasium, aged thirteen. His parents said he was big for his age; a fine, strong specimen. He never felt big. Do children ever? He was in his Ancient Greek class and copying sentences from the board. The genitive absolute. Wonderful. A concise concoction, separate and clear. οἱ ἄνθροποι τιμῶσι τους θεοὺς εν τῷ ουρανῷ ὄντας. *Whilst the gods are in heaven, men worship them. With the gods being in heaven. Since the gods are in heaven. As the gods are in heaven.* Look up. Memorise. Write. Translate. Look up. Memorise. The routine was heavenly. Language worked as it should. Only those students in the class who did not complete their studies at home, who ignorantly glossed over constructions, found the language difficult. It was easy, really. One logical step after another.

Something hit him in the back of the head. This was not unusual. His immature classmates tried to distract him all the time. He ignored it. Best not to react. This is what his father had said. Best not to give them anything to work with. He continued, progressing, whilst they wasted their time. Another strike. A pebble bounced onto the floor. Michail blew through his mouth. An obvious signal, he thought, that he was displeased and trying to concentrate. But it happened again. This time the pebble bounced off a bone on the top of his neck. 'Oh!' he cried, regretting it immediately.

Fits of giggles erupted from the back of the classroom. Even the keen students sitting at the front laughed behind their hands. Michail shoved his head down and translated the sentence he had just written. *Once the city was destroyed...*

'Michail?'

The teacher tapped on his desk. Michail stopped writing, wishing this unwanted attention would disappear.

'Look up when your teacher addresses you,' she said. He knew it was a simple request. Easy enough in theory. But his rhythm had already been broken. The translation was unfinished. Best to be a good student. Best to finish the sentence quickly so that he could prove his academic prowess. He began to write again.

'I said look up!' The teacher's voice was so loud. If she would just pay his books some attention, instead of him, then she would be impressed. She had not yet seen how much work he had completed. He did not know what to do. He tapped his page, quickly, trying to alert her to all the good translation work he had finished. However, his tapping did not have the desired effect. Instead, his teacher grew angry.

'Michail Mikras, I have asked you to look at me whilst I am speaking.'

A chant began from behind him. The teacher shushed them, though she sounded half-hearted. '*Kamaki, kamaki, kamaki!*' They called him a flirt, which made no sense. They said he was playing hard to get. He just wanted to be left alone. '*Kamaki, kamaki, kamaki!*' Michail felt his cheeks grow warm. He was certain he would not be able to muster the courage to face his teacher now; not with the added pressure of the chanting.

He stared at his desk and focused on the rhythmic movement of his right leg. There. He breathed.

Back and forth. Predictable and kind. Back and forth. Back and forth.

He felt a searing pain across the back of his hand, his writing hand, with which he had been translating. And again. And again. The ruler did not break his skin. It was like it burnt it. His hand was on fire. But Michail bowed his head and looked at his desk and recited the grammatical rules of the genitive absolute in his head. He could remove himself from any situation he wanted. It was just a matter of concentration. The mind was stronger than people thought.

As a grown man lying, damp, on his apartment floor, Michail did not agree with his thirteen-year-old self. It was not just a matter of concentration. Especially, he thought, when the problem one was trying to forget was caused by oneself. He had never thought he would be guilty of lack of attention to detail. That was something reserved for other, less diligent, officers; the ones who laughed and ate lunch easily with one another. He had always made sure to work hard, to be the very best. He massaged the back of his right hand.

The English lady's feet teetered down the circular stairwell and stopped outside his door. Michail listened to the three familiar knocks without moving from the floor. 'Michail?' The woman's voice tremored in broken Greek. 'I heard... noises? Is everything all right?'

'Yes,' he called.

'Will you let me in?'

Michail, who had been awake for almost twenty-four hours wanted more than anything to fall asleep in his damp clothes precisely where he lay. However, his neighbour was persistent.

She liked his company, he assumed, and did not like to take no for an answer. He often found her waiting in his corridor when he got home from a late shift; she claimed to be checking in on his whereabouts. He sighed, eyes stinging, thinking of his father who had always insisted on kindness to elders. 'One moment, Moira,' he called.

He unbolted the door, turned the lock, and unhooked the safety chain. The old woman narrowed her eyes, evidently wondering why he felt the need for such excessive security. His stomach sank as he imagined telling her that, because of him, a potential murderer was on the loose. Perhaps he ought to urge her to install better locks?

He stepped aside from the door and gestured to his couch, which was now bathed in the rosy morning sun. She shuffled in and took a seat, beaming at him. In this light, she did not seem as old as he had previously imagined. She had only ever been in his apartment after dark, usually after work. Her hair hung grey and long and her shoulders were beginning to hunch, but her face was moderately smooth. She did not look much older than his parents, perhaps mid-seventies or so. She eyed the scene beadily, as she always did. Michail admired her attention to detail; she viewed everything, even the menial things, as if viewing a work of art. She would, he thought, have made a better Hellenic police officer than him.

'Moira.' He closed the door behind her and fiddled with the locking system, hoping that it would not alarm her. 'I am afraid I am very tired. I must sleep, quickly, and then return to the station.'

'In this light, it is magnificent,' she replied in her best Greek, gazing out of his window.

Michail nodded, suddenly aware of the fact that the Acropolis was the most public of crime scenes. Especially here in Thissio, where it was difficult to avoid. It is why he had stretched himself – beyond financial rationale – to rent an apartment here. He had never regretted it: the view was worth the majority of his payslip.

'Sit with me?' Moira patted the sofa. Too tired to protest, Michail sat down, placing a hand on each knee.

'You know, the ancients did not always plan to build such a commemoration. After the Persians sacked their city, they swore an oath to leave the Acropolis sanctuary as rubble. A ruinous memorial. I always wonder what they intended to remember. War? Defeat? It certainly did not stop them fighting.'

She had a knack of diving straight into conversation, which Michail appreciated. He leaned back, beginning to relax. Her voice was both monotonous and melodic at the same time. She had written a few books when she had been a scholar in England. He enjoyed her expertise. She now lectured at the British School at Athens and gave tours of the city to visiting students. She continued, 'They placed temporary tents, linens I imagine, over the images – the statues – of the gods. Even without the proper structures, they believed their gods needed a home, a proper resting place.'

Michail thought of the forensic tents the police erected over cold bodies.

'It was over thirty years before Pericles commissioned the rebuilding project,' Moira finished.

Michail replied slowly, inhaling her floral scent, 'Athens became ashamed of their mess. They wanted to show competency, their power. If one has an unkempt appearance, then it is safe to assume that the brain is unkempt.'

Moira turned to observe him. She wore her usual thick-rimmed glasses, which she tended to treat as microscopes, pushing them closer to her eyes when she wanted to peer at something in more detail. She looked at his stained and dampened uniform with a raised eyebrow. Michail did not feel the need to explain himself.

'Tidy desk, tidy mind.' Moira smiled. 'But I came to check in on you. Like I said, I heard some disturbances. The ceiling is not thick.'

'I am sorry–'

'Not at all.' She reached across and placed a hand on his knee. Usually, he would have been highly disturbed, but she seemed confident in the gesture and Michail did not have the energy to argue with her. 'I know young men – *have* known – they can become lost and angry at themselves. It sounded... it sounded like you were in pain, Michail.'

Michail put her forwardness down to the language barrier. He removed her hand from his knee. 'I have been on private police business.'

'Oh?' She did not seem concerned about having her gesture rejected. 'I have heard, as most have in the city, about the murder yesterday.' She leaned closer to him. He smelled peppermint on her breath, and underneath it, red wine. 'Most terrible, isn't it? They say that Hephaestus...'

'It is a private, ongoing police investigation.' Michail stood. 'Now, if you do not mind–'

'There was a young boy's body on the Acropolis yesterday.'

Michail clenched his fists, then released them. It was perfectly plausible that she thought she was making good conversation. There was no reason why she would know or even assume that he was on the case. Perhaps the police in England were more candid. He made a mental note to ask Ms Sampson.

'How do you...?'

'He was English, on a school trip. They are staying in the area. I was awake last night, the sirens, lights, there was a crowd, too, you must have noticed? I went out to see what the hullabaloo was about. His teacher was, as you might imagine, distraught. He was waiting for the parents to arrive.'

Again, all plausible. Statements were to be taken from the school group today, the teacher included. Michail rubbed his eyes.

'You are exhausted,' she said.

'Yes, I have not slept yet, as I said.'

'You should take better care of yourself.' She pointed to the Parthenon. 'Even the greatest of structures take their time. No point pressuring yourself.'

'Thank you for stopping in. I hope the book is going well.'

Moira turned to him, a wide smile forming across her face. 'Oh yes, very well indeed, Officer Mikras. The myths are all around us, this is becoming clear.'

With that, she pushed herself off the sofa, releasing a small 'hmph' and padded, barefoot, to the door. 'Robust security,' she commented, fiddling with the bolt.

'You can never be too safe,' Michail said, watching her nimble fingers work the locks. 'Thank you for visiting me, Moira. Speak soon.'

It was only after she left that Michail noticed something strange, though not necessarily significant. He put it down to her being an academic, but as he pulled off his wet uniform, he could not shift it from his thoughts. *Most terrible.* He agreed, of course, that murder was most terrible. But she had not used the modern Greek word, *tromeros*, instead using the Ancient Greek, *deinos*. He pulled down his fold-out bed and fell into it. *Deinos.* It did translate as terrible on occasion; he was certain of it.

However, a thought niggled like a worm in his brain as he fell into a fitful, grateful sleep. Because he also knew that it translated as something else. *Deinos* was also used to mean marvellous, miraculous, awe-inspiring. As he fell into semi-consciousness, he regarded an image of Moira, giving a tour of the Acropolis hill, springing from rock to rock, barefooted, gesticulating at several mutilated and bloody corpses that were strewn about the site. Her audience clapped and cheered as she said, 'Marvellous, they are, just marvellous. A brilliant specimen of how the gods persist! We should be grateful for them and worship them as our own!'

Michail awoke to another woman knocking on his door. This time it was a careless hammering. He rolled over without delay, reaching for his phone. 8.45am; he had managed two and a half hours' sleep, at least. Katerina's voice sounded from the hallway. 'Michail! I have coffee! Open up!'

The mention of coffee was enough. He folded down his sheet, stepped out of bed, folded the sheet back up so that it was tucked neatly in, and pushed the mattress against the wall. The mechanism clicked satisfactorily.

'Michail! Come on!' she shouted as he worked his way through the locking system again.

Michail thought Katerina looked surprisingly well turned out, all things considered. There were subtle bags beneath her eyes, but she smiled brightly as she handed him his coffee and pushed past him into the apartment. She eyed the wet clothes hung over the chair. 'You've got spare, right?'

'Of course.'

The mention of his uniform made him very aware that he was standing in nothing but his underwear. Surprisingly, this did not seem to bother Katerina. 'Great view,' Katerina announced. Michail grabbed his dressing robe from the back of the bathroom door.

'You know my address?' he asked, wriggling into the robe.

'Easy to find.' Katerina faced him. 'And I thought we could go to work together.'

He took a long sip of coffee and swayed slightly. He was light-headed, still exhausted. 'Ms Sampson is furious with us.'

Katerina narrowed her eyes. 'Sofia was unprofessional, Michail. She should have never... she should have controlled herself. I hung about when you ran... after you left. She apologised to me. I think the body... spooked her. She was rabbiting on about a message, you know, one of the social media comments. She reckons she missed a clue. She thinks she could have stopped the boy's murder–'

'Murder?'

'Yet to be confirmed, I know. But this social media post about an olive branch, which is what killed him, has got people excited. Then there's Laurence-Sinclair. Oh, and the axe murder, it's in the papers...' She dug into her handbag and produced the day's *Hellenakratia*. 'Front page – look.'

In large, capital letters, the headline read: *THE AWAKENING: GAY PROSTITUTE IMMIGRANT DIES BY HAND OF GOD.* The accompanying photo showed the Hephaestion axe, covered in blood, attached to the temple. Michail shook his head in disgust. 'I would hardly call this a real newspaper.' The image of the publication's darling editor-in-chief, Christos Panagos, beamed at him, showcasing a smug smile. What sort of an editor put their photograph on the front page?

'Not the point,' Katerina replied. 'Some people do call it a real newspaper and buy it every day. This is what they're reading.'

She shook the paper out and read, 'The young man, thought to be an illegal immigrant squatting in the Exarcheia district, is alleged to have been a sex worker and to have dealt in illegal drugs. Rebel freedom-fighter organisation, The Awakening, has suggested a religious theory: that the goddess of our city, Athena, has arisen and will purge us of the "filth" and "unholy", who reside and infect our city. The theory is based on the nature of the crime which imitates...'

Michail laughed. 'Nonsense, obviously, Katerina. They don't even know our victim's name! Let alone know his sexual orientation. This is right-wing hate, as expected from such a publication. It does not even make sense. Hephaestus cut Zeus's head open to help him, not to punish him.'

Katerina nodded. 'Agreed on the right-wing hate stuff. But they claim to have a name: a Marius Zamfir, Romanian. And they are suggesting that the birth of Athena is the beginning of some sort of string of events. They are calling it a "symbolic awakening". They obviously have some contacts at The Awakening organisation, whoever they are.' She shrugged, exasperated. 'I don't like it either, but there are more leads here than anything we came up with yesterday and we need something.'

'How do they know his name?' Michail shouted over his shoulder, rushing to shower.

'No idea,' Katerina replied, taking a seat at the dining table. 'But maybe this will help us find Laurence-Sinclair, and if there's one thing that will get us back in Sofia's good books, it will be that.'

Snake

Katerina waited at the café below Michail's apartment building for him to get dressed. The smell of freshly baked bread made her stomach tighten; she was exhausted, and the idea of eating was nauseating. Bright-pink flowers bloomed in wooden tubs at the entrance. Katerina imagined spending a day sat amongst the flowers, sipping coffee and thinking of nothing in particular. She could deceive her mother, who would no doubt be waiting for her, as usual, in the kitchen, when she arrived home. *Another productive day, Mama, they have chosen me for the most important tasks.* Her mother would praise her cleverest of daughters, but ask for no further details, no matter how fatigued Katerina seemed. No matter how late she returned home. She knew what her mother was really interested in. *He called again today. Such a nice man. A good man. Katerina, please tell me you have regained your senses.* The day stretched ahead of her like an impossible feat.

Michail's apartment was only a short walk back along the Apostolou Pavlou road where they had parked the car last night. She was surprised that Michail lived so centrally. Rest assured, it was a lovely place to be. Even if his flat was tiny. Katerina found herself wondering how on earth Michail would find room for a significant other in there. Was it intentionally small, for that reason? She tried to picture the type Michail might go for but drew a blank. Had he ever had a serious relationship? She imagined him getting ready for bed – a private moment reserved for the eyes of lovers. He would fold down his bed, plump the pillows, she was sure. He probably slept on his back... feeling herself blush, she distracted her thoughts by counting pedestrians. Clearly, she was more tired than she thought.

It was certainly a vibrant street. Though wide and immaculately kept, without any traffic, it was almost constantly full of tourists heading to the Acropolis. Michail struck her as a man who appreciated peace and quiet. But then there was that uninterrupted view of the Parthenon, a building for which he maintained a strange reverence. She supposed it was impressive – knew it was, she had been told – but Michail looked at it with love, like a child's admiration for a parent.

Katerina frowned at the sound of two elderly women sitting at the table next to her. They were smacking their lips, glossy with thyme honey, and speaking loudly. She noticed they had a copy of *Hellenakratia* spread across the table.

'What is the world coming to, Dimitra? Not metres away from where we sit?'

'Inconceivable. So violent! You see...' she pointed at the article, 'it says his head was sliced. Like a lemon. The murderer has not been found.'

Her friend gasped, one hand on her chest, one hand mopping up honey and butter from her plate with a wedge of bread. 'My God! What are we to do? This isn't some back alley, this is the Plaka!'

'Yes, yes. They've brought nothing but crime and fear. Lock the doors, I say. If that makes me a bad person...'

'Absolutely not! It's just good sense. You don't see Greeks

running about getting their heads sliced in half. This man,' she pointed at Christos Panagos's photograph, 'he speaks sense: *As if a goddess herself intervenes to help the city of Athens...*'

The woman nodded as she recited the words carefully, her nose millimetres away from the paper. She chuckled, leaning back in her chair. 'This city deserves a bit of divine attention, intervention.'

'I agree, I agree. Bring back greater days! The golden years!'

'Yes, I like the idea. This man, Panagos, he had friends in high places too, I hear. He'll bring change, perhaps. A new Pericles!'

'Change!' Her friend clapped, chuckling.

There was no point in intervening and, anyway, they were doing nothing illegal. They sounded so righteous and proud of their views. It occurred to Katerina that this was the sort of conversation that would once have been held in private. Women like this would have slandered the foreign and blamed their problems on the needy between their own walls. No more. These ideas were becoming more commonplace. Katerina stood, making sure she cleared her throat loudly. The women noticed her.

'We were just reading about the murder, officer, do you know anything?'

Katerina shook her head. 'Nothing to do with me. Have a good day, both of you.'

Michail walked out into the street, looking more refreshed. He straightened his belt and clapped his hands together three times. 'There is no time to chat, Katerina.'

The old women exchanged a hard glance.

The traffic on the Leof Alexandras road was already busy; Katerina leaned back on the headrest, willing herself not to close her eyes. Michail drove with his back straight and his chin pointed forwards.

Katerina turned up the air-conditioning and yawned loudly.

'We must remain focused today. There is no room for further mistakes,' Michail said, without looking at her.

She closed her mouth and looked out of the window. The apartment blocks that lined the thoroughfare all had their shutters closed. She supposed she would keep them closed all day too if she lived on this noisy road. Most of the shops on the ground floor were open. A corner café by the subway, a travel agent – who even used those anymore? The trees made it more bearable. The leaves were calm against their bustling backdrop. She took another long sip of coffee and fidgeted in her seat, urging her body to remain wakeful.

Michail must have cried out beforehand but it was not enough warning. The car lurched to a sharp halt and Katerina was thrown forwards and back at force, spilling her coffee. Horns blared around their now stationary car. 'What the hell!'

She waited for the electricity in her chest to abate. Michail checked over his left shoulder, seeming irritated that the cars behind him were causing such a fuss. Shouts began to pour out of the car windows. It seemed that even police cars could not escape the wrath of morning commuters.

'What on earth are you doing?' she shouted, pulling the steaming shirt away from her skin. 'Michail! Why did you brake like that?'

He did not answer, but instead indicated right into a small, shaded street lined with parked cars. She did not bother asking where they were going, as Michail seemed fixed in determined concentration. He would enlighten her soon enough, she thought. She did, however, allow herself a loud, pointed sigh.

'We need to demonstrate extreme observational rigour,' Michail said, pulling over to park.

Katerina clambered out of the car, swearing at the dark coffee stain running down the front of her shirt. He was already marching back towards the steady flow of traffic on the Leof Alexandras. Katerina pursed her lips. If he wanted to ingratiate himself with Sofia, being late into the office was not the way to do it. At the corner of the street, which Katerina noted down as Patriarchou Ieremiou (she would show him observational rigour), next to a second-hand electronics shop and between two large air-conditioning vents, was a square space of wall covered in graffiti. As it happened, Katerina was a fan of good street art. The most promising murals, of course, were famously found in Exarcheia, where the police rarely patrolled, and many urban artists lived. What she and Michail looked at now, however, was not that type of street art. The wall was filled with half-hearted sprayed tags and logos, evolved in a random web of blues, yellows, reds and black. It was the type of wall that made an area feel unsavoury.

Michail turned to her. 'You see?'

'Please tell me you didn't just almost crash the car because of some rubbish graffiti?'

Michail walked up to the wall and pointed to a white square at the top. Katerina squinted at it. Inside the square was a stencilled black axe, with the words '*She wakes*' written on its handle. Katerina stepped closer, placing a hand on the paint. Wrapped around the handle of the axe were two entwined snakes. It was intricately done, to be fair; their scales were formed in tiny diamonds.

'Is it fresh?' Michail asked, glancing up the street.

She shook her head. 'Not sure, spray paint dries quickly. How did you see it from the road?'

Michail frowned. 'I have already said that we must miss nothing. You should have seen it from the passenger seat.'

Katerina placed her hands on her hips. 'You could have killed us, or someone else.'

'I was confident that there was enough space behind me to avoid a collision.' Then he smiled. 'I admit, I may have been a little rash.'

It was good to see him smile. She laughed. 'Perhaps. I'll get a few photos. You think it has something to do with Laurence-Sinclair?'

'There are snakes on his ring.' Michail sniffed, looking at his feet.

'Don't worry, Michail, we'll find him.'

'Correct.' He looked back up at the graffiti. 'There is no use in worrying, only in rectifying the problem.'

Katerina leaned against a cabinet with her notebook poised for the team briefing. Sofia thrust herself into the conference room with brisk momentum, her small frame commanding what Katerina now realised were signature black heels. This fresh demeanour struck her as a stark contrast to Sofia's performance last night. Her infamous 'directness', as people called it, had truly revealed itself. In Katerina's mind, a random social media comment was hardly anything to get bogged down by; it was most likely a coincidence; a tenuous link at best. Sofia, however, had reacted as if she was being eaten from the inside out. She had blamed herself – and those around her – without hesitation. This was someone who did not like to fail. Important to remember, Katerina considered, as she opened her notepad: it was good to know how to impress the boss. Sofia observed her team, clearly waiting for silence.

Just before she began to speak, the conference-room door swung open and through it lumbered six constables. Katerina jumped as one of them – Theo – eyed the room. 'Sorry I am late, Ms Sampson.' He gave Sofia a cheeky bow as his friends laughed. Katerina glanced at Michail, who was fastidiously studying his notepad, and then back at Theo.

'What are you doing here?' Katerina could not help it. Theo was a local constable; he had no business here. He was also her ex-fiancé, which meant he certainly had no business here.

Sofia held out a silencing hand to Katerina, narrowing her eyes. 'I echo Officer Galanis's question, though,' she said. 'What are you doing here, constables? This is a private meeting. Should you not be at your stations?'

'Special orders from the top,' said Theo, nestling into a corner.

'The top?' Sofia took a step forward, folding her arms.

'The police director,' replied Theo, ignoring Sofia and eyeing Katerina smugly. He thought that this would impress her, did he? He thought that this is what she wanted? That they could work as a team now? Katerina buried her head in her notepad.

Sofia looked like she might say something else, but thought better of it, and regained her composure. She bowed her head, looking away from the new arrivals. 'Thank you, *everybody*, then. Yesterday was a challenging day for the department and so you have my gratitude for your hard work. It is, as you know, far from finished.' She pointed the remote control at the screen. A photograph of yesterday's first murder appeared. A low mutter emanated throughout the room. Sofia continued, 'As most of you will know, a sector of the press thinks they have identified the first murder victim as a Marius Zamfir: that is yet to be confirmed. As soon as we can identify the body then we can begin to investigate possible motives. I think, however, it is prudent to assume that this was a hate crime of some sort: something meant to send a message.' She clicked the remote again to the image of the axe.

'The initial autopsy has confirmed this as the murder weapon. No prints have been found and forensics are still going through the DNA samples, though they're not throwing anything up.' The head wound appeared on the screen again, this time in a detailed close-up. 'The only discrepancy is the nature of the wound. There is a clear inward blow to the forehead.' Sofia pointed at the screen, tapping it with her nails. 'But also an outward motion around the site of the wound, as if a force has been pushed from the inside of the head.'

'The birth of Athena!' one of Theo's friends shouted. A few others jeered.

Sofia narrowed her eyes. 'We're all aware of the... hype being spread in popular media. I'd ask that we, as people of fact, do not get carried away. It's possible that the murderer went to pains to make it seem like, um, the mythological birth.'

Quiet laughs petered through the conference room. Yiorgos stood, nodding to Sofia. Katerina straightened herself; he wore a fixed and stern expression. 'I echo Sofia's sentiments, team, we cannot allow ourselves to be swept away with fairy tales. A man's life has been taken: that's the reality. Sergeant Mikras, Officer Galanis, I need you to look into Marius Zamfir, find out who he is, whether he's missing, anything relevant.'

'Understood,' called out Michail. Katerina nudged him in the ribs.

Yiorgos observed them both. 'Excellent.' He looked down at his notes. 'Ah, yes, the security footage has been corrupted, sections of the tape are missing.' The room gave a collective sigh. 'But it's being looked into as a matter of urgency. In terms of suspects, we have only one so far: a Dr Laurence-Sinclair.'

The man's photograph appeared on the screen. Even in a

still frame, his eyes managed to linger inappropriately. Katerina held Michail's arm still, feeling him grow restless. She noted that Sofia pressed a hand to her mouth.

'Michail and Katerina met him on two occasions. Firstly, by the agora site and secondly when they spotted him on the Acropolis hill last night. He works for the Acropolis Museum, recently promoted to managing curator. His ring–' the signet ring, giant and brash, flashed onto the screen, '–was found on the quickest passageway to the sanctuary on top of the hill. His colleagues say that he keeps himself to himself. The word "eccentric" was banded about. He hasn't been in touch with any of them since last night, as far as we know, and he wasn't working at the Acropolis Museum last night, that's confirmed by the museum's security.'

Yiorgos switched the slides to what looked like an old photograph of a hippy. 'Cursory research has thrown up a few relevant details. Laurence-Sinclair made a name for himself in the 1970s in London by running a small... cult, I suppose.' The slide changed again to a close-up of Laurence-Sinclair's hand. 'You can see he is wearing the same signet ring here, decorated with two snakes. According to old university publications, he was sacked from his position as a postgraduate researcher for "luring and corrupting" his students with illegal substances. The records don't specify, but it doesn't take much creativity to imagine the type of parties he was running. Anyway, things go quiet for a few decades, until he accepts an appointment at the Acropolis Museum in the late 1990s. That's what we've got, although Sofia's working on some contacts back home. Which brings us to our second body of the day.'

He smiled, sadly. The teenager's corpse appeared on the screen. 'Oscar Mathers, a student of St Edmund's Cathedral School. He was on a school trip. Sofia and I interviewed his classmates this morning. They all confirm that they snuck out of the hotel at approximately 11.30pm to play on the Acropolis. Their stories add up. There was a dare to see who could climb the highest up the Erechtheum and Oscar accepted. However, none of them actually saw Oscar fall. They only heard him struggling once the olive branch had impaled him, after the impact. We are treating his death as suspicious, given the circumstances.'

'Circumstances?' The same man who had called out earlier raised his hand. 'What circumstances?'

Theo chuckled and Katerina felt his eyes burning against her skin. She would not meet his gaze.

Sofia pursed her lips. She stood again, taking the remote from Yiorgos and replied, 'On all the major social media platforms is a relatively new group calling themselves The Awakening. They have a small following, though it is growing quickly. Some of them were chanting at the bottom of the Acropolis hill last night. We have reason to believe they are posting announcements of potential crimes before they happen. There was a post containing some details about the Temple of Hephaestus body before the murder itself.' She paused. 'There was also one about an olive branch.'

Katerina glanced at Michail, who was tapping his thumbs repetitively. Sofia continued, in a softer voice, 'Cyber are on it and will update us of anything relevant. It would be worth following the groups yourselves, though I urge caution.'

Michail raised his hand, rigid and purposeful. Katerina almost pushed it down, thinking he ought to keep a low profile this morning, but she was too late. 'Go on,' said Sofia, batting an errant strand of hair behind her ear.

'Thank you for such a clear and concise breakdown of events,' Michail said. The room was silent. 'The myths, as much as the notion of the gods arising again must be disregarded, all feature the goddess Athena. The murders obviously happened in salient locations. Her "birth", to use the phrase, happened next to the Temple of Hephaestus, the god who eventually cut her out of Zeus's head, and the olive branch death happened next to the sacred olive tree, the one Athena is supposed to have planted when she conquered Poseidon. It is not yet technically a pattern, but it is notable. Should we further consider myths featuring this goddess? It may help us locate the next event.'

'Absolutely not,' said Sofia, seeming agitated. 'We work with facts, Sergeant Mikras. I only mean for my team to be mindful of social commentary.' A few short laughs played about the room, Theo's the loudest; people began to stand, notes in hand, fuelled with coffee and ready for the day's work.

Katerina was sure she heard Michail whisper, 'Incorrect.'

Theo grabbed Katerina's arm on the way out of the meeting, dragging her to a quiet corner of the corridor. 'What the hell are you doing?' she hissed, tugging her arm away from him. 'We cannot be seen together here.' This was beyond the pale: she thought that her promotion onto this case meant that at least she no longer needed to work with him. As she stepped back, she saw that agonising hurt in his eye. She shrugged, looking behind him to check the team were out of earshot. 'Look, I know this is hard...'

'Hard?' Theo sprung towards her again, taking her waist. There were tears in his eyes. 'It's agony for me, Kat.'

Katerina couldn't see there was anything else she could do but comfort him. His emotions were well-known for running out of control. 'Theo, we spoke about this. It's not that I fell out of love...'

'That's what it feels like, Kat. That's what it looks like to everyone!'

She hushed him, bringing his head close to hers. 'This is not the place, Theo. This is not the place.' She stroked his hair as he held her, peering over his rippling shoulders. Luckily, nobody seemed to be paying them any attention. Eventually, he heaved himself off her, wiping his eyes.

'But the wedding?' he said.

Katerina could not bear to hear the word. She shook her head.

'We were planning it together...' Theo continued, his eyes deep and swollen with pain.

She nodded quickly. 'I know. I know, Theo. Please do not think this is easy for me. But we are at work.' She looked at him squarely. 'You did not request to be moved.' It was a statement because she wished it not to be true.

His eyes widened. 'No, no I said. The police director made the call. He thinks that more hands are needed on the ground.'

She watched his face, so familiar, so needy. 'Okay. Okay, I believe you. I need to get back to work.'

'With Michail?' Theo's lips curled upwards.

Katerina pushed past him briskly. 'Yes. With Sergeant Mikras.'

The morning was disappointingly unproductive. They were given a small, windowless room from which to work. Katerina, who was used to writing minor incident reports, usually connected to petty theft and traffic offences, experienced a terrifying realisation of the responsibility she held. She had tried to broach the topic of Theo's arrival, but Michail had simply said, 'The police director reserves the right to use human resources as he wishes.'

Her fingers poised over the keyboard, she looked sideways at

Michail, like an errant student who had not revised for an exam. Instead of researching the *Hellenakratia* articles, he was scrolling through a website about Greek mythology. Before she could speak, he said, without looking away from his screen, 'Yes, Katerina, I am aware of my insubordination. Please investigate Marius Zamfir; this will not take long.'

Smirking, she typed the name into her server. She could not remember a time when Michail had broken rules, not even unimportant ones. Predictably, the screen flooded with search results from various publications. Frustratingly, Sofia had instructed her not to contact the *Hellenakratia*'s editor-in-chief, Christos Panagos. 'A delicate dance,' she had said. 'Don't contact him without consulting me.' However, feeling like she was hitting a wall and knowing how busy Sofia was, Katerina had already left three messages on the newspaper's answerphone.

Other than that, Marius Zamfir's name brought up no previous criminal record, nor useful information. Unfortunately, it seemed it was a relatively popular Romanian name. After hours of reading about an esteemed cancer doctor in Sibiu, a lawyer in Cluj-Napoca and a teacher who been awarded a prize for exceptional mathematics lessons in Bucharest, none of whom looked anything remotely like the victim, she banged the keyboard with her fists. 'We need to speak to that newspaper, Michail, this is useless!'

Michail nodded, looking at a map on his screen. 'I agree. You are wasting your time.'

Katerina blew through her teeth. 'You think I don't know that?'

Michail held his index finger up to her face, marking something down in his notebook. 'Interesting,' he said. 'Very interesting.'

'What are you doing?' Katerina rolled her chair across to get a better look at his screen.

'Nothing... yet,' Michail replied, turning to face her. 'But it is obvious you must visit the newspaper offices. They are not returning your calls.'

'But Sofia said...'

'Ignore her.' Michail said the words in a strained manner, as if his tongue was stuck. He crossed his arms and looked her directly in the eye. 'In an unprecedented turn of both my professional and personal ethics, I am suggesting that Ms Sampson, our superior, is lacking in judgement.'

Katerina raised her eyebrows. 'Sergeant Mikras!'

'You must not do the dance delicately, as she suggested. We are the Special Violent Crime Squad of the Hellenic Police Department. There is no time for dancing. My suggestion is to go straight to the newspaper and demand to see the editor as a police matter of mortal importance.'

'Right! Wait, what are you going to do?'

Michail looked back at his screen. 'I have important research to complete.'

Katerina swung around. 'What do you mean?' Michail furrowed his brow and leaned closer towards his keyboard, typing in short bursts. 'Michail?'

'Yes, I heard you,' he said, evasively.

She jumped up from her chair to stand behind him. His spine straightened and she caught the last imprint of a tab before he closed it. Something to do with textile mills. 'Michail, we're supposed to be partners and I'm getting nowhere.' Michail sat in silence, clearly considering his options. 'Michail, will you just tell me!'

'All right. Just checking something through...' He clicked the mouse and the printer whirred into action. 'Here, you will see all possible myths relating to the goddess Athena.'

Katerina retrieved the document from the printer tray and sat beside him. Indeed, Michail had collated and summarised a comprehensive list of the goddess's myths, together with detailed comments along the side of the page. She vaguely knew most of them. There was the birth of Athena, of course, then the battle for the patronage of Athens against Poseidon, the Arachne myth, a blinding of a man named Tiresias, and a long list of appearances in the Homeric epic. She took a breath. 'So...'

'Yes, precisely.'

Katerina looked back at the document again. She bit her lip, scanning the notes he had made, wishing she could think of something relevant to say. She agreed they should be looking into all possible avenues. She was surprised Sofia was opposed to the idea.

'To me, it makes sense.' Michail loaded the mythology site back onto his screen. 'The trick is making an educated guess about which one. If I can cross-reference these myths with the social media posts, then it is possible we might predict when and where the next murder will take place.'

'Is that not a bit... presumptuous?' Katerina asked, disappointed. She had hoped he had found something concrete. He ignored her, scrolling down his screen. She felt herself grow impatient. 'Fine, I'll go to the offices alone.'

Without thinking, she reached to touch Michail's shoulder. Michail leapt up, lurching away from her, knocking the keyboard to the floor with an uncomfortable, prolonged crash. They both stood, staring at the keyboard, entangled in a mess of wires and leads. The office suddenly felt very small. The soft hum of the air-conditioning unit pondered upon the moment, filling the space between them with stale air. She bent down and picked her way through the mess, placing the keyboard back on his desk. Michail nodded, the tension around his eyes softening.

'Right then,' Katerina said, aware she was growing warm. 'See you for lunch? Your *spanakopita* is in the fridge.'

This seemed to cause Michail even more consternation. He rocked gently from leg to leg, flexing his hands into fists and then releasing them. Eventually, he settled, and arranged his face into an expression that Katerina could only recognise as something between extreme stress and gratitude. 'Thank you, Katerina. Good luck at the newspaper. And remember, no dancing.'

Katerina nodded, smiling. 'Right.'

The *Hellenakratia* office was to be found behind a ramshackle of cars and bins on the long central street of Charilaou Trikoupi. Katerina stood on the opposite side of the road, checking she had got the address right. The building was a peeling mess of 1970s architecture and the glass on the narrow entrance door was smashed, held together by what looked like masking tape. Katerina found it hard to believe that the brash publication was made here, and it was even less conceivable that Christos Panagos, who seemed to manicure his public image so masterfully, worked from such a building. She rolled her eyes: the press at its best – never presenting anything as it was. Slippery. She was glad she never had to see another one of these newspapers again. Theo had read the *Hellenakratia* voraciously, idolising Christos as some sort of modern saviour.

Taking a deep breath, Katerina marched across the street. The bins stank in the afternoon heat, rotten and thick. She wrinkled her nose and pressed on the buzzer.

'Yes?'

'Hello, Katerina Galanis, Special Violent Crime Squad.' She flashed her badge at a video camera. 'I've left a few messages for Christos Panagos. I'm looking for information on an article you ran today.' She was pleased at the confidence of her voice; she sounded commanding. The intercom crackled and the door eventually buzzed open.

Katerina entered a tired corridor, decorated with cracked beige tiles. 'Up here!' a woman's voice sounded from above. The staircase was narrow and lined with a wobbly, iron handrail. Katerina ascended two steps at a time. She smiled when she saw the owner of the voice: a woman probably in her mid-forties with brassy hair, tied up in a knot at the centre of her head. The lobby followed a similar colour scheme of yellows and beige and the woman's desk was a fold-out table, with a laptop and some pamphlets arranged on the top. She flashed her badge again. 'Special Violent Crime Squad, is Christos here?'

The woman looked Katerina up and down. Katerina stood very still, wondering what sort of assessment was being made. 'Like I said–' she began.

'You're with the police?' the woman interrupted, raising a thin eyebrow. Katerina nodded, waggling her badge before putting it away. 'You work for Sofia?'

Interesting, Sofia was known even to the receptionist. 'Yes, Sofia Sampson is running the investigation.' Katerina hoped the name would carry some weight.

The woman took her time lighting a cigarette, leaving Katerina standing in the middle of the room. Eventually, she puffed out a cloud of smoke and gestured for Katerina to take one of the plastic chairs arranged along the side. 'You can wait here.' Katerina nodded and took a seat, covering her mouth with the back of her hand. She watched the woman write a text message, cigarette hanging from her mouth. In a few moments, the woman's phone buzzed with a reply. 'Go through, then,' she said, pointing to a flimsy door with a frosted plastic panel.

'Thanks.' Katerina smiled, glad to be leaving the haze.

To her surprise, the door led down a long, windowless corridor. When she reached the end, she was met with two doors on either side of the stone walls. Neither was labelled. 'In here,' a voice rang out. Opening the right door, Katerina was met with Christos himself, in a deep-blue suit, sitting on a red beanbag, a laptop on the worn carpet before him. His long legs were bent at an almost ridiculous angle, causing his trousers to ride up, exposing fuchsia socks. He peered up at her through a fringe of thick dark curls. 'Police?' he purred, through a delicate smirk. He leant back on the beanbag, folding his arms. 'Won't you take a seat?'

His demeanour was enticing, Katerina allowed herself that. She immediately saw how this man – not much older than her – had managed to slither his way through the upper echelons of Athenian society. His smirk made one feel that he was peering into your heart, massaging your darkest secrets with soft hands, embracing them. Katerina folded her arms and scanned the small room. Again, no windows. She fought the urge to check over her shoulder, thinking of the narrow stone corridor outside. 'I'm good standing.' She held her hand out, stiffening her chin. 'Officer Galanis, Special Violent Crime Squad.' She eyed his mobile phone, which lay beside his laptop. 'I've left you a number of messages.'

Christos shrugged; his shoulders languid beneath his jacket. Katerina narrowed her eyes at him. 'Apologies,' he said. 'Busy morning, as you might imagine. A lot of... excitement in the air. But I am glad you took the initiative to visit.'

So, he had been playing hard to get. Katerina observed the dingy, stark office space. 'Glad I came.'

'You were expecting luxury, Miss... ah, Miss Galanis?' He straightened out his legs, placing one over the other.

She shrugged. 'I don't know. Seems a bit... bare.'

He let out a soft laugh, tilting his head ever so slightly

backwards, so that Katerina watched his smooth neck convulse with the sound. 'Ideas are my business, Miss Galanis. I do not require physical distractions. I work for the people, their interests. I assure you my mind,' he tapped his temple, 'is an abundance of riches.'

'I see.' Katerina realised she was holding herself awkwardly. She released her arms to her sides, willing herself to seem relaxed. 'You named a victim of ours as a Marius Zamfir and suggested that you have information regarding his identification.'

He cocked an eyebrow at her. 'Yes.'

He was going to make her say it. Katerina pursed her lips. 'I need that information: who he is, where he lived.' She shifted from foot to foot, her throat was growing dry. She added, in a less commanding voice than she had hoped, 'You are legally required to give us anything you have.'

Without making an effort to reply, Christos pushed himself up from the beanbag and stepped towards her. He was tall and she was forced to look up at him, as if in worship. She took a step back, wishing she had forced Michail to come with her. 'Do you have it? A file?'

Christos nodded slowly, his smile simmering hot and ready. 'Sofia draws a blank, then?'

Katerina frowned. 'You know Sofia?'

'I know everyone.'

Katerina shook her head. 'Will you give me the information or not? We are in the middle of a murder enquiry.'

'Murder?' He raised a finger to his chin in mock confusion. Katerina was beginning to grow irritated.

'Yes, murder, as you are aware.' She took another step towards the door. Perhaps this had been a mistake. Christos Panagos seemed only interested in wasting her time. He chuckled, this time low and deep. The vibrations caused her belly to tighten.

'There are some who would say that it is not murder at all, but divine intervention. There are some who say our city's goddess awakes.'

'You are right, there are some crazy people out there,' she replied flatly. She turned her back on him, ready to leave. Sofia had been right: a waste of time and now he knew that the team were on the back foot. How stupid of her. And Michail. She began to walk towards the lobby as quickly as possible, happy to be leaving this strange office building.

'Lena will give you the file,' Christos called after her.

'What?' Katerina almost hissed the word, turning on her heels. Christos was framed between the narrow walls, legs spread widely, his face beaming.

'Lena, the receptionist. She will give you the information you require. Arrived yesterday on my desk. No idea who from, like magic.' He bowed his head and Katerina hurried down the corridor. 'Send Sofia my regards. She will be pleased to hear from me, I am sure.'

Katerina rested her head against her mother's front door and wondered how long she could stand there, head hung limply, pressure growing pleasingly on the front of her skull, before being classified as clinically mad. She twitched her lips, encouraging her face to move into a pert smile. There was a theory about smiling and the positive effect it had on the human brain. Something to do with the muscle memory tricking the frontal cortex into thinking it was happy. It was not something she had ever had to consider before. She was just tired, that was all. All things considered, she was coping quite well. There were good things in the world, in her world, upon which to focus. She liked the song the neighbours played, even though her mother would be complaining about the noise as the synthetic beat dropped in bulbous waves through the floor. It imitated Katerina's pulse, which had grown loud in her ears. She listened to her insides for a bit. Pictured the blood, encased by fibres, pumping through her veins. Always pushing, always in a hurry, working so relentlessly in constant flow.

She pulled her head from the door.

It was still there. *Flat 2* written in gold. The white panelled door could have done with a lick of paint since before her father passed. There was laughter from within the apartment; her mother on the telephone. She would be pleased to see her youngest daughter at a sensible hour. Tomatoes were baking, the unmistakable sweet and acidic aroma wafted under the door. Her mother would be prodding them with the spatula, careful not to break their skin, minding not to burn them. She would be pleased to nourish Katerina, to wash her clothes, to encourage her to bathe after the long, hot day. There was everything to be grateful for.

Katerina's phone buzzed: Sofia, scheduling a meeting for first thing tomorrow. No doubt to discuss what the history was between herself and Theo, as well as to tell her off for going to the *Hellenakratia* offices. There was also a note about how Sofia's London contacts had uncovered some extra information about Laurence-Sinclair. Sofia had sent through a menagerie of documents. *Obviously, I've read them*, Sofia wrote, *but a second pair of eyes would be useful. Michail has them too – use Google Translate if required.*

Katerina pushed the key into the lock. The door was well over a hundred years old, same as the building. The key was the old-fashioned kind so the mechanisms of the lock stuck and crunched as it turned.

'Katerina!' her mother called from the kitchen. Like most of the apartments in the area, her mother's was a cavernous, spacious surprise. The entrance hall housed a tall mahogany display cabinet, full of blue and white ceramics. The hallway was abundant with paintings: her mother was not a picky woman. Biblical scenes, cheap oil replicas, photographs of sculptures, friends, prints of unknown artists interested in the modulations of the human form lined the walls.

'In here!' shouted her mother again. 'I am doing the supper, come sit!'

Katerina noticed the living-room lights were off. Lola and Kalle were not here tonight. Perhaps they would be joining later. Or perhaps they were on late shifts.

'Katerina!' her mother's voice cracked towards the end of her name. 'By God! I forgot the herbs!' Katerina listened to her mother skate across the kitchen in – no doubt – her open-toed rubber slippers. 'It will be no good without the herbs!'

The kitchen was full of the daily mess. Her mother was incapable of cooking and clearing away at the same time. Her father had tried to improve the catastrophe of pots, pans and jars that routed the kitchen nightly but her mother had always said, 'A mess in the workspace is a delight in the mouth. I am not a boring cook, my darling.' She said the latter whilst pointing at him, moving her finger in a circular motion, her grin as wide as their love.

At the large kitchen island, set in the centre of the room, sat Theo. Katerina stopped in the doorway, one hand steadying herself. He looked at her, his dark eyes soft, his hands clasped firmly on the counter. He wore a tight black T-shirt so that his arms bulged indulgently through the stretched material. His police gun remained attached to his hip.

'Oh, Katerina.' Her mother kissed her on the cheek.

85

'Theo?' Katerina asked, without looking at her mother. 'Mama? Did you invite him? I have work to do.'

Her mother, clearly adamant that she would avoid the question, returned to the stove. 'A better day today? No more bodies?' Her laugh was strained and inappropriate. 'Ah, I mean, you did not need to work so late today. I was worried last night, Katerina, you have no idea what a mother's imagination is capable of...'

Ah, there. The first reference to motherhood of the evening. Katerina made for the fridge and grabbed a bottle of beer. Her mother narrowed her eyes but did not say anything. Sighing and despite her better judgement, she held a bottle out to Theo, careful not to graze his fingers as he took it.

'Thanks,' he said, in a tone her mother would call humble and Katerina would call saccharine. He had no shame.

She held her beer to the ceiling. 'Well cheers, then,' and took a long, gulping sip. 'Theo has told you, Mama, that we are on the same team again?' Katerina opened her laptop on the kitchen counter and found Sofia's documents. 'He turned up to our meeting today.'

'Oh,' her mother began, eyeing her daughter's drinking with small and disapproving eyes. 'Well, that is... good news! Theo has come over to share a meal with us. He telephoned me, can you imagine? Think of the moral fibre a man possesses to telephone his *pethera*–'

'You are not his *pethera*,' Katerina said flatly.

Her mother ignored her, speaking rapidly over the sizzling tomatoes, '...the bravery, the *remorse*.' She had rehearsed this. Katerina took another long swig. 'He is a man of courage, Katerina. He has come to make amends.' Her mother turned to her, spatula in hand. 'What could I say? Did you want me to push him back onto the streets? Alone? They are not safe nowadays...'

'Metaxourgeio?' Katerina could not help smiling. 'Afraid a guerrilla gardener will chase him with a spade?' She ate her smile. 'And Theo can handle himself, he's a policeman too.'

Her mother smirked at her, widening her eyes innocently. 'Your cases have spooked me, what can I say?'

Katerina sighed deeply, beginning to read a university transcript from 1972. Laurence-Sinclair was intelligent, it seemed. He had scored almost full marks in his final-year examinations. He had been a star student. She clicked on a file entitled *'Written reports'*; the screen loaded and she swore aloud.

'Daughter!' her mother scolded.

'Sorry, Mama. I need to read this, Sofia has asked me to, but it is a scanned document written in English.'

'You should have focused on your English studies.'

'I know, Mama!' Katerina took another swig of her beer. 'But I need to read this now. I need to impress Sofia. I have a meeting with her in the morning.'

'I wouldn't tie yourself in knots trying to impress that woman,' Theo said.

'Oh?' Katerina's mother raised an eyebrow. 'Katerina speaks very highly of Ms Sampson.'

'I suppose if you like that sort of thing. Are all English women that tarty by the way? There are plenty of Greeks who need jobs, and here she comes, landing direct from London and pretty much falling into one of the most senior positions in the force.'

Katerina squinted at her screen, trying her best to block Theo out. 'She's half-Greek,' she said, distracted by the document. 'I think she is wonderful; she deserves your loyalty. That's the end of the matter.'

'Wonderful!' Theo burst out laughing, causing her mother

to jump. 'I'm sorry, Mrs Galanis,' he said. 'Your daughter is precious!'

Katerina took a steady breath and opened another document, trying not to pay attention to Theo. This one was an old newspaper clipping, again, in English, though Sofia had encircled a few phrases in what Katerina recognised as ancient Greek with a question mark. One of them being γλαυκῶπις. 'Interesting,' Katerina said aloud.

'What?' Theo's head moved towards her screen as she closed it shut.

'Nothing,' said Katerina, exiting the document. 'Theo, I feel that we have said enough. You are welcome to stay to dinner if Mama has invited you, but if we are to work together, then we must... respect each other's space.'

She crossed her arms as Theo began to speak. 'I would rather we spoke in private.' He looked at her mother's back, nudging his head towards the hallway. Of course, he preferred privacy.

'You can say anything in front of Mama that you want to say to me. She knows everything.'

'Everything?' His eyes twinkled. She did not rise to his bait. 'The wedding is in two months,' he began.

'The wedding *was* in two months,' Katerina corrected him. 'We have had this conversation.'

Theo drained his beer and squeezed the empty bottle in his hands, flexing his muscles. Even now, he could not resist a chance to show off. Her mother turned around at the noise of glass grating on her slate countertop and frowned. 'Another?' Katerina asked him, attempting to keep the peace.

'Um, yes, please.' He did not offer to get up himself.

Opening his beer, he continued, 'I know I made a mistake, I have said a thousand times that I am sorry, Katerina!' He banged his fist on the counter; tiny glassy vibrations filled the air. Her mother, back still turned, moved sideways towards Katerina, and began inspecting the bread oven. Theo composed himself, unravelling his fist. 'We cannot continue like this. I am glad you did not just roll over. You showed strength of character in moving out – but it's gone too far, Katerina, we must move past this. We can, I know it.'

Katerina narrowed her eyes at him as she tipped her head back to finish her bottle. He could make things so difficult. 'I'm very busy, Theo. I don't have time to reorganise a wedding, even if I wanted to.'

His face creased with indignation. 'With work?'

'Yes.' She shrugged.

'She is always busy,' her mother added, turning to put an arm around her daughter. 'She works hard, like her father.' Katerina placed a hand on her mother's plump and dark forearm.

'She should know her allies,' Theo said.

Katerina frowned. 'I thought we were on the same side.' Theo said nothing, shrugging his shoulders.

'Please, Theo.' Katerina was suddenly overcome with exhaustion. She needed to finish reading Sofia's notes before their meeting tomorrow, as well as come up with a sensible explanation for breaking her word. 'Can we do this another time?'

He chuckled. 'Need to call Michail?'

'No.' She shook her head. 'I need to work and then sleep.'

'You like him, don't you? I saw you together today, beavering away, looking at graphs, having the time of your lives. Jesus, Kat, he used to be our joke.'

'Enough.' Katerina stood, red in the face. 'That's enough, Theo, please.' Then, because she was tired and needed him to leave, 'I don't owe you anything else. It's over.'

Theo drew himself away from her abruptly and chucked his

beer bottle into the bin. 'I can see I have overstayed my welcome,' he said. Her mother looked like she might reply, but Katerina shot her a look. 'Don't work too hard, Kat,' he said, seeing himself out. 'You can dig too deep, you know.'

'Tomatoes?' her mother said, offering the plate.

———

As she slipped into her bed, the same single bed she had slept in as a child, Katerina's face was lit up by the light of her phone. She hugged her knees to her chest, nervous about her meeting with Sofia tomorrow. She hoped Sofia would not have a problem with Theo; it was over between them, after all. And visiting Christos Panagos? Well, this she was less sure about. She did feel a certain pride in her own tenacity; this sort of forthrightness was surely what a good police officer needed? Sofia was bound to understand that. She had done what was required. Now they had a proper lead.

She moved over to her desk and ran a finger over the file, laid open. Here were photos of Marius Zamfir in various locations, all seemingly in the Exarcheia district. There was a long shot of him sitting smoking in a makeshift artists' café, there he was spied through a window, his beautiful profile distracted, unaware. There he was passed out in the corner of a warehouse, his lips gently parted like they had been on his corpse, sleeping, intoxicated. It looked as if someone had stalked him. Who had given the *Hellenakratia* these? A handwritten note accompanied the images:

'A portrait of a parasite' or any other title you wish to invent. Recent events have certainly 'awoken' public interest. Send the Hellenakratia's regards to the Special Violent Crime Squad. Christos Panagos (Editor-in-Chief).

Arachne

Sofia was furious. She fought the tiny convulsions in her neck, observing the girl from her leather chair, her fingers gripping its arms. Her department had been sucked straight into Christos's twisted power games, despite her extremely clear and direct orders.

'Did you not hear me?' Sofia attempted to seem calm out of professionalism but was aware of the angry tremor in her voice. Katerina Galanis's mouth was wide open. 'Close your mouth, girl!' Sofia cried, holding a rigid finger up to Katerina's face so that she didn't say anything that would make her even angrier. The file was placed open on her desk. Photographs, details, his place of birth, his family – all deceased. There was just enough information to tantalise but nothing concrete: no address or anything like that. She snapped it shut.

'You mean to suggest a newspaper does better work than us? That simpering Christos Panagos,' she said the name through gritted teeth, 'is better than my team?'

'No, Sofia–'

'Quiet!' Sofia sat back in her chair, her mind calculating, pacing. 'I should have you off the case.'

'Sofia, please–'

'I said quiet!' Sofia ran a fingernail across the thick brown file containing Marius's details. There was no innocent reason why that man would have released this information to Katerina; he had no fear of the law. Christos was forever scheming. This was a message. A taunt. 'They let you in, no questions?'

Katerina shrugged. She did not seem to comprehend the severity of her actions. 'I went to their offices and buzzed up. The receptionist, Lena, was frosty at first but then let me through. He is...' She held her hands out.

'If you say enchanting, I will sack you immediately.'

'No!' Katerina's eyes widened. 'No! I meant to say that he is creepy. It is like an invasion, the way he speaks. I... I can see how he has gained such popularity. If I didn't know better, I could be mesmerised by him.'

'He is dangerous.' That was all Sofia was willing to offer the girl. She nodded curtly towards the file. 'And he gave you this without so much as a greeting?'

'No. He spoke about divine intervention.' Sofia rolled her eyes. 'And he mentioned you.'

Sofia was very careful not to flinch. She squinted across her desk at Katerina. 'Me?'

'He said he knew you.'

Sofia nodded. Katerina seized the silence. 'It was easier than I thought. You are not pleased?'

Sofia massaged her temples. 'Too easy,' she replied, clicking her tongue. Katerina said nothing. Sofia sighed. 'Must I explain to you why we do not exchange information with the press, let alone that sort of press?' She noted that Katerina had dark circles beneath her eyes. Sofia tried her best to understand. She had been young once. She had mistaken stupidity for tenacity. This was no ordinary case. The girl had justice in her heart, at least. And she did not know that justice was as rare as tanzanite, even in the special force. She continued in a softer voice, 'We do not know for whom they work. Our agenda is to bring safety to the streets, to hold people to account–'

'Then why don't you?' The girl's shoulders were held back, her chest pushed out. The young ones were full of confidence. 'It is hard to know what to think when you ignore the obvious lines of enquiry. Corruption is everywhere: those were your words! I remember them from the Academy lecture. It is hard to know whom to trust, Sofia. I went with my instincts and, look!' She scooped the file from the desk. 'I was right. They have an entire file on him, this will help us.'

Sofia waited for the end of the girl's speech, which no doubt she thought was righteous. She pursed her lips and stood, holding a steady eye. She moved her mouth purposefully, as if it was separate from the words she spoke. Each syllable hung stagnant in the air as she said, 'You came very close to accusing me of something, Officer Galanis. I have always striven for justice. I can speak for myself. The press – the *Hellenakratia* in particular – are the mouthpiece for all sorts of unsavoury organisations, as you know. My department will not work with them; we cannot trust them. I would treat the information in that file with caution and I would warn you against accusing your superiors.' She flared her eyes at the girl. Such insolence could not be tolerated.

To Sofia's surprise, Katerina held her ground. She spoke with an energetic fluency, her brow furrowed with concern, without thought, it seemed, of the consequences. Perhaps she thought that the damage was already done. 'You didn't want to look into the myths, like Michail suggested. Everyone is talking about it, not just the press. There are signs popping up all over Athens: #SheArises... the list is endless. Even Christos mentioned it. There are graffiti axes all over the city – like the murder weapon – wrapped in snakes. Michail says this is a symbol of Athena. Look at the bloggers: there are conspiracies popping up everywhere. Some are even saying that Athena herself is behind The Awakening. We should not ignore–'

Sofia raised her voice. 'All stirred up by the press whom you eagerly consulted! All a distraction from the facts at hand.'

Finally, the girl seemed crestfallen. Her head dropped, defeated. A few seconds passed. Their breaths punctuated the dead office air in syncopated intervals. Sofia sat down again, sinking into the warm leather of her chair. She kicked off her shoes, usually something reserved for late afternoons. She reminded herself that the girl did not know the history behind this man. There was no way, however, that she would go into that now. 'Look,' Sofia began. 'It's good that we have found – *think* we have found – the victim's identity. See if anything in the file is verifiable. Go to Exarcheia with Michail tomorrow and try and find out more. Remember that Christos would have revealed his source if he had really wanted to help us. This is... well, it is not straightforward. Like I say, tread carefully: it suits them for us to have this information, that much I know. As for the Athena myths...'

Sofia could hardly believe she was entertaining the idea. Intuition was one thing, but to bend to the fancies of the public, to the vomit of extremist press; it was a descent into chaos, surely. Yet, they were struggling. There had been no success in tracking down The Awakening and its support was growing every hour. Katerina was correct, new conspiracies were beginning to surface, clouding the cyber team's search. However, if the police enquired into such claims, then they would legitimise them, give them fuel. The two bodies materialised in her mind's eye. The murdered man, the boy's death, both somehow taking the public's imagination by storm. She would be answering to the police director tomorrow. She needed momentum. She needed direction, at least. Katerina gripped the file, still standing before her. She was irritating, certainly. She was also bold. Sofia decided she liked her.

'No news on Laurence-Sinclair's whereabouts?' Sofia asked. Katerina shook her head. 'Very well,' Sofia said. 'We navigate uncharted waters. I give you permission to pursue any line you see fit. The same goes for Sergeant Mikras. Where is he?'

The girl shifted from one foot to another, gesturing to their shared office where, no doubt, Michail was already meticulously elbow-deep in his myth research. Sofia frowned. 'Let him know then. But Katerina, do not defy me again, or if you decide to, please inform me of your intentions beforehand.'

Sofia could not help but smile at the look of unbridled delight on the girl's face. 'Oh, and Katerina?' Sofia lowered her voice. 'I don't have anything to worry about between you and Constable Theo Kounos? I noticed... a certain tension yesterday.'

'Nothing at all,' Katerina replied. 'Ancient history.'

'Very well.' Sofia nodded, gesturing to her office door. 'I can tell you that workplace relationships are always a disastrous idea.'

The news of Ms Sampson's change of heart did not come as a surprise to Michail because it was the obvious and logical direction of inquiry. He was only sorry about the inordinate amount of time she had taken to reach this decision, forcing him to work covertly, which had only delayed things. At least now he could converse at length with his colleagues about his provoking and potentially groundbreaking theories. He had been busy cross-referencing a spreadsheet of key mythological words with suspicious social media posts. So far, references to spiders – and the Arachne myth – had been littering the comments. Much as it filled him with dread, Michail was sure he had identified the basis for another murder being plotted. The next trick was to decipher the specific details. He stared at his tablet, which was propped up behind his lunch tray, thinking that it would be useful to have someone to bounce ideas off.

Unfortunately, a familiar scene had unfolded before him in the canteen, which had resulted in his new colleagues suffering from a case of temporary blindness as they scanned the communal tables for somewhere to sit. Despite him nudging the chair next to him suggestively (he had not yet summoned the courage to wave), he remained alone, picking his own brains.

But this was not the only déjà vu about today's lunch. Much as he tried to ignore it, a fiery voice, thrown from the far end of the canteen persisted, forcing him to break his concentration.

'Mikras! What are you doing sitting alone? Mikras, come here, come here!'

Michail knew he must be polite and reasonable. Theo had been transferred here under fair circumstances. Even if Michail thought it went against all the protocol and meritocracy upon which the organisation rested, then he must make sure that he kept it to himself. Michail blinked twice at the gesticulating man.

'I said join us! Don't leave us waiting!' Then the mock crying act began: Theo did not even bother to come up with something new. 'Boo-hoo, don't leave us waiting!'

A roaring laugh followed. Michail looked at his plate. He only had three mouthfuls left – four at most: this was a perfectly manageable situation. He had, after all, been hand-picked by Ms Sampson to serve her in the elite Special Violent Crime Squad. A yob like Theo no longer needed to bother him. He could not help but wonder, as he always had, what Katerina saw in the man. But that, of course, was no concern of his.

Michail chewed with a methodical and thorough technique, compromising on neither speed nor digestion. His eyes focused straight ahead to avoid distraction and accidental eye contact with Theo. A howl of laughter sounded from across the canteen. Michail swallowed hard, attempting to speed up his *spanakopita* intake and, unfortunately, choked. He gripped the table quickly, knowledgeable of what to do in such a circumstance, opened his mouth wide and thrust his head forwards. Laughter rung in his ears. This was most unsatisfactory. His eyes bulged as he realised his windpipe was still blocked. He clutched the table, reminding himself not to succumb to panic.

'Oh my goodness!' A pair of hands clenched his midriff from behind and pulled backwards in a strong, swift tug. There was a soft popping sound as the pastry dislodged from his throat and landed back on his plate in an unappetising clump. Michail wheezed, hanging his head forward, enjoying the pleasant feeling of oxygen rushing back to his brain.

'Michail?' Ah, Katerina. 'Are you all right?'

'Thank you, Katerina. Yes, I am fine. Just an errant bite of...' His voice trailed off as he realised she wasn't paying attention; a typical trait, he had to admit. 'Katerina?' She was looking towards Theo with an expression of unadulterated rage. A strange expression to reserve for a fiancé, Michail considered.

'Was he bothering you?' She looked down at Michail, as if he had done something wrong.

'No, Katerina. I was merely enjoying my lunch when your fiancé...'

'What?' She looked momentarily confused and then sighed. 'No, no sorry, Michail, we split up. I thought that was obvious. Long story...'

'No need to tell it then,' said Michail, picking up his tray and tablet. Though a peculiar feeling fizzled in the base of his stomach. He hoped the *spanakopita* was not off.

Katerina stared at him. 'He shouldn't treat you this way.'

Michail shuffled on the spot. There were many things he wanted to say in response; namely, that he was not sure he had the authority to decide how a man of Theo's size and popularity treated him. 'It is not a concern,' replied Michail. He was about to ask her to critique his latest assessment of the murder investigation when Katerina marched off towards Theo's table. Michail was unsure whether to follow her, so settled upon staying put, watching intently from a distance. He hoped she would not cause an unnecessary hullabaloo.

'Theo!' she shouted. 'Theo, what do you think you're doing? He almost choked!' The men sat around him jeered at her in a most disrespectful manner. Michail could not help but admire the way she ignored them. 'Answer me right now,' she demanded coolly. 'And apologise to Michail.'

Theo made a show of standing up tall, towering above her. She stepped back, hands on her hips. 'Doesn't suit you, Kat, this mood. Something got you rattled?'

Michail watched as Katerina's face darkened. She looked from Michail to Theo. 'Apologise,' she said. 'We are a team now.'

'I'm aware of that,' replied Theo, suddenly very serious. 'I am happy to be playing for the right side.' He walked over to Michail smoothly. 'I'm interested, Mikras, what are you working on there?'

Michail was certain that Theo was, in fact, not interested at all and gripped his tablet tightly. 'As Ms Sampson has now permitted, I am attempting to forecast the next murder, if there is to be one.'

Theo seized the tablet before Michail could do anything about it. He looked to Katerina, who shrugged. He supposed there was no harm in sharing information with the team; it would be wrong to let personal grievances obstruct a collaborative effort. 'Spiders!' Theo exclaimed, bringing his nose close to the screen.

'Correct.' Michail nodded as Katerina joined him. 'The numerous references to spiders affiliated with the so-called Awakening, coupled with it being a well-known Athena myth, suggest that the next murder will be Arachne... themed. She was turned into a spider by the goddess after a cloth-spinning contest.'

'I know,' Theo snapped.

'Apologies,' said Michail quickly, thinking it best not to reveal his surprise.

'All very detailed,' Theo said, twiddling his fingers over Michail's spreadsheet. 'Seems sensible to me.'

'Stop it, Theo,' Katerina warned.

He laughed. 'Kat! What? No! I'm being serious. Listen, I know I give you a hard time, Mikras.' Theo jabbed his shoulder in what Michail knew should be a friendly gesture but somehow felt threatening. 'But you know it's all fun, right? You know I don't mean it?'

Michail was not sure how to respond so was glad when Katerina held her hand out for his tablet. 'We'll be sure to keep you updated, then,' she said to Theo, retrieving it.

'Great. Like you said, we're a team.' Theo looked as if he was about to rejoin his friends, when he said, 'So what's the problem, then? What's stopping you from following the lead? Anything we can do to help from the ground?'

'Come on...' Katerina began to lead Michail away. However, Michail considered the logical benefit of utilising the human resources available to him. He was also excited that somebody, even if it was Theo, had shown interest in his theory.

'The problem is knowing *when* the murder will take place. I have a few ideas about the location, but I am struggling with pinpointing a time frame.'

Theo nodded; his arms crossed thoughtfully. 'Well, send me your stuff and we can take a look. The more eyes on it the better.'

'Yes,' said Michail, again unsure of how to interact with this new and helpful Theo. 'It is possible to send you the file.'

'Great,' Theo called, already walking away, leaving Katerina and Michail standing bewildered.

The Gorgon Swastika

At 5am the next day, Exarcheia Square was already abuzz with a public breakfast, accommodated by the café on the corner. *Tiropitas* and bread were spread across a communal table upon which the sun was already beginning to beam. The owner of the café leaned against a wall, smoking heavily with one leg bent up. The breakfasters helped themselves to the food, none of them taking more than was polite, Michail noticed. A few of them glanced at him nervously. He sat on the bench opposite them, Katerina at his side, who appeared to be trying to hide her yawns by covering her face in the crook of her arm. Neither he nor Katerina seemed to be viewed as a threat. Neither of them was in uniform, as instructed by Sofia. This was the best time of day to investigate Exarcheia. It was easy to infiltrate these communal breakfasts with little suspicion, so Sofia had said. This way, they might be able to find out where Marius Zamfir had lived, or at least who his friends were. Asking in uniform was not an option: most of these residents hated the police.

Thick trees squatted in the sandy ground at the square's centre, their curling roots decorated with cigarette butts. Michail liked the street lamps here: bulbous globes supported by thin and stretched metal arms that extended out as if in greeting. The square was enlaced with spray paint. The façade of the café by which the breakfasters sat covered in graffiti and slogans. Rudimentary silhouettes of angular figures were placed behind red capital letters reading: *'Fuck the police'*. An impressively realistic (and decapitated) woman was painted above the café's canopy. She held her own head in her hands, facing front on. From her severed head erupted fat and rounded letters: *'Stand up, rise up'*. Figures in police uniforms ran in the shape of swastikas all around her head. *'You can't kill a movement'* read another slogan in pink letters. Image moved into image with lurid, colourful ease. Michail found it difficult to look away from the walls. Once he began, he found he could not stop; one word led into another. Here, ideas grew and evolved from the ramshackle walls, as if thoughts themselves could keep the brickwork from crumbling. 'Stop staring, you look dodgy,' Katerina said, nudging him in the ribs.

The breakfast group's main congregation point seemed to be the middle of the street on the edge of the square. Michail was almost sure that most of the attendees were Afghans, based on the snippets of quick Pashtu he thought he could identify. He had been on patrol in the area only a handful of times before. The orders from his superiors had always seemed somewhat murky. *Maintain order* or *Watch for trouble!* They were simple instructions but never really explained the full story, especially when interlaced with vague and inaccurate comments about *violent foreigners*. Michail had never really got to the bottom of quite what was meant by this term: his superiors should have known to be more specific. Katerina sunk down low into the bench. 'All looks very peaceful to me,' she said quietly, as if reading his mind. Michail nodded, watching the crowd.

'*No pasarán!*' the group chanted. Michail recognised the

phrase, which meant 'They will not pass'. He had heard it before at a squat raid, part of a wider police 'clean-up', when the residents had levelled it at them. It was an exclamation of freedom, originating from the Spanish Civil War. Hearing it again, he was transported back. '*No pasarán! No pasarán!*' they had shouted, their hands bound behind their backs as they were led out of the building and to the police vehicles.

This *Breakfast For Resistance*, as it was known, looked both legal and ordered from where Michail was sitting. He listened to the gentle chatter and laughter, the scrape of plates and the glugging of water as it was shared around. There was certainly no sign of the illegal activity the police associated with the area; again, much as it irked him, he was forced to question whether the Hellenic Police Force had got it right when it came to the people of Exarcheia.

The 'clean-up' had been a success on paper; this was true. Several refugee squats had been disbanded and many drug operations had been uncovered. However, he remembered that the reports had been unclear and messy. Crimes had not been compartmentalised as they should have been. For example, drug use and refugees seemed to have been treated as synonymous issues. This could not be the case: he had heard that many of the refugee squats had strict anti-drug policies. He also noticed how the young, fashionable twenty-somethings, with their expensive haircuts and trainers, were never targeted for their recreational drug-taking.

Michail watched the breakfasters carefully, waiting for an appropriate moment to approach. The breakfasters began to sing a slow, mournful song in a language that was both familiar and alien. The singing stopped and there was a convivial round of applause. Michail joined in, standing to show his appreciation. Katerina followed his lead, clapping enthusiastically. She should be careful not to be so overexuberant, he thought, patting her on the arm.

Pushing himself from the bench, he walked towards the breakfasters who were beginning to pack away, Katerina by his side. The first man who caught Michail's eye was crouched low to the floor. He appeared to be holding a black marker in his hand, with which he was drawing a picture onto the low wall that surrounded the grassy area. Again, he used those swastika-shaped figures to symbolise the police. As Michail drew closer, the man said, '*No Pasarán*.' Michail nodded, brisk and firm, before being beckoned by a second man who was clearing away the breakfast table.

Michail clenched his hands tightly in his pockets and moved towards him. Smiling, the man held out a *tiropita*, presented in the centre of his palm. Michail unfurled a hand and lifted the oblong pie up carefully between two fingertips. 'For me?' he asked.

The man's teeth were yellow. His smile widened and fine lines danced across his face. 'Of course, for you.'

Michail nodded, feeling embarrassed about taking this man's food under such dishonest circumstances.

'For you,' repeated the man. '*No pasarán*.' Katerina accepted the food with a kind smile. She was good at this sort of thing. Michail looked to Katerina and nodded. It was time to broach the topic of Marius. These people were obviously gentle and might know something.

He forced his face into a grin and returned to the man who was drawing on the wall, hoping Katerina would follow. 'Nice drawing,' he said, careful to sound casually interested. He knew the most effective way to elicit information was by tricking the target into thinking they were engaging in an innocent conversation. The man who had given them the *tiropitas* walked over to join them.

'Police.' The artist pointed at the swastika figures. 'The people.' He pointed at an individual stick-figure who was drawn as fleeing from the police.

'Hmmm.' Michail nodded, wiping crumbs from his chin. 'Very effective. Down with the police...' Both men remained silent. 'I-I have seen that pose before.' Michail amalgamated his arms in the shape of the swastika, bending his elbows at right angles and standing on one foot. The men laughed. This was excellent; he was successfully establishing rapport.

'Certainly,' said the artist, pointing at the similar police figures on the façade of the café. 'They are all over Exarcheia.'

'Ah.' Michail smiled, thinking furiously. He relaxed his limbs and resumed his casual pose. 'Obviously, you are fans of art?' He had identified a mutual interest, which was an effective practice in such undercover operations.

The man nodded. 'Of course. Art is free here; so are we.'

Michail took a step back, considering the man's drawing intensely, tilting his head to one side. 'It reminds me of a famous temple,' he said.

'A temple?' The artist frowned, looking towards the drawing. He laughed. 'It is meant to be no temple. It is police.' He raised his arms and mimed shooting a gun. 'Police.'

'Ah, yes,' Michail agreed quickly. 'The police scum, absolutely.' He felt Katerina shift next to him. 'What I meant was the shape you have drawn. You see?' Michail pointed at the figures. 'The limbs, um, of the fascists, fall in right-angle shapes. It reminds me of a sculpture on a temple in Corfu. The pose is a replica, really. You know Medusa?'

The artist's friend – the *tiropita* man – waggled his arms around his head. 'Snake lady!'

'Correct,' said Michail. 'The pose is prevalent in representations of the fleeing Medusa all over Greece. She is shown running just like that, in that very pose.' Michail pointed at the police figures. The men began to speak to one another in bored voices; he was losing their attention. Michail shrugged, laughing. 'Medusa in Exarcheia, who would have thought?'

They shrugged, exchanging a look with one another. Michail calculated that it was his cue to leave; the signals were obvious, but he was struggling to uproot himself from the spot. There was more to uncover here – he was sure of it. Katerina shifted impatiently next to him, no doubt wondering where he was going with this line of enquiry. Perhaps it was worth being more transparent. He smiled again, looking up to the sky. 'Crazy rumours. You heard about the murder near the Plaka? You know what some people are saying?' Michail was careful to keep his voice low. His palms began to sweat. He widened his smile. 'Crazy, eh?'

There was a slightly longer pause than what seemed usual. Michail breathed out. 'What people believe...'

The men stood. They were not smiling. The artist twiddled the black marker between his fingers. Like a snake. Michail cleared his throat. He was suddenly very aware of the shuttered buildings surrounding them, the alien graffiti looming like a colourful maze. He retreated, a quick step back, willing his hands to stop trembling. He heard Katerina take a sharp breath. The men's eyes were dark, quizzical. He should not be afraid. An afraid police officer was an ineffective one.

The artist broke the silence. 'The murdered man?'

Michail coughed, attempting to loosen his throat. 'Ah, you heard?'

'Who didn't?' The artist took a step towards Michail, his eyes burning.

'Ha!' Michail took another step back. 'There you go! The news is everywhere!' His voice sounded unusually high-pitched.

The artist squinted at Michail. 'You knew him?'

'No,' Michail replied too quickly. He looked at his feet, gathering himself. 'You?'

The *tiropita* man prowled closer, cocking his head. 'Where are you from? I have not seen you around here before.'

Michail reminded himself of how it was possible to control the biological mechanics of his body. He instructed his neck to straighten, ordered his eyes to meet the men's.

Katerina jumped in. 'We're local, just interested, that's all. Anyway, *no pasarán*. It is time for us...'

They began to back away. Michail cried out as he stumbled on a twig, lurching backwards in three flailing leaps. Katerina managed to catch him and began tugging him away from the square. A small crowd had by now gathered around them. Michail noticed the owner of the café observe the scene, put out his cigarette and return inside. The sound of bolts closing tinkered through the square. Michail laughed, as any normal human might after an embarrassing fall. 'Excuse me! Good day...'

Katerina joined in. 'Clumsy fool...' she said, her eyes on the circle of people surrounding them.

Michail felt a hand on his shoulder. He noted that Katerina positioned herself out of the way. She had not yet reached for her gun, but she had a clear shot. Shooting was an absolute last resort. Michail held her gaze, knowing that she understood. The hand resting on his shoulder was stained with black ink. Michail turned towards the hand, meeting the face of the artist. Up close, he looked young. His beard was thick and glorious, full of lustre. Michail placed a hand on his. 'Ah, thank you. Just a little stumble, that's all.'

The artist accepted the gesture. 'We did not mean to frighten you.' Then, he nodded slowly and said, 'There is a shrine.' He pointed to a narrow street running off the square. 'If you are interested... then you can go there.'

Michail bowed his head, a deep sign of thanks. The artist squeezed his hand. The hold was harsh and lingering; fingernails pressed against Michail's skin. He jerked his head up, but the artist held him there, and winked slowly. Michail sensed the other breakfasters gathering, nudging. Despite Michail's attempt to remain casual, he felt his eyes widen. Finally, the artist released his hand and stepped back. 'Be careful, both you and your friend,' he said.

The narrow street was also decorated by colourful painted shutters. The paintings, whether they were crude or skilled, all sang the same unanimous song. The oversized boot kicking in the face of a fascist. The larger-than-life ragged man sleeping on his side, one shrewd eye open and glaring; the watchful owl whose wings were inscribed with the word *'freedom'*. *We will not be defeated. We will not surrender without a fight.* Michail had never considered himself the enemy. He did what he was told; trusted that he worked for the good of Athens. But this art did not play into his narrative of himself, nor of the police. This art suggested he was a part of the oppression, upset, unrest. His stomach lowed deeply. He was aware of his fists tapping the side of his thighs. He closed his eyes and counted, slowly.

'That went well,' Katerina said. Michail was unsure whether she was being serious or not.

'Yes,' he replied. 'An illuminating conversation.'

'The Medusa pose?'

'Correct. They are using the swastika shape to symbolise the police, I know. But...'

'There could be a link between Medusa and the snake graffiti from yesterday? Because of the snakes in her hair?'

Michail was impressed. 'Exactly! Not to mention the

connection with Athena: she was the one who helped Perseus kill the gorgon Medusa. It is another reference to an Athena myth.'

'And there's Laurence-Sinclair's snake ring,' Katerina added, gravely. They nodded in unison. Michail turned to observe her profile. She wore a concentrated expression, her brow creased with thought. A quiet calm hummed through his limbs. It was nice to have his partner at his side. It was nice that she took him seriously.

The artist had been right: the shrine was obvious. About five-hundred metres along the street, on a doorstep leading to a pull-across red metal door, was a photograph. His sandy hair, blue eyes and perfect nose were unmistakable. The symmetry of the face was marred somewhat by a tiny crookedness of his smile, but it was him. *Forever Marius* read a makeshift wooden plaque, the words stencilled out and white against a black background. There were a few dead flowers scattered about, and letters, lots of letters. Michail sat on the step and picked through them. *Always in our hearts, Marius, sleep well. Beautiful boy, now forever beautiful. The good die young. Shine on, Marius.*

As the artist in the square had indicated, spray-painted swastika-shaped figures decorated the concrete of the steps. Michail placed his hand over them. The snake-haired gorgon, Perseus the gorgon-slayer, aided by Athena. Athena, goddess of the city, goddess of the crimes. The running gorgon. The fascist police. The ring. The shrine. For Michail, it felt like falling at a terminal velocity. Every time he tried to form a theory, it was as if it slipped his mind. The dots were not yet aligning. But he had found Marius, at least. And it looked like there were those who knew him well enough to celebrate his life. That thought brought tears to Michail's tired eyes.

Katerina placed a hand over her crucifix necklace and

Michail saw her lips move in quick, silent words. As futile as it was, he suspected she was praying. However, despite his apathy towards religion, there was something respectful about the way she made time for this dead stranger. Finishing with a swift 'Amen,' Katerina opened her eyes.

'Good,' Michail said, nodding towards the red door.

A single doorbell lay to the left of the red metal. Michail pressed it three times: short, sharp, and purposeful. He heard muffled shouts through the metal. Then some shuffling, the scuttling of shoes against cranky staircases. It seemed the household was awake. Or, at least, expecting to be woken. Michail was not an advocate of using the threat of weapons as force, preferring the art of persuasive conversation; however, he reached for his right thigh instinctively.

Katerina placed a hand on his arm. 'Last resort,' she reminded him.

Bolts sounded on the other side of the door. Michail straightened himself up. There was a short pause as the person behind the door, Michail assumed, inspected them through the peephole. Michail smiled in order to seem relaxed and at ease. The door did not slide across its tracks easily. It screeched loudly as two hands, knuckles white, fingernails purple, dragged it back, grunting and groaning. A man was revealed behind the door, similar in age to Marius, with thick, curly dark hair, a blue bandana hung loosely around his neck. He wore a tight vest-top and was decorated in various pieces of silver, including a chunky necklace that pressed heavily against his collarbone. He was, Michail suspected, what would be described as 'cool' or whatever word was being used these days.

'Yes?' the man said, in an accent that sounded initially Italian. 'What do you want?'

The man squinted searchingly at Michail, and then at

Katerina, sniffed heavily and wiped his nose against his forearm like a cat.

Michail cleared his throat. 'The shrine.' He stepped to one side and gestured to it. 'For Marius. We have some questions.' Michail paused, considering how to proceed. He added, 'Was he a friend of yours?'

The man shuffled towards Michail, stepping through the threshold of the door. The sunlight seemed to bother him, causing pimples to erupt over his slim arms. He folded them close over his chest. 'Who wants to know?' he asked.

Michail's badge sat heavy in his wallet. He lifted his chin, meeting the man's eye, remembering his training. He must seem unperturbed: confident and natural. There was no reason for them to be suspected as anyone other than friends of Marius.

'Katerina,' Katerina replied, holding out a steady hand. 'And my brother Michail. We knew Marius, quite a while ago now.'

The man did not budge. 'You are Greek,' he said.

'Yes.' Michail nodded. 'From Athens.'

'How did you know Marius?'

Michail was aware that he must avoid exhibiting the signs of lying. However, he could not seem to regulate his heart rate and was nervous of his pupils dilating. He breathed through pursed lips, hoping the gesture would be interpreted as some form of grief. At least he knew what to say. Katerina and he had practised it many times over. It was a sensible story; the *Hellenakratia* was the only lead they had. 'We were close,' he said, forging a soft smile. 'Marius and I were very close.'

'I am here for moral support,' Katerina chimed, giving Michail a sympathetic pat on the shoulder.

The man narrowed his eyes but took a step to the side, shrugging. 'Then come in,' he said. Close to Italian, but not quite, Michail thought. The vowels were too open for Italian; perhaps he was Montenegrin? They ascended the steps and entered a wide corridor lined with empty plant pots. The walls were decorated with graffiti resembling the art outside the house. Michail noted the running swastika made more appearances, as well as a large, coiled snake, which wrapped around the grainy walls towards a metal staircase.

'Do you mind? I am sorry.' Katerina grabbed her phone from her bag. 'I'm into art and...' She gestured at the snake on the wall, flicking her hair over her shoulder. 'I'd love to capture it.' Michail held his breath; she was being too pushy. It was not necessary to have a photograph.

However, the man nodded, pushing his bottom lip out. 'Knock yourself out.' Then, he said to Michail, 'Up there, to the kitchen.' The man pointed past the snake. 'I am Risto, by the way.'

Michail peered up the staircase and followed the snake's elongated head, which stretched up the wall elaborately as Katerina snapped away. Its tongue stretched out garishly, licking the brickwork. They emerged in a long warehouse kitchen without any windows, lit only by a long fluorescent light. A workman's bench, complete with rusted nails and a chipped finish, stretched almost the whole length of the room, with mismatched plastic chairs and stools pushed underneath it. A dull drip sounded erratically from a steel sink. The air was sweet with the smell of vegetables nearing rot and fresh herbs planted on the workspace. Michail wondered how they survived without sufficient natural light. Risto slunk past, his feet padding against the stone floor, a toe ring scratching against the surface. Michail took a seat at the table, asking, 'Were you a friend of his?'

Risto laughed, rubbing his eyes, which Michail noted were tinged with red around the edges. 'Yes, we were friends. It is easy to make friends here.' He looked to the ceiling. 'Never much privacy.'

Michail nodded, observing the space. It seemed like one of the standard shared warehouses in the area. By the looks of the walls, a group of artists lived here. They were covered in intricate murals. These looked to be created out of enjoyment, love, rather than any political motivation. A thick jungle of trees was painted on the far side of the room, with different animals camouflaged in clever ways. The face of a monkey was blended into the bark of a tree. Michail was pleased to see that Katerina kept in character as an art lover, running her hand over the mural as if enraptured. As he looked more closely, he began to see other objects hidden in the foliage: a plastic mobile phone cover served as a boat for ants on the river. A water bottle hung like a banana from a tree. 'Did you paint this?' he asked Risto.

'A collaboration.' Risto leaned back, his hands stretched behind his head. 'Marius too. He did a lot of it.'

'It's wonderful,' said Katerina, raising her phone again.

Risto smiled, evidently flattered. 'Thanks.'

Michail looked at his hands, trying to think of how to move the conversation forward. Surely art was the obvious topic? It was a beautiful piece. The amount of skill present in the execution was evident: these were talented professionals. Yet the Hellenic Police would rather treat them as criminals. And for what reason? It occurred to Michail that if these people had been treated with respect, then they would have trusted the police and reported Marius as missing on the day of his murder. He would have been identified immediately. Time would not have been wasted.

'Take your time.' Risto laid a supportive hand on Michail's wrist, although Michail noted his eyes lingered on Katerina's back.

He reminded himself of his cover story and did his best to tearfully exclaim, 'How could this have happened?'

Risto's face darkened. 'Those in power don't care for people like us. We are...' He searched for the word, looking about him until his eyes rested on the open bin. 'Trash. Waste.'

Michail remained hunched over, his face in his hands. 'You know who did this to him? I read that it was brutal. Who would do such a thing to Marius?'

The sound of people moving in the rooms upstairs distracted Risto. He stood up and filled the kettle on the side of the counter. 'Have you had breakfast?'

'Yes, thank you,' Michail said carefully, thinking how best to revert Risto's attention. 'It was a horrific thing to do.'

Risto placed the kettle back down and turned towards Michail. He ran his fingers through his hair, breaking up the curls to form a soft bed of waves. He narrowed his eyes again. 'Yes. Awful.'

There was more movement from upstairs. Chairs scraping, clatters, the sound of locks being opened and closed. 'They'll be down soon,' Risto said.

Katerina joined Michail at the worktop, leaning over the counter casually. She looked back at the mural. 'Are you all artists here?'

'Yes, most of us. We all create.' Risto stirred a large pot of coffee. He dipped a finger into the steaming water and tasted it. 'Hot!' He laughed. 'So, when did you date Marius?' He turned to Michail. 'I have never met you.'

'A while ago,' Michail replied. 'No, I don't think we met. I saw his name in the paper and... I don't know, I wanted to pay my respects, I suppose.' He gulped a mouthful of air in an attempt to relax his vocal cords. His words must not come across as contrived.

'It has been a difficult couple of days for us,' Risto replied, sliding over a cup of black coffee to Michail. 'We are in shock, as you can imagine.'

'My brother too,' Katerina said.

'Of course.' At that moment, three more housemates entered the kitchen. A woman and two men. They carried themselves with the same style as Risto, a lackadaisical aesthetic that Michail was sure must take longer to perfect than it looked. His eyes were immediately drawn to a tattoo on the smaller man's arm. He wore a loose-fitting linen shirt, buttoned down to his navel, sleeves pushed up. A snake tattoo coiled around his left elbow and his neck, the head resting on the top of his close-shaven head. The fangs hung low past his eyebrows; the slitted eyes rested on his forehead. He looked as if he was shedding skin: half snake, half man.

They jostled about, finding cups and plates and eventually sat at the table. 'Friends of Marius,' Risto said, though they did not seem in the least bit interested. Through mouthfuls of toast, they mumbled half-hearted greetings. Michail pushed his chair back, thinking that their time was up. Questioning so many people at once would arouse suspicion.

'You're not staying?' Risto asked, surprised.

'It's, ah, it's strange being here... more difficult than I thought...' Katerina stood, following Michail's lead.

'Stay,' said the man with the snake tattoo. 'You want to talk about Marius? We're the people to speak with.' He seemed confrontational, Michail noted that the top of his chest was flushed and pink. Michail remained seated. Katerina straightened her back.

Michail spoke carefully. 'I did not mean to offend–'

'You didn't,' Risto interrupted, shooting a look at his housemate. 'Mani is just upset. We all loved Marius.' The last sentence was directed at Mani, who took a long gulp of coffee.

Michail seized the change in tone. 'The papers said Marius was working as an escort.' He felt Katerina tense beside him. He agreed: the question sounded forced. It would be prudent to leave as soon as they could.

Risto blew through his lips and exclaimed something in his mother tongue. 'Sorry – no, it's typical no? Suits them to label him a prostitute, a criminal. The city's pollution.'

Michail nodded in agreement. 'Fascist press.'

'Fascist police,' said Risto, holding Michail in a hard stare. 'And there are idiots who believe such things.'

'Only idiotic until proven true,' Mani whispered, sneering at Risto. Risto opened his mouth as if to say something, but instead turned away from his friend.

Michail watched them carefully. 'I-I can't help wondering who would do such a thing, though. Marius was gentle. I can't imagine how he would have got caught up in anything dangerous.'

A silence descended upon the kitchen. Michail remained quiet as Mani watched the others with an intense stare. Since they were friends, it should have been the look of a lion protecting its pride. However, Mani glared at them hungrily. The others bit their lips and busied themselves with menial tasks.

'We know no more than you about that,' Mani said.

'Of course,' Michail replied, standing. This time, Katerina was ahead of him, paving their way to the exit hurriedly. 'I thank you for your time...'

There was a bang on the metal door from downstairs. Mani swore loudly and checked his phone. His eyes widened. 'He's early. You must leave now.'

'Mani, we said no more–' Risto began.

'He's here, what do you want me to do?' Mani snapped, his eyes darting about the kitchen. Michail detected an excitement in the man's face. 'It's my turn.'

'Your turn...?' Michail began to ask before being pushed out of the way by one of the women who were piling up the plates, tossing away unfinished pieces of toast and gulping their coffee in what seemed like a brisk panic.

'It's no problem,' said Katerina. 'We were going anyway.'

'Ignore him,' hissed Risto, as the banging on the door became more urgent. 'I don't trust...'

Mani laughed, almost hysterical, but did not reply. Michail backed away from the commotion towards Katerina, feeling uneasy. 'We will be leaving then.'

'Yes, I am sorry, Michail. It is best,' Risto said, taking Michail by the arm and leading him to the steel staircase.

'Get them out of here!' Mani said. Michail took a final look at the kitchen, taking in the scene, before he hurried down the stairs, his feet clanging against the metal.

'Send him up!' Mani yelled from the kitchen in response to more thunderous banging on the door. Michail glanced at Risto, who looked irate.

When they reached the hallway, Risto grabbed Michail's arm and pulled him close. 'Listen,' he whispered, his eyes wide. 'You are police?'

Katerina was already halfway down the corridor. Michail heard her reach for her gun, ready to protect them.

'What? No–' Michail spluttered.

'Shut up.' Risto shoved a finger against his lips. 'You are, I noticed from the way you carry yourself, and your hair... I've seen enough of you around here.' He glanced at Katerina. 'Put it away, I'm not going to hurt him.'

Michail began to shake. Risto loosened his grip. 'I won't harm you. Listen, please. Marius was part of some group, deep into it, the same as Mani.'

'The Awakening?' Katerina stepped forward.

'I don't know.' There was another bang on the door, Mani shouted again from the kitchen. Risto whispered rapidly, 'They started to meet here, frequently. It is like a weird club, or something. He brings them here, mostly foreigners, refugees. I hear them through the door. It sounds fine, like just any other gathering, but then...'

'What?' Michail was breathless.

'People started to disappear; Marius wasn't the first.' Risto pointed at the door. 'Him. That's who Marius left with the night he was killed. He organises the gatherings. He tried to involve me, but... I don't trust him.'

Michail stared at Risto. 'We need to question you further; we need more information.'

Heavy footsteps sounded from the top of the stairs. 'Let him in, Risto!'

'Go.' Risto moved away from Michail. 'You will see him now, pretend like you don't notice him. But... you're police, remember his face or something. Tell someone. I'm afraid for Mani.'

Mani appeared at the bottom of the stairs. 'What's this, a lovers' meeting?' He barged past the two of them, pushed Katerina to one side and tugged at the door-handle with both hands, throwing his body weight backwards to slide it open. Michail watched expectantly, his heart thudding impossibly inside his ribs, eyes fixed, afraid to blink, afraid to miss a single detail.

Behind the door stood Laurence-Sinclair.

There was a moment of absolute silence, or at least, that is what Michail experienced. Laurence-Sinclair's grey-blue eyes registered him, drank him in as if counting each pore on his face for an excruciating, long second. Then Michail experienced an electric jolt through his body. And another. Adrenaline. Nature's way of spurring him into action.

Michail lurched forwards, his arms extended out before him. 'Stop!'

'Michail!' Katerina's voice sounded behind him. Laurence-

Sinclair backed down the steps, kicking over the offerings to Marius on the floor. Michail heard a scuffle behind him, someone shouting, 'Run!' He did not need telling. Laurence-Sinclair was already on the street, his old legs pumping on the dusty ground.

'Stop!' Michail shouted again, following him. 'Laurence-Sinclair!'

'Police!' Laurence-Sinclair shouted over his shoulder. His voice heaved as he ran. 'Undercover police! Help me!'

As if he had uttered a spell, angry bodies appeared out of the shutters. Michail did not deter his gaze from Laurence-Sinclair, who was running with difficulty, but also with surprising speed, towards the square. Screams and shouts arose in cacophony throughout the narrow street. Michail belted forwards, his arms set into an efficient sprinting position as Laurence-Sinclair hurled himself into the square's centre. Michail pursued him, annoyed that the trees provided Laurence-Sinclair with a place to hide. He scanned the green area, sure that Laurence-Sinclair would be recuperating nearby.

'Police!' he heard Laurence-Sinclair shout again from a clump of dense bushes. 'Undercover – they are here!'

Furious voices blared out in reply and hostile faces appeared in the opening. Michail froze. A sinking dread fused him to the spot. He was surrounded. Laurence-Sinclair had all the backup he needed here. He had to find him before he escaped again. A rustle caught his attention, but before Michail could react, Laurence-Sinclair's heaving body catapulted out of the bushes, bundling past him, almost knocking Michail off his feet. Catching his breath, Michail swung around shouting, 'Stop! Stop that man!' Of course, no one did.

Michail took a deep breath and propelled himself forwards for another chase. However, it seemed the street had suddenly become unusually crowded. People milled about aimlessly, stepping in Michail's way, pushing past him rudely.

'Excuse me...' Michail cried weakly. But it was no use; as he attempted to push through the barrier of people, he realised they were protecting Laurence-Sinclair. 'No,' Michail protested. 'You don't understand. He's–'

'Fascist police!' one woman called. Her words were echoed around the square. Michail hung his head, listening to the cries. '*No pasarán! No pasarán!*' they repeated, ensuring that Michail could not follow Laurence-Sinclair into the back streets. Michail shook his head as Katerina caught up with him.

'Where is he?' she asked. 'Did you get him?'

'No,' Michail replied miserably, casting a dark look at the determined blockade of faces. 'He has escaped again.'

Katerina observed the human barrier, which had now begun to disperse. She raised her eyebrows. 'If they knew who they had just helped to escape...'

Michail nodded, again unable to shake the feeling that if the police had behaved differently in the past, then Laurence-Sinclair would not have escaped so easily for a second time. As he began to catch his breath, Risto ran towards them. He seemed alarmed, his face quivering and twitching.

'Is everything all right?' Katerina asked, leading the three of them to a less public position.

'No,' Risto replied.

Michail blew out of his mouth deeply and closed his eyes. He knew what Risto would say before he said it. His housemate Mani had seemed impatient, jumpy. He had been expecting Laurence-Sinclair. If it had not all happened so quickly, then maybe he and Katerina could have stopped him.

'Mani has gone too?' Michail asked, cautiously scanning the square, though he knew it was pointless. Michail observed Risto, who looked as if he were about to break. Understandable: friends were precious, so everyone led him to believe.

Risto nodded, his eyes wide. 'Yes, Mani. With *him*, I'm sure. It is the same as Marius. Oh God!' Risto stiffened his arms and clenched his fists as if he wanted to punch someone. 'Please,' he said, his dark eyes beginning to swim. 'You must find him. I am afraid that...'

'You believe him to be in danger?' It was a sensible assessment. Michail felt his own arms stiffen at the thought of another victim: *one point six one eight. One point six one eight. One point six one eight.* Still, chaos reigned. He ran through the facts: Mani had been expecting Laurence-Sinclair, he had been eager to see him, to let him in. Michail suddenly grabbed Risto by the shoulders.

'Michail!'

'No, Katerina, this is of the highest importance. Tears will have to wait.' He looked at Risto, waiting for him to calm down. 'I am sorry for being direct, Risto, however, if we are to find your friend then we must act quickly. You said Marius, like Mani, began behaving strangely before he left with Laurence-Sinclair. How so?'

Risto shook his head, grinding his back teeth. 'I don't know... it was like he was obsessed. He started saying strange things like...'

'Like what?' Michail tried his best not to grow annoyed, but this man should have spoken to the Special Violent Crime Squad a long time ago. He had withheld essential information and hindered the investigation.

Risto grasped his chin: at least he was attempting to be rational. 'He started saying that we'd got it all wrong–'

'Who?'

'Us, all of us.' Risto gestured around the square, where people had begun to move on. 'The Exarcheia residents, us: the artists, the refugees, the activists, we're a family. We were, until...' Michail tensed as Risto's eyes grew dry with fury.

'The raids?' Michail offered, feeling his face grow hot.

Risto nodded. 'The attacks,' he replied.

Michail shifted uncomfortably. But this was not the time for apologies, nor for political debate. In any case, he did not speak for the whole of the police force. His imperative was to gather as much information as possible, without scaring Risto into silence. 'What did Marius think you had wrong?'

'Same thing as Mani,' said Risto. 'That the police were, *enlightened* – that was the word, enlightened. Imagine saying that, after all you've done to us.' Michail crossed his arms defensively. 'He said Laurence-Sinclair had another way; a way free from pain. They said that our way of life only caused trouble. Marius wanted to submit to a greater, purer cause. That's what he said. Mani started to use the same phrases. His whole way of thinking changed!' Risto began to pace about the square. 'I should have stopped him!'

Michail concurred, 'Correct, that would have been useful–'

'Michail!' Katerina interrupted.

Risto stopped still, glaring at Michail. 'I knew Laurence-Sinclair was trouble, even when he first started sniffing about. Giving out money, offering odd jobs here and there. He brought pills into the house, a man of his age!'

'He never showed you any interest?' Katerina stepped forward.

'Of course.' Risto laughed darkly. 'I was just his type.'

'His type?'

'Young, poor and foreign,' Risto spat.

Katerina pressed on with impressive vigour. 'You weren't interested in what... he had to say?'

'I was tempted by the money, who wouldn't be? But no, there was something off about him. He was always rubbing this snake ring he wore, getting people to paint snakes around the house. That's weird, right? He was obsessed with the things. You saw Mani? That monstrosity of a tattoo? He was talked into it by *him*. The doctor – Laurence-Sinclair – spoke about reclaiming the real meaning of the snake, whatever that meant.' Risto sighed, shrugging. 'He had his favourites, and I wasn't one of them. This is just what I picked up. He and his friend...'

'His friend?' Michail almost shouted the question.

'Yes, he sometimes brought along another man.' Risto hesitated as Michail's mouth twitched. 'He didn't look like he was from around here. He was a thug, if you ask me. No idea what he had to do with anything. He was out of place here, that's for sure.'

'What did this man look like?' Michail's heart beat hard and steady.

Risto held up his hands. 'I never saw him up close. It was always night-time and I made a point of leaving the house whenever Laurence-Sinclair was there. Dark hair, tallish...'

'Anything more useful or specific?' Michail demanded.

Risto's eyes widened. Katerina stepped forwards. 'Can you give us anything to go on?' she asked in a soft voice. 'We just want to help.'

Risto shook his head, his eyes welling with tears once more.

'Don't worry,' Katerina said. 'But if you think of anything, will you let us know?'

Risto nodded, his eyes panning searchingly between the two of them. 'Promise me you will find Mani?'

Miasma

Sofia had never enjoyed meetings with police director Basil. He treated each one like some sort of extravagant date, a pleasure he did not reserve for the rest of his staff. Yiorgos, however, had been very keen to join their meeting.

'And what will you tell him?' Sofia had quipped wryly. 'That you have completed, what, three successful press conferences? And that whilst you have been preening yourself in preparation, you have made no progress at all with the multiple murder case.'

Yiorgos had seemed hurt, which was exactly how he always seemed when he wanted to get his own way. But Sofia was certainly not that gullible. She did not feel compelled to massage a grown man's ego. Yiorgos certainly didn't go to the trouble of massaging hers. 'I just thought you might want moral support,' he had said. 'Another voice in the room.'

She had promptly reminded him that she could handle herself. However, as she waited alone in the restaurant, fiddling with the edges of the linen tablecloth, she considered that it may have been judicious to bring Yiorgos along. It was unfortunate, but, much as she had appreciated Michail and Katerina's efforts, they had lost Laurence-Sinclair yet again. On top of this, another young man named Mani was also presumed missing, likely to have followed Laurence-Sinclair into considerable danger. The whole thing, to use the technical term, was a total mess. Yiorgos would have been a good balancing weight: a levelling distraction. She shook the thoughts from her head, smacking her lips to make sure they were full and ready for delicate conversation.

She heard Basil before she saw him. 'Thank you, thank you,' he said. Sofia had never found peace with his unusually high tone. It was the voice of a yapping animal, she often thought, rather than of a man. He approached their table, walking as he always did, in powerful steps, a purposeful swing of the midriff, as his fists, aimed towards her, punched through the air. Good grief.

'Sampson!' he shouted, kissing her on both cheeks. 'Sampson!'

'Basil,' she said, standing. She gestured to the other side of the table. 'Please.'

He moved around the table as if doing some sort of dance, drumming the surface with his hands. So, he was excited. 'What have you got for me then?' The waiter brought him over a large glass of red wine, and he slurped it through his teeth. 'Excellent, excellent. Sofia, tell me. This case is bigger than anything I can remember.' He placed both hands on the table, tapping them eagerly.

Sofia sipped her water and thought about all of the things that prevented her from believing this buffoon was actually her boss. She sighed and reached into her bag for her notes. There was a lot to cover and it would be better to get it over and done with.

Basil enjoyed another gulp of wine. 'I've ordered ahead for us,' he said. 'Tasting menu. Only the best for Sampson.'

Her heart sank. They would be here for hours. She smiled primly. 'Thank you. So, the case–'

'Ah!' he interrupted. 'Been hearing a lot about it, all over the press, everywhere.' He lowered his voice, wiggling his eyebrows. 'There are those who say these are not entirely tragic occurrences.'

Sofia, who had been organising her notes, allowed a tingle to climb up her spine and settle at the base of her neck. Looking at her papers she responded in a voice that she meant to sound playful, but unfortunately sounded furious, 'The death of a child? That is not tragic?'

'Oh!' He guffawed into his wine glass, blowing air through his nose. 'Oh that, that, of course is...'

'But not the murder of Marius Zamfir,' she finished flatly, now watching him carefully as she drew her nails over the ring-bound notes. Basil held her in silence for a moment. She watched those grey eyes harden beneath the jocular demeanour. Tilting her head to one side, she invited him to respond. His cheeks dropped slightly, giving the impression of a thinner, more sullen face.

'You know what I mean, Sofia. He was not, at least he was not...'

'Greek?' She arched an eyebrow. 'I thought the force had moved on from such opinions.'

Basil sat back in his chair; his round belly proudly presented. Placing his hands over his midriff, he observed her for a few moments. She held his gaze, happy to entertain him, if that's what he wanted. Eventually, he said, 'I hope I have not misrepresented myself.'

Sofia pursed her lips. He continued, 'I would not want you

– Sofia Sampson of the Special Violent Crime Squad – to think that I am aligned with anything, anything... noxious.'

'Noxious?' She refilled her water glass, enjoying the glugging sound it made coming out of the carafe. She would let him explain himself. It was important to let people have their say, their whole say, she had learned this many a time before. She peered at him intently. He shifted in his chair; she supposed it must be difficult to get comfortable with such a poor physique.

'Sofia.' He settled in his chair, leaning forward with his elbows on the table. 'Considering your... history... I can see why you would be, shall we say, hyper-aware of certain sensibilities.'

'I would have thought a hyper-awareness of extremism would be a good trait to have in my role,' she clipped. 'Continue.' Anger flashed in Basil's eyes. She could tell she had overstepped the mark. Despite her feelings, she knew that provoking him was neither sensible nor useful. 'I apologise, Basil, I mean to say I am interested in what you mean.'

The first course arrived as some sort of raw, fishy foam. Sofia sniffed it and pushed her plate to one side. Its timing, however, distracted Basil. When he had finished slurping his last mouthful, he resumed, 'Nobody has forgotten, Sofia. It was a huge risk, a woman in your position, to take on the establishment those few years ago. The names you published, many were grateful...' He did not need to complete his sentence; she knew how it ended: many were not. She remembered the looks. She remembered the retorts. They had tempered over the years, but back then they had been vicious. 'Witch!' they had called her. 'Lying bitch! Take your barks elsewhere! Woof woof!'

Sometimes, she thought it had been worth it. She had exposed corruption, drawn attention to the extremism that existed in the force. She had wanted to pave the way for a better future. She wanted young officers to benefit from working freely, with a pure, just cause. But she had not caught everyone. How could she have? As a result, she had inflamed the remaining embers. They had nothing on her, of course, which meant she had kept her position. But she was rendered unapproachable. Marked. This, she could live with. What she could not live with were the unsolved murders, the unnamed bodies that lay broken and forgotten. So perhaps it was not the worthy act she imagined it to be. As long as corruption existed in the force, justice would not be served.

Basil was still talking. 'You must understand that there are those who do not see everything as black and white. Things are not always wholly right, or wholly wrong. There are decisions to be made, Sofia. For all of us.' He reached across the table to grab a napkin and wiped his brow. He was nervous about something. She hoped it was her. 'You arrived with a job to do; I get it. But you must start seeing how we do things here...'

'Decisions?' She poured him a glass of water and slid it across the table. 'For us, the only decision is to serve the people, to maintain safety on the streets, surely?'

'If it were so simple...'

'It is. To me. I would hope the same is true of you.'

He took a deep breath and lowered his brow. 'Times are forever changing, you know this. We have said it before. What was right and true centuries, decades, years ago, even, is not right and true now. Our country emerges from – is still existing in – extreme financial strife. We Greeks, we get things done. We always have; we are skilled! This is our national pride. We pass skill after skill down through the generations. The fear is we become diluted. The fear is we weaken ourselves. And for what? In the name of liberalism? What's that? And so some dare to ask the question: what can we do? There are people suffering, Sofia. And there are some, you will be aware, who attribute their suffering to people like Marius. We can't support ourselves, let alone foreigners – *not* my words. But there is some truth to them, surely you can see that?'

Sofia was very still. The air-conditioning blew tiny particles of dust through an oblong of yellow light which, from where she was sitting, sliced through Basil's chubby face. 'This is a murder investigation, Basil.'

He breathed and the particles erupted in a volcanic dance around his jowls. 'I think you will find it is much more than that.' Then, before letting her reply he added rapidly, 'And we have met the challenge by expanding your team's human resources.'

Sofia narrowed her eyes. 'Yes. I'm grateful for the extra... strength in numbers.'

'Ah,' he said. 'Good, good.'

She stood, ready to leave. 'Apologies, as you will imagine, time is of the essence.'

'Hmm.' Basil gurgled the wine in his throat, taking his time. 'Best be off then, Sampson.' She nodded and made for the door. 'Oh wait,' Basil said, blocking her with his arm. Sofia looked down at him. He was a pathetic excuse for a man, his puckered face mooned up at her. 'Here.' He handed her an expensive-looking envelope.

'What's this?'

'An invitation to the *Hellenakratia's* annual gala. Christos wanted to give it to you personally, but...' Basil smirked.

'Why would I want to attend that?'

'You're the head of the Special Violent Crime Squad, Sofia. The crème de la crème of society will be attending. Christos is a good person to, well, get back on side.'

She snatched the envelope, shaking her head. 'He's done nothing to deserve my attention.'

'I don't know, he cares deeply about our citizens. I would

have thought that common ground.' His eyes darkened. 'You will go. It's time to make amends.'

Sofia ground her teeth and left without another word. It was only when she was outside that she noticed the envelope was sealed with the stamp of an axe and a snake.

The Active Medium

oira had made herself comfortable, once again, on Michail's sofa. It had been a long day, especially considering the early start. When he and Katerina had returned to headquarters, Theo had been waiting for them. It seemed that Theo and his constables had spent the morning scouring social media and had noticed a new hashtag emerging alongside the spider posts. It appeared to provide a clue as to when the next murder would happen. Michail found it difficult not to be delighted at Theo's support: perhaps this was a sign of a new beginning? This #ThursdayBites was certainly illuminating and pressing, today being Tuesday. Sofia had agreed to meet Michail tomorrow to discuss it.

On top of this, Michail had experienced a brain wave whilst looking at the photographs Katerina had taken of the snakes in Exarcheia: he had a qualified interpreter of art living above him! Thus, he had followed all the required social protocol with the aim of inviting Moira to his apartment for an enthusiastic session of brain-picking. A bottle of wine was placed on his coffee table, along with some *baklava*. Then, he had knocked on her door and in his most alluring voice invited her down for the evening.

'Goodness, is everything all right, young man? You seem strained.'

It was not the response he had expected, but he dealt with it admirably, immediately switching tack and demanding her expertise as a matter of national security. She had chuckled (which, again, was not the expected response) but she followed him down the stairs. And so the first stage of his mission was a success.

The next hurdle was ensuring that Moira did not indulge in too much wine before she had proven herself useful. Therefore, Michail took it upon himself to be the symposiarch for the evening, pouring her a small measure every time she said something of note. So far, the plan seemed to be running smoothly: this old woman liked to talk.

'You know,' she said, 'I visited Athens as a youngster, well, young compared to how old I am now.'

'Go on...' Michail replied, the bottle of wine held firmly in his hand.

She looked at him carefully and smiled. 'I was about your age and my husband, well, he was here too.'

'I did not realise you had a husband,' said Michail.

'I don't, not anymore,' Moira replied. 'Don't look so sad, Michail! It happens. We had a good life. He was a classicist too, that's how we met. He was one of my students at the university...'

Michail's hand tightened around the neck of the bottle as he thought about her flagrant abuse of power as a lecturer.

'Oh, Michail! No need to look so shocked. He was an adult when we met, I was a mere handful of years his senior *and* it was the seventies.'

'Did you… see some nice art on your visit?' Michail asked. It sounded forced even to him.

Moira held out her glass. 'I'll be needing more if you want specifics. Come then! What is it you want to know? You mentioned my expertise.'

Michail relented. Whilst he poured her another glass, he explained, 'Obviously, I will not be sharing any specifics of the case.'

'Of course not.' She nodded, smirking.

'This said, there have been a number of… events in the investigation so far that have led me to believe that art or, more specifically, the use of art, is important.'

'Art is always important.'

'I agree. But particularly to you. Greek art and myth are your specialities?'

Moira nodded, taking a worryingly large sip of wine. 'Yes, that's me.'

'Excellent. I need to know if you have any knowledge of art – specifically mythological symbols – being used to spread a word, or an idea.'

'You are talking about #awakening?'

'No.' Michail sighed, frustrated. It would be obvious what he was talking about – there was no use pretending it was a secret. The Awakening was spreading like a plague of locusts online. 'All right then, yes. But you did not hear that from me.'

She sat back and stared at the Parthenon, smiling. 'I feel as if I am in one of my lectures.'

'Please.' Michail gestured for her to begin.

'Well, the holiday to Athens with my husband, Andrew his name was, is a good place to begin, I suppose. We didn't rent here, it would have been far too expensive. No, we had an apartment right on the Piraeus harbour. I remember the balcony overlooked the ships, in and out, in and out they went.' She mimicked the motion with her hand. 'Andrew said ships were the lifeblood of the Greeks – both in ancient times and then. I don't know what a young, modern Greek like you would think about that! Anyway, that's when I learned to speak Greek. We were enamoured by this place. We loved the tavernas, one in particular. It was on the corner of the harbour, a small place, no idea if it still exists. The owner would pull *peynirli* straight from the bread oven with a wooden stake. You couldn't order if you didn't speak the language! That's also when I learned to drink, ah.' She raised her glass to Michail, and he begrudgingly topped her up. 'After the beers and the red wine and the shots, he – Andrew – would scoot his chair up close to mine, his cheeks flushed from the heat and the sea and the alcohol and whisper that he wanted to dance!'

Michail saw that the old woman was lost in her memory. Irrelevant as this all was, he did not have the heart to interrupt. She continued, 'And so we would – dance. He took my hand, and we danced all night, our lungs filled with laughter, until the owner closed his shutters for the night.' Moira's chest heaved. Michail wondered whether he ought to say something, offer a consolation of some sort, but she smiled, her eyes teary. 'But you want to hear about the art.' She shrugged. 'Living, life and art, they are the same. That's the thing to crack, young man.'

Michail nodded, even though he was not entirely sure what Moira meant by that. 'In Piraeus, we developed a joint obsession with some bronze sculptures. They hadn't even been out of the ground for two decades, discovered in the late fifties. I wrote a lot about them.' She pointed to the ceiling. 'It's all up there in my books.' She counted her fingers. 'There is an archaic Apollo, two statues of Artemis and – this is the one I want to speak about – an imposing Athena.' Michail sat up straight.

'Glad you're interested.' Moira laughed. 'This bronze Athena – you can still see her now, in Piraeus – she sparked all sorts of conversation between us. Obsessive conversation, Michail. That's the first point: art gets the conversational juices going. Think about it; there is no language barrier, no requirement of sophistication, nor intellect. It is purely in your face. If people are talking, then it's working.'

'People are talking about the graffiti around the city,' Michail said.

'Indeed,' said Moira.

'But can an image, or a statue, control specifically *what* a group of people think? For example, can an image brainwash people? Make them... think in a way they didn't before?'

'Why, that happens all the time.' Moira shrugged. 'Today and throughout history. Let us take the bronze Athena at Piraeus. She is known as the "approachable" Athena. Her arm is raised towards the viewer, she draws you in with a serene and kind expression. However, she is dressed for war, she has her special cloak, her aegis, decorated with snakes,' Moira raised an eyebrow as Michail sat straighter still, 'and she would have carried a shield and a weapon. This is a goddess ready for a fight. In my book I argue that this rendering of Athena, simultaneously kind and aggressive, was sculpted to incite men to go to war for their city. She cradles them with kindness and then inflames their minds, without them knowing, with feelings of power, rage and, of course, patriotism. I call it the Active Medium: the effect art has on its viewers. I have felt a draw to her all my life. Athena is powerful in this respect, specifically, I think.'

'Good at stirring up nationalism?'

'Or patriotism,' Moira replied softly. She wiggled her glass for another drink.

Michail held up the bottle. 'It's finished, I'm afraid.' Walking to the kitchen, he said, 'Are you familiar with the running gorgon swastika?'

Moira turned to look at him. 'The Temple of Artemis, Corfu?'

'Correct. But she also appears throughout Exarcheia?'

'Yes, yes.' She nodded. 'It's on one of my tours: Modern Classics in Athens. The resistance uses the image of the running gorgon to criticise–'

'The fascist police, I know.' Michail returned to the seating area with another bottle of wine. Opening it, he pondered. 'It's similar to another symbol cropping up in the city, one that is also appearing online: the axe and the snakes. They both refer to Athena and snakes.'

'You think they are connected.' Moira's eyes glowed in anticipation.

'No,' Michail said. 'Maybe.' He clenched his eyes, willing himself to concentrate. 'The swastika gorgon, one evocation of Athena, is used by a left-wing rebellion, who are, ultimately, fighting for equality. The other, the axe and the snakes, alluding to Athena's birth has cropped up in support of this "Awakening", who have publicly claimed two deaths and want to "purify" the city, whatever that means.' He lowered himself back into his chair and reached for a glass of wine himself. 'I don't know what to think.'

Moira swilled the wine about in her glass, sniffing at it. 'Art is free for the taking, remember. The most powerful images throughout history are stolen and adapted. The Christian god is Zeus, the virgin Mary is Artemis, the Nazis used the Roman eagle. Art has no imperative to be faithful, remember; it is truly free.' She gestured to the Parthenon, now shining brightly against the black sky. 'Bright-eyed Athena, to use her ancient epithet, belonged to Golden Age Greece, she had nothing to do with our politics, nothing to do with our notion of modern equality. It is possible that the city is stealing her back by modifying this liberal, Exarcheian use of her image. Perhaps the axe imagery is a revision of the running gorgon.'

'The city?' Michail was growing tired.

'The Golden Age of Athens, our goddess's great reign, was as pure – as nationalist, as you put it – as it can get. The great statesman Pericles would be embarrassed by Athens's current state of affairs.' She drained her wine but asked for no more for the time being.

Michail nodded. He remembered learning at school about the pride in 'pure' blood that the ancients had prized. He had studied the Citizenship Law of Pericles, which stated the son of an Athenian father must also have a full-citizen mother to be classed as a legal Athenian citizen. He shook his head. 'Well, let us hope that is not what The Awakening really wants. That thinking is best left in the past. My fear is that if we don't find out who is behind this soon, there will be another murder. A young man.'

Moira sighed and looked at him with kind eyes. 'Some things are beyond your control, Michail. Do not worry yourself trying to fight what you cannot.'

He nodded, following her gaze towards the Parthenon, thinking of Laurence-Sinclair and Mani, wherever they were. The building did not comfort him as it usually did. Instead, he imagined the goddess Athena ebbing from the marble, in a grey and dusky haze. Moira's phrase 'bright-eyed' irritated him for some reason. He had read the epithet at school many times; γλαυκῶπις, gleaming-eyed. However, the description twinkled at the forefront of his mind as he eventually bid Moira goodbye, thanking her for her help, before folding down his bed.

The Weaver

S ofia was almost certain she had entertained the idea for
long enough. For once, Yiorgos shared her opinion: that
this was an unholy waste of time. She had only agreed because
she had promised she would give her new recruits more
responsibility, being short on ideas herself. The urgency
presented by the missing Mani character also mounted the
pressure. Again, he was practically untraceable in official
records: an invisible man. Michail had arrived at her office
yesterday enthused and prepared for their meeting. It had
seemed a good idea until he began to explain his theory. He was
of the opinion that Laurence-Sinclair was plotting a string of
murders, all inspired by the myths of the goddess Athena, in a
pledge to purify the city of foreigners.

'It is clear that he strives for the ideology of Golden Age
Athens. He must be The Awakening,' he had said, breathlessly.
Sofia could not deny that this was a reasonable extrapolation;
Laurence-Sinclair was a scholar of that period, although it
seemed an enormous undertaking for one man, especially one of
his age. Also, Laurence-Sinclair did not seem the type to elicit a
successful social media campaign. Then there was the question

of motive. 'So, obviously it follows that we must look at the remaining textile mills in Athens, of which there are four.'

'And why is that?' Sofia asked, completely nonplussed.

Michail immediately dove into a laborious retelling of the Arachne myth, the weaver who offended Athena, hung herself out of shame and ended up metamorphosised into a spider. He was speculating: a fact which he wholeheartedly disagreed with. 'It is logical,' he insisted, his chin pushing low and his brow slanting forwards. 'It is a popular though incorrect assumption that the simplest explanation is usually correct. This is why hindsight is so illuminating. What was thought of as unlikely becomes likely when the facts are presented in the correct manner. The truth becomes clear. Look...' He presented her with his mobile phone. 'Scroll down. This is the next attack; I am sure of it. *The spider's nest is due a shake? #AthenaProtectUs from the damned and the strangers... next instalment to be woven into history?!?! #WeaveYourMagicAthena. #Awakening about time #TraditionalValues were woven back into society #irl #throwback #purge!! #ThursdayBites.'*

'My God, who are these people?' Sofia squinted in disbelief at the screen.

'This type of online behaviour has been growing in popularity since the first murder,' Michail replied. 'It seems that some people are quite taken with this... narrative. But see, there is a recent penchant for weaving in these posts. I can't find the original blog post anymore–'

'That's right, cyber says it's been expunged. They are most likely operating a targeted social media campaign now. Apparently if they are creating multiple fake accounts and then deleting them just as quickly...'

'They are impossible to track down. Constable Kounos brought this particular hashtag to my attention: #ThursdayBites.

There are variations: #SpinningThursday #ThursdaySpins, see? They began last week.'

'Thursday is tomorrow,' Sofia said.

'Precisely. And the weaving mills are my best guess as to a location. Now, I have contacted the owners and, taking shift timetables, cleaning rotas and machinery supervision into consideration, any time from 5pm would be a good time for Laurence-Sinclair to strike.'

'You think we can save Mani?' she said.

'It's worth a try,' Michail replied.

Sofia had handed back Michail's phone and closed her eyes. She had to be seen to be doing something, not only by her colleagues, but by the press and the public. The cyber team had already told her that the #awakening movement was growing exponentially. The press were rampant: *Are you #AwakeYet?* one headline asked that morning. This was no longer contained to right-wing publications. Not to mention the graffiti popping up on just about every corner of the city. Snakes and axes, the same imagery pushed over the untraceable social media channels, free for everyone to share and share alike. So, she had agreed to co-ordinate four separate units across the city to wait outside the weaving mills. Two units in the suburb of Nea Ionia, one in the suburb of Acharnes and one in Ilisia, where she waited.

'This is stupid,' Yiorgos mumbled. She took a step away from him as a cloud of cigarette smoke billowed from his mouth. She tutted and readjusted her weight, watching his right hand with interest as it tapped subtly on his phone, held loosely by his right hip.

'Maybe,' Sofia replied, straining to see who he was messaging. There had been no mention specifically of these locations online yet, give or take a few fanatics who were making it their game to locate the next murder.

She had briefed the force that this would be an entirely closed operation. Not even family members were to be told about the plan, if it could even be called that. 'Make it airtight,' she had repeated to the teams. 'You are looking for anything suspicious at all. Whatever you do, do not cause alarm. Do not add fire to #awakening.'

The mill was a large lemon-coloured warehouse. As dusk drew in, a trick of the light made the windows turn a deep shade of black, obscuring the view of the factory workers inside. A few workers left through the car park entrance, buzzing their employee cards against the gate. They spoke excitedly, pointing at the collections of police cars outside their place of work.

Yiorgos exhaled. 'Great employment for foreigners when our own people can't find work. That's progress, we are told.'

Her radio crackled. 'Sampson?'

'Yes, here.' She turned her back to Yiorgos, irritated that Basil's constables had addressed her so informally. They had probably picked up the habit from Yiorgos.

'We have an unidentified vehicle in the car park. A Moto Guzzi V7 motorbike, we've spoken to the manager and he doesn't recognise it.'

Sofia looked past the security gate to where she had stationed two men at the car park entrance. 'Investigate it.'

'Will do.'

'Probably nothing.' Yiorgos yawned. Sofia ignored him. She watched the two men approach the vehicle through the gates. The security guard waved at her. The sky behind the mill had turned a bright pink. Sofia usually loved such colours but tonight the hue reminded her of blood, inky blood, spilling its way through the innocent clouds.

'How are they doing?' Sofia jumped as Yiorgos spoke. She looked to the gates nearest them where the mill's security guard sat in his checkpoint box. Katerina and Michail obediently stood on duty next to it. Michail nodded in their direction and Yiorgos raised an arm at him. 'A weirdo, no?' he said, as he waved.

'He is dedicated,' Sofia said tersely. 'And he has attention to detail.'

'So did Rain Man,' Yiorgos replied, throwing his cigarette butt to the floor.

'Who are you messaging?' Sofia asked, irritated.

Yiorgos narrowed his eyes. 'Private matters,' he said.

Sofia's radio reignited. 'Ms Sampson, you might want to check this out.'

'What?' Sofia had already begun to stride towards the motorbike. She heard Yiorgos's plodding feet behind her.

'In the luggage hold, there's some sort of package.'

Sofia beckoned for the rest of the team to standby and motioned for Yiorgos to keep up. 'On my way,' she replied, gesturing to the guard to open the gate.

The car park was dimly lit, in that half-hearted way that car parks are when it is neither day nor night. The windows of the factory, lit from within, now glowed a pale orange. A few cheap cars were scattered in random spaces but other than that, it was empty. It was easy to see how the manager would have spotted an unfamiliar vehicle. She walked to the far corner of the car park where the motorbike was parked. The two constables leaned over the hold.

'Let me,' she said, waiting for them to move. One of them held a torch as she peered inside. A parcel of white cloth, tied up with string, was tucked tightly into the carrier. A large, almost perfectly circular pool of dark blue emerged from its centre.

Yiorgos hovered from the opposite side. 'Best have a look,' he said, gloves already on.

Sofia let him lift the package carefully onto the ground.

'Careful,' she whispered. The liquid flow was not so substantial that it dripped; it looked sticky; the substance was thick. 'Is it heavy?' she asked.

Yiorgos shook his head. 'Not really.' The string was tied in a neat bow on the upper side of the cloth. Yiorgos's large fingers worked their way around it, pulling at the knot delicately. Slowly, he removed one strand of the string and held it up to be bagged. Then, he rotated the package around and unwound the other string, moving in large, expanding circles. Finding an edge, which looked tacky with the blue substance, he peeled it back. Sofia clicked her fingers to the man with the torch who, peering over, had allowed his arm to droop. Yiorgos's gloved fingers revealed a mess of thin, angular legs and rounded bodies.

'Hold it up,' Sofia demanded, her voice calmer than she expected. The night was growing thicker. In an act that would have looked from afar like a sick votive offering, Yiorgos held up the contents of the cloth. 'Are those...'

'Spiders,' Yiorgos said. 'Dead. Looks like they've all been skewered, ugh.' He looked away. 'I hate spiders.'

Sofia leaned closer. 'Blue blood,' she said quietly. 'Of course.' She kneeled, her nose millimetres away from the wiry mound, her knees stinging against the tarmac. 'There's a note.'

'What?' Yiorgos wrinkled his nose.

'A note.' Sofia snapped her head up, pointing to the centre of the package. 'I can see the corner of it there, in the middle.'

Yiorgos sighed, holding out his gloved hands, which were stained with the dark blood. He used two fingers to push the spider carcasses out of the way, groaning. 'This is repulsive.'

Sofia watched intently as he fished out a tacky note on heavy-set paper, decorated with thick black ink. 'What does it say?' she asked, shuffling forwards. Yiorgos stared at it, his face inscrutable. 'Yiorgos, what does it say?' Sofia repeated.

Suddenly, a power surge sang through the factory complex:

the windows, the street lamps and the light in the security booth all flickered out. The torchlight illuminated Yiorgos's face, which seemed unusually stricken. He looked at Sofia and then back down at the note. Sofia undid the top button of her blouse, suddenly excruciatingly warm. She steadied herself. 'Read it to me.'

Yiorgos cleared his throat. 'It's the nursery rhyme: *The little spider goes up with difficulty, the rain falls and it goes down again, the sun comes out, dries the rain, and the little spider starts from the beginning.*'

'Spiders,' Sofia said. 'More bloody spiders.' Looking back towards the gate where Michail stood guard, she watched him methodically move his torchlight through the darkness, searching square metre after square metre. Katerina's torch dangled at her feet: that girl still needed polishing.

Sofia began to ask Yiorgos to bag the note when a commotion from within the security booth interrupted her. The guard was gesturing wildly, his torch sending frantic signals over the car park. 'Come!' he shouted. 'The system is down. I can't see anything.'

Sofia pushed herself up from the tarmac and ran towards him, bellowing, 'What do you mean?'

The guard shook his head in dismay, tapping at his computer keys uselessly. Before him, the small square monitors glowed a deep grey. 'They blew up,' the guard cried. 'Like there was a fire.' Sofia looked towards the factory. There was no sign of fire. She remembered the bright light from the corrupted security footage before.

Yiorgos was already radioing for backup, his gun ready in one hand. 'Security is down. Stand alert.'

All over the car park, dizzy beams of torchlight fumbled through the darkness. She had men at every entrance. Except the door leading into the car park. Heat rose quickly in her chest and over a ragged intake of air she breathed, 'It was a distraction; the motorbike! They distracted us. They're in there. They played us.' She pointed to the door, already hurrying towards it.

Behind her, Yiorgos bellowed into the radio, 'Entry team deploy, now! Arms ready! I repeat, deploy the entry team. Guards, do not let anyone out of the building.'

As Sofia reached the door, she was plunged into a bright blindness. She stopped, stunned. The emergency power supply had kicked in. Blinking into the newly lit corridor, she grabbed her gun and leaned against the wall, beckoning her team to go ahead of her. They filed up the stairs in long, fluid strides. 'Hurry!' she shouted. But that was when the sound came. It wove down the stairs seamlessly. High and mighty. They screamed as one, the people in the factory, because they found her as one. It was lamentation that Sofia heard; that ancient sound of beating and tugging. The wail echoed through the stone walls as her team belted towards its source.

This one was difficult. Yiorgos had reached the scene before her. He had overtaken her on the stairs whilst she was removing her heels. As she had reached the main mill room, he had placed a hand on her shoulder. A warning to turn away, not to look. He probably thought it was his duty to protect her. Sofia had batted him off and stepped forward, barefooted into the mill. It was much more modern than she had expected. Stupidly, she had assumed that the workers would be kept in the old style, pushing the looms back and forth monotonously, sat on low stools. Instead, enormous rolls of cotton hung from the ceiling, the threads stretched in long, colourful diagonals across the space, reaching towards the bellies of large, round metallic pods. Carts of sample fabrics and ends were parked at the end of every line. She supposed this is what the employees pushed about as they worked.

The machines had been halted, and for good reason. In the centre of the room what looked like a cocoon was nestled into one of the oversized, hanging bobbins. It took a while for Sofia to piece together the macabre puzzle in her mind. She wondered whether the process would have been easier if it had been Mani – whom she had been expecting. Two feet stuck out of the end of the cocoon, shoes still on. At the top of it appeared a woman's head, whose neck hung from a thicker thread looped into a noose. She swayed in the air softly, the bobbin still retaining its mechanical rhythm. Her body was bound tightly by the cotton. It looked like her arms were pinned painfully against her chest. She had struggled at the last moment, Sofia imagined; she had writhed against that cotton cocoon. But this was not the worst of it. The woman's mouth was open like she was still drawing her last breath from the stale factory air. Whoever had done this had not thought her hanging corpse sufficient. Instead, they had poured what must have been hundreds of spiders down her throat. They erupted from her mouth like a writhing black and brown stream.

'Sergeant Mikras,' Sofia said into her radio, her hand visibly shaking.

'On guard, Ms Sampson. No sign of–'

'You were right. It's the myths. We have a hanging weaver with spiders clambering from her mouth.'

'Affirmative,' Michail's voice crackled over the radio.

The Myth-Buster Unit

I t would have been Michail's dream role in the Hellenic Police Force, were it not for the grisly murders befalling his fellow citizens. He was put in charge of what had become known as the Myth-Buster Unit. It consisted mainly of him and Katerina, though they had been given a larger space from which to work and commanded briefing privileges, which Michail had made full use of since he had accepted his new responsibility seven days ago. His duties were threefold: to research and record any suitable Athena-related myths; to monitor any references to these on social media (since the cyber team had done such an insufficient job thus far); and to view the modern city of Athens through the spectrum of the ancient myths, casting reasonable projections for where the next crimes would take place. Since Michail had already been doing all the above, running the Myth-Buster Unit was neither a challenge nor a hindrance. Although, he appreciated the recognition, and Katerina seemed impressed with him.

As any self-respecting Athenian knew, there were numerous myths involving Athena. She had been the divine protector of many heroes, of course. And she featured heavily in the Homeric epics. Michail attempted to look at them from the point of view of a murderer: which of them would create the most sensational scene? He found that if he viewed the concept of murder as a work of art, he could envisage the bodies without feeling queasy. Unfortunately, he had no insight into the mind of Laurence-Sinclair – whom he was convinced was the orchestrator – apart from him being an older, upper-class English man. In many ways, Laurence-Sinclair reminded him of Moira. With a penchant for snakes.

'Suppose Laurence-Sinclair used these meetings at the warehouse to lure young foreigners to him?' Katerina suggested.

'It certainly makes sense,' Michail replied. 'They would feel safe in Risto's house.' He looked at Sofia. 'Have we any news on the woman at the cotton mill? Could she have been a part of Laurence-Sinclair's club?'

Sofia looked up from her phone. 'Just, Yiorgos has messaged. Syrian refugee, Iman Samaan, lived in Exarcheia.' She exchanged a meaningful look with them both. 'Again, no family to speak of. Again, no prints or DNA from forensics.' She sighed and rolled her eyes. 'It's like the bodies have been touched by the hand of a goddess.'

'Or like they positioned themselves willingly,' mused Katerina, remembering how she had noticed the ritualistic placement of Marius's body.

'So it seems,' said Sofia, nodding encouragingly at Katerina. 'Iman must have been willing, to an extent, for the perpetrator to string her up in the factory so quickly, even if she struggled towards the end. But why would she do that? Why would any of them?'

'Drugs?' suggested Katerina. 'Risto mentioned that Laurence-Sinclair brought pills into the house.'

Sofia nodded slowly, rolling her shoulders back and forth. 'It's possible.'

'And wasn't Laurence-Sinclair sacked in the seventies for distributing drugs to his students?'

'Yes,' said Michail. 'Recreational drug use was confirmed by toxicology for Marius, were there any hallucinogens in the report?'

Sofia shook her head. 'No, but we will test Iman.'

'All right.' Michail saw no point in labouring over the matter before the facts were confirmed. 'The other question is raised by Oscar Mathers. He was a child, only visiting Athens on a school trip. No drug use, not an immigrant, he did not live in Exarcheia. Even his body,' Michail clicked his remote and Oscar's photograph appeared on the screen, 'bears no resemblance to the other bodies; it is not as... artistic.'

Katerina agreed. 'It looks as if he died as the result of an accident.'

'I agree.' Sofia nodded at the screen. 'This doesn't match the pattern. There is no extravagance here.'

'Correct,' affirmed Michail, watching Sofia, who had seemed distracted for most of the meeting and now appeared to be deep in thought.

'You know,' Sofia began, 'social media aside, there is no reason why Oscar's death should be treated as suspicious. His witness statements were all solid. Coincidences happen and there are only so many Athena myths. What if the olive branch post was just as a whimsical message and gained more traction after Oscar's accident?'

Katerina stood and began to pace around the room. Excellent, Michail thought, she was proving herself proactive in front of their superior. Katerina began, 'Terrorist groups claim random deaths as their own all the time. If that's what this is, and it seems so, then...'

'Who informed them about Oscar's body?' Michail finished, getting her drift. 'There were supporters chanting at the bottom of the Acropolis that night. And Laurence-Sinclair was near the site of the accident.' He grinned at Katerina. 'Officer Galanis found his ring.'

To Michail's surprise, Katerina did not seem grateful for the reminder of her triumph. She stopped pacing and looked at the ground. He continued, 'Almost as if he wanted us to find him, or at least find his ring...' Michail thought back to that night. The rain had been torrential. Was it possible Laurence-Sinclair had planted his snake ring as a way of claiming Oscar's death? The snakes on the ring strongly resembled those on the graffiti being photographed and posted to #awakening. 'Perhaps he only meant us to find his ring and the storm slowed him down, resulting in us finding *him*. We were "off the beaten track". He would have expected us to go directly up to Oscar's body.'

'But how did he know about Oscar's accident?' Katerina asked, crossing her arms tightly. 'He must have been there before we were.'

Sofia hunched her shoulders, massaging her temples. She seemed agitated. 'A tip-off,' she said quietly. A silence followed.

'Surely no one would have...' Katerina spoke slowly, as if she did not want to believe it. An awkwardness descended. The whirr of the air-conditioning unit clicked and pushed out a new current with a dense rhythm.

'You suspect a mole in the force?' Michail asked. He looked over his shoulder at the closed office door. He thought about how he recently felt part of an effective, coherent team. The infiltration of a poisonous officer was an almost unbearable notion.

Noticing Sofia hunched further over, drawing restless, repetitive circles on the screen of her phone, Michail clicked his remote and his whiteboard screen changed to a detailed Myth-Buster Table that he had prepared earlier. It was best to press on for now. 'Let's focus on the myths for the time being. These are the murders,' he drew red crosses through Athena's Birth, The Olive Tree Victory and Arachne, 'that The Awakening – likely Laurence-Sinclair – has claimed. These,' he drew a large circle around a larger list of myths, 'are still possibilities.' He let Katerina and Sofia, who had become drawn and pale, consider the options.

'The blinding is an obvious one,' Sofia said, gesturing to a bullet-pointed myth at the centre of the board. 'The Tiresias myth. Forgive my crudeness, but that would be a nice murder to stage. Artistic, as you say.'

'Agreed,' Michail said, circling the Tiresias myth in green. 'He was punished for happening upon the virgin goddess bathing naked. So perhaps... a brothel?'

'Maybe.' Sofia nodded, making a note.

'The gorgon myth,' Katerina said. 'Maybe something to do with the snakes, like how the spiders were used at the mill?' She walked closer to the screen. 'There are more snakes here, who's this, the Erichthonius character?'

Michail zoomed into where he had written: *Erichthonius, Athena's son.* 'Half man, half snake. She kept him in a box on the Acropolis so that nobody could find him until...' Michail noticed that both Katerina and Sofia suddenly seemed very sombre. He continued, 'Until he was found by the daughters of the king at the time, Cecrops, one of whom threw themselves off the hill in horror when she laid her eyes on the serpentine man. Interesting fact,' Michail raised his finger into the air, 'not many people know that a statue of a snake used to be behind Athena's statue in the Parthenon. It was meant to represent Erichthonius, her hidden, lethal son.'

'Half snake?' Katerina confirmed.

'Correct,' Michail said, scribbling on the board. Despite the circumstances, he felt the blood rushing to his brain. This was good! This was his forte; he was pleased to show off what he was made of. His hand beat excitedly against his thigh, but he breathed, remembering to keep himself retained. 'He was kept in a box until the big reveal on the Acropolis. An important story for the city of Athens: it was crucial in building the physical and emotional identity of Athenians. The Erechtheum is actually named after him...'

'Michail.' Katerina was standing next to him, looking between the screen and him.

'Yes, Katerina? You need clarification? If you let me finish—'

He was interrupted by an almighty groan. 'Are you unwell?' he asked Katerina, concerned.

'Oh please, Michail, will you think about what you are saying? Half snake, half man? Remember Mani's snake tattoo? Risto said he got it under Laurence-Sinclair's orders.'

Sofia frowned, nodding. 'And the box, hidden away, you say? That sounds dramatic, as does the Parthenon. It would garner attention, which is what these murders seem to be aiming to do.'

Michail stepped back from the board, hands on his hips. He studied his meticulously labelled set of notes, designed to draw the eye to the most salient pieces of information. He blew out in three quick puffs, conscious that his slowness had irritated his fellow Myth-Buster Unit team members. Then, the pieces on the whiteboard moved into a sturdy order; his brain hummed as they fell pleasingly into place. He said in a quiet voice, 'You think Mani is being kept hidden somewhere? You think the next murder will be in the Parthenon?'

Both Michail and Katerina turned to Sofia, who was now tapping ferociously at her screen. Michail was pleased to note that she had downloaded all the relevant applications, as he had advised. 'Look for the hashtags,' he reminded her. 'Try *hybrid, perversion of humanity, snake-man, hidden son,* anything like that.'

'Got it.' Sofia tapped the screen with quick and erratic flicks of the finger. Katerina settled back into her chair and looked at the ceiling, her eyes wide. Michail turned away from them both and studied the board again. It would be unacceptable to miss the next murder. This was merely a challenge of intellect and logic; one that could be solved by the practice of methodical thought. He checked his phone for any new social media trends. The Arachne murder dominated his first search, accompanied with a new hashtag that was gaining speedy traction: #MythMurders. There were the irrelevant speculators: members of the public with too much time on their hands trying to play detective. However, a growing number of commentators seemed to be entertaining the idea that some sort of revolution was taking place. *The time has finally arrived. Athena arises. Cleanse Our City. #MythMurders. #SheAwakes.* It was a worrying sentiment. Scrolling through the comments, Michail frowned at the amount of people who agreed with it. Was this merely morbid excitement or genuine conviction? The belief in an ancient goddess rising to purge a city was madness. Though, he considered, it was no madder than a belief in a Christian god, or any other higher being. Humans showed an endless capacity for the irrational.

'A few #SnakesArise #EntwinedInSnakes #MythMurders but nothing specific,' he said to his screen. Katerina approached him from behind and leaned over his shoulder.

'Whoever is posting the clues might have stopped,' she said. 'We were close in the weaving mill. Maybe we spooked them.'

'They wanted us there,' Sofia said, raising her head. 'They knew we'd be there. They were toying with us. The spiders were a message: they are one step ahead.' Michail turned as Sofia snapped her phone case closed and stood, sighing. 'Someone within this department must have tipped them off. I kept the mill locations watertight. There is no way they would have had time to prepare the spider package without warning. God, perhaps they only followed through on the Arachne murder because they knew we were coming.' That made Michail feel nauseous.

'Perhaps it is the same person who notified Laurence-Sinclair of Oscar's accident,' Sofia mused. 'I had not considered that until tonight.' Michail understood why Sofia had looked so pallid. This was confirmation of a mole in her team, not just the force.

'I can't imagine anyone here who would...' began Katerina.

Sofia held a hand up to her forehead. She looked pained, hurt. 'As you said, Katerina, the police force has not always been on the right side. I have my suspicions and I have had them before.' She levelled her eyes at them both. 'But it is no concern of yours. Focus on what you are good at, leave this to me. We cannot have another murder in this city; give it everything you have. We need to find Mani – and Laurence-Sinclair – before it is too late.'

Sofia left the room with a noticeably depleted swing in her hips. Michail turned back to his screen when he felt Katerina's hand on his shoulder. He froze. There it was in the pit of his stomach again. An urgent discomfort, prickly and excitable. He shifted to one side, but she leaned in closer. She must have been millimetres away from his cheek. Michail felt the heat from her neck conduct through the narrow space of air and settle against his skin. He stared at the screen.

'A mole.' Katerina's voice sounded thicker this close. He could hear the movement of her lips; the short, shallow breaths between syllables. He never usually paid attention to such things. The best course of action was to continue as normal. Katerina would surely be perturbed if she knew that he was thinking about the soft, warm details of her lips. It did not seem professional.

'Yes,' he replied, conscious of the quick undulations of his vocal cords. 'But I believe Ms Sampson when she says she has it under control. She has proven herself fallible, but she has also conceded to our superior analysis of the murders. I therefore trust her with this.'

Her hand tightened on his shoulder. He cleared his throat and stood, careful not to push her away. She was in a strange mood. He must remain consistent and rational. He walked back to his whiteboard and stood before it again. 'So many stories,' he said. 'So many possible ends.' He checked his watch.

'It's late,' Katerina said from behind him. He turned. She was wearing an odd expression. He would have described it as a smile, but it protruded more than her usual countenance, her lips tensed and crooked. Her eyes also seemed less sharp, the lids drooping slightly.

'You look tired, Katerina. It is time for you to get some rest. I shall see you tomorrow when we can recommence our Myth-Buster Unit investigation.'

Katerina looked at the floor. It appeared he had said the incorrect thing. He transferred his weight from foot to foot, thinking through what he ought to say. He did not want Katerina to be unhappy. He would be able to find the correct verbal remedy if he concentrated fully. Luckily, Katerina made a helpful suggestion. 'We could work from your apartment,' she said. 'That way I will have a break from my mother and that view of yours might provide us with a bit of inspiration.'

Michail nodded, moving swiftly across the room to grab his bag. 'Good idea, Katerina, a change of scene sounds promising.'

The Gala

Sofia would normally have enjoyed a rooftop view, and this one was undeniably spectacular. The Acropolis rose out of the darkness, behind the cobbled charm of the Plaka steps, like a mighty standard. But the site of Marius's murder lay hidden and forgotten in the quiet shadows below, it seemed, between the laughter and the champagne. She would also have normally enjoyed the formal dress code, were she not concerned about seeming too feminine in front of Basil. The black backless number she had opted for rose to the challenge nicely; high-necked, revealing her muscular back, and contrasting aggressively with her bright-red lips. She took a sip of champagne and eyed the crowd gathered below the balcony. There were some professional camera crews, reporting on celebrity news, as well as a large crowd of fans. She had not realised Christos had become such a famous figure. Of course, she was not surprised that he was late to his own party.

Basil approached her, carrying three canapés on a small plate. 'Sampson, Sampson, you made it.'

She narrowed her eyes, attempting to smile. 'An offer I couldn't refuse.'

'Indeed, indeed.' Basil chewed loudly, moving his head along to the string quartet playing on a platform in the centre of the room. His eyes beetled over the attendees.

'Looking for someone, Basil?'

'Why, yes, yes. The prime minister is here.'

Sofia nodded; the good and the great of Athenian society could not resist a party, it seemed. Even if it was thrown by an egotistical psychopath. There was a huge cheer from below the balcony. Sofia watched a huge surge in the crowd as Christos stepped out of his car. He was magnetic, Sofia thought, their bodies were drawn to him. A bodyguard on either side of him, he waved at his fans, stopping to pose for selfies, greeting his adoring crowd with lingering kisses.

Sofia leaned further over the side, frowning. 'Is that... that's Theo Kounos, and... my team!' Indeed, Basil's new recruits escorted Christos Panagos up the red carpet, radios engaged, eyes alert, hands poised and ready by their right sides.

'What?' Basil had suddenly become very interested in a stain on his napkin.

'What are they doing? Basil! Why the hell are my team working as bodyguards for Christos? This is against all protocol. Nobody informed me of this.' She allowed her drink to be topped up by the waitress, straightening her spine as Basil faltered.

Eventually he stumbled upon the words, 'It's for Christos's protection. Now, now, he is not a statesman, *I know*, but he has more than the popularity of one. It seems right that he is afforded...'

Sofia did not wait to listen to the rest of his drivel. She wafted her hand at him, making sure to walk away with her head held high. This party was a waste of time. She stormed past the string musicians, who were playing a particularly unimaginative rendition of Vivaldi's *Spring*, and made for the marble staircase which led outside, wrinkling her nose at the abundance of flower arrangements. The money spent on this sham was extortionate. Clearly, Christos had directed his magic at donors with deep pockets. The *Hellenakratia* had wealthy supporters. Making her way to the door, she stopped when a hand was placed on her shoulder.

'Sofia Sampson.'

The voice was the same as she remembered it, curled and delicate, as if it had plotted its way carefully before sliding off the owner's tongue. His hand was warm and dry against her bare skin. She arranged her face very carefully as she greeted him. 'Christos.' She nodded to the entrance outside, where his name was being chanted excitedly. 'You leave your fans wanting more.'

His henchmen flanked him like two giant columns. She raised an eyebrow at her employees, and they mumbled a greeting, dropping their chins close to their chests. Sofia enjoyed the fact that she could intimidate them, at least, even if it seemed they ultimately followed Basil's command and not hers.

'You are spellbinding,' Christos mused, his eyes following the length of her figure. 'I don't think I have ever seen you so... put together.'

Sofia crossed her arms and took a step closer to him. 'Some of us have better things to do than play the well-dressed sycophant.'

Christos laughed gently and raised a hand up to her hair, pushing a strand behind her ear. She stood firm; she would not flinch at the touch of this traitor. 'Still so angry, Sofia...'

She seized his wrist in a calm but firm movement. His bodyguards stepped forward. 'Stand back,' she said in a hollow voice. 'That is an order, constables.' Unsure of what to do, they hovered at their master's side.

Sofia glared into Christos's eyes. They seemed older than they had been when he had worked for her. The youth had been drained from them: the pursuit of power will do that, she thought. 'Do not speak to me about anger.' Her voice quivered. She swallowed heavily, digesting the memories. 'You never even grazed the depths of it.'

Looking over his shoulder, she noticed Basil at the bottom of the staircase, twiddling his fingers. She let go of Christos's wrist, forcing herself to slow her breathing. Christos was not worth her time nor care. He was briefly distracted as a couple entered the building and greeted him. Turning back towards Sofia, he offered her his hand.

'I am leaving,' she said, shaking her head.

'Come, Sofia, for old time's sake.'

She shook her head, a shard of ice emerging behind her ribcage. He cocked his head, allowing his eyes to dance in that way they always did. They spoke of secrets; they always spoke of secrets. 'Go on, take a bite. The forbidden fruit is often the most succulent.' His tongue stroked each syllable, delicate and fatal.

'That makes you the serpent,' she said, feeling her face turn to stone. Christos did not reply but instead elongated his fingers further towards her. He knew she would not turn him down now. He was offering information, toying with her or not, she could not ignore him. Giving a stony stare to Basil, who seemed delighted with her decision, she took Christos's arm and was led once again up the marble staircase, into the snake pit.

To Michail's initial disturbance, the change of scene distracted Katerina. She helped herself to a glass of red wine and, for reasons undetectable, poured him a glass, even though he had made it clear that he needed his wits to be sharp. It seemed that Katerina was set upon telling him the minutiae of her personal life. He had to admit this was not entirely unwelcome, although slightly surprising, as they had never ventured into such territory previously. After four attempts at steadying the course and focusing her mind on the murders at hand, Michail desisted and took a seat next to her on the sofa, where she sat cross-legged and barefooted.

He picked up his wine glass in a bid to seem nonchalant when the topic of Theo came up. 'I do not understand, Katerina, why you allowed yourself to suffer. You have proven yourself impressive. He is unimpressive and unlikely to prove himself as such. It was an insufficient pairing.'

She laughed and he noticed that her lips were stained a faded purple. 'That,' she giggled, 'is what is so great about you, Michail.' He smiled, prepared to accept the compliment, but she suddenly looked hurt, her eyes misty and private. 'But it isn't so simple. It's complicated! I hate that phrase... don't you, it's *complicated*? But it's true. It must be so easy to see the world so simply like you do. Have you never wanted something stupid, Michail?'

'Everything is simple once you break it down,' Michail said, his tone more serious than he had intended. He surprised himself in wanting to share a memory with her. 'As a child, I wanted my mother to return. Impossible, of course, because she was dead. I had the idea that if I was perfect – if I achieved perfection – in my studies, the house chores, if I could be the perfect child, then she might come back. I made lists. I ticked off everything I thought I had to do. My schoolwork was always done on time, checked over ten times before handing it in early. I polished my shoes over and over, threw away any clothes that had even the tiniest stain on them. My father once found me scrubbing the kitchen tiles in the middle of the night. But I knew, really knew, if I made life perfect, then she would obviously want to come back to me.

'I could not work out what I was missing, Katerina. After eight months of achieving perfection, she still had not returned. So, I embarked upon a thorough self-assessment. My grades were perfect, I was clean to the point of rawness, I looked after the house meticulously. One night, my father was watching one of his soap operas and I caught a few minutes of it. I don't remember what it was called, but there was a scene portraying a family sat around a large dining table. The mother was asking about her children's day; except for one, she wasn't. The extra child was her son's friend, who had been invited over for dinner. That was it! The detail I had missed! In order to achieve perfection, I needed to source myself a friend!

'That night, I came up with a plan. I drew a longlist, based on compatible qualities of the individuals at school I would consider. By process of elimination, I produced a shortlist of peers with which I equipped myself on the next day in school. It did not go to plan, Katerina.' He looked away from her; it was silly to allow the past to haunt him. He knew better than this. 'Some children were kind, at least. They offered a sustainable excuse. Others... well, they were not so understanding. I was not able to achieve the perfect life. My mother did not come back. A ridiculous notion, I know.'

He looked to the Parthenon, which was lit up, as he knew it would be. Katerina allowed him a moment of silence, which he appreciated. 'Even the most complex constructs are rooted in simplicity. It is a way of seeing things, piece by piece, in their correct order and turn.' Michail bowed his head, aware that the motion may seem strange, but also relaxed enough that he did not feel he had to restrain himself. 'That's how I moved on. Everything – everyone – has their time and place.'

'And where do you fit in?' Katerina asked. 'Piece by piece?'

The small double sofa vibrated softly as she moved closer to him. 'Just here,' he said, smiling. 'This is my place.'

Katerina stretched her legs out and placed them over his thighs, yawning. 'Not a bad spot to be.'

'No,' he said, staring at her ankles. He took a quick sip of wine.

'Sorry,' Katerina said. 'If it's uncomfortable...'

'No!' he started, embarrassed by the volume of his voice. 'No, no, it is okay.' And then, in cold contradiction to the warmth he was experiencing in the pit of his stomach, 'But perhaps we should turn our attention to work.' He stood, leaving Katerina on the sofa. 'As colleagues, I think it is best to... remember our place.'

He stared out of the window, listening to Katerina rearrange herself on the sofa. This was the correct decision; he was sure of it. He had read enough about break-ups to deduce that Katerina's emotional behaviours would be affected for a considerable amount of time. If she was in need of the 'rebound', then a colleague was not the person for the job. Especially since Theo was now working in the same building as them. Yes, despite the empty and desolate feeling now yawning inside of him, this was the correct decision.

For a moment, he thought he noticed a small, flashing light from the top of the hill, but it disappeared: possibly the optical illusion of exhaustion. Waiting for Katerina to respond, he reached for one of the books Moira had left him to read, entitled *Reading Athena: Deciphering Athens' Protector*. It had proved highly illuminating, especially Moira's arguments about the various epithets surrounding the goddess, as well as the argument that her mythology had shaped the building scheme of ancient Athens. So far, though, he had come across nothing that told him anything new about #TheAwakening, nor Laurence-Sinclair. He flicked it open, glancing at Katerina, who was sitting in an extremely rigid stance on the sofa. 'My neighbour's book,' he ventured. 'She works at the British School at Athens.'

Katerina shook her head, as if bracing herself, and stood. Michail did his best to maintain a neutral expression. 'Let me see,' she replied, taking the book from him. Michail watched her scan the pictures of various sculptures, casting her eyes over the long paragraphs of descriptions. 'It's very specialised,' she said, frowning. 'My English is terrible.' Then, her head jerked forwards and she pointed at one of the pages.

Michail leaned over. 'Athena's epithet, you might know it,' he said. 'In Greek it is normally translated as "grey-eyed", but it seems English academics prefer the translation of–'

'Bright-eyed Athena,' Katerina finished, squinting in concentration.

'Precisely,' replied Michail.

'I have heard that before somewhere...' She paced about the small apartment, the book hanging from her hand. 'Wait!' Reaching into her pocket she pulled out her phone and began searching frantically. 'γλαυκῶπις! That's the word! I recognise it from the Laurence-Sinclair documents Sofia sent us. She circled the word – I guess she didn't know what it meant.' Katerina showed Michail the old article, containing a photograph of a group of serious-looking undergraduates. 'I forgot all about it...'

'Yes,' Michail said, irritated that he had not picked up on it. 'γλαυκῶπις!' He looked through the article in more detail. 'It looks like it is describing Laurence-Sinclair's club members. γλαυκῶπις – Bright-Eyed. See here, it's written in English too:

he called the students the Bright Eyes! Obviously, as academics, they preferred using the Ancient Greek.'

Katerina clapped the book shut, nodding. 'This could prove a historic obsession with Athena,' she said. 'It's almost a motive.'

'It certainly strengthens his affinity with the #awakening movement,' Michail replied, looking to the Parthenon again. 'But why resurrect his club here in Athens now, decades later? And why would he want to murder his new Bright Eyes?'

———

Christos handed Sofia a fresh glass of champagne. The quartet were now playing a sombre tune. It struck Sofia as inappropriate for the situation, mournful almost. The notes were unpredictable, as if they refused to be caught. 'You like it?'

She faced Christos. 'They are talented. I am not familiar with the piece.'

He smiled, taking a quick sip of his drink. 'Frederick Delius, *Daybreak*, I believe?'

'You believe?' Sofia did not think for one minute that every detail of this meeting was not contrived. Feeling as though she was being watched, she swivelled around, realising she was the object of a few fluttering, furtive glances.

'They're jealous,' Christos said in a hushed tone. 'Everyone wants to be you, stood beside me.'

Sofia looked at her feet. She experienced the implacable sensation of morbid curiosity. Here he was: Christos Panagos, the centre of this pomp; adored, coveted. It was unbelievable, yet, perfectly believable. 'How do you do it?' She observed him carefully, stepping closer. 'How do you do... this?'

'You mean, despite my charm and good looks?'

Sofia drew a sharp breath. He always had the ability to draw her in, focus her most serious attentions, and then drop her with a throwaway comment. She snapped, 'You were sacked from the force, disgraced.'

'And yet...' He leaned closer still, so that their faces almost touched.

'Yet here you are, commanding attention. Rising ahead. It is not right. People's memories are short.'

'Or perhaps they are not.' He stepped away from her, inviting her to walk around the string players. She followed him. 'Look at how they play,' Christos said. 'It's a miracle, is it not? Their arm moves the bow, which in turn moves the string, which causes tiny vibrations and, somehow, our eardrums receive the sweetest, most pure sensation of sound. See how the players relax? The tension is held by the strings. The players, however, allow their necks to soften, their arms to slacken because this produces the best timbre. A stressed player will mar their music.'

'I know. I used to play.' She had not meant to say it, had not meant to give him anything of herself.

'In London?'

She grimaced, seeing his excitement at having caught her. 'Yes. It wasn't a big orchestra or anything like that. We met on Thursdays, in a church in Marylebone. It was... lovely, really.'

'And yet you left?'

She nodded. 'Yes.'

'You miss it, your home?'

She narrowed her eyes. 'This is my home now, Christos.'

'Ah, Sofia.' Christos's eyes penetrated her. 'But I know you have never felt like Athens is your home.'

Sofia stiffened; he had no idea what she felt. 'I don't know what you mean.'

Christos bowed his head forwards. 'There is a difference between home and a hiding place. Whatever you ran from in London, it will follow, eventually. Ghosts always do.'

Sofia took a long sip of champagne. 'You don't know me,' she said. She looked at the musicians. 'What's your point, anyway, Christos?'

'You fight your instrument,' he replied, beckoning a champagne waitress to fill up her glass. 'You want to control everything, you cannot, just let the tune find its way. That is why it never worked between us.'

'Oh really? I thought it was because you were implicated in right-wing extremist groups whilst working for the organisation that is supposed to protect its citizens.'

He laughed, raising his glass to the guests who were watching them with interest. 'You felt betrayed?'

Sofia closed her eyes, unwilling to participate in this line of conversation. 'Yes, Christos, because I was betrayed. Both professionally and personally.' She did not want to be transported back to that fateful night, alone in her office, reading the secret email threads. She remembered how she had ticked off each employee's name, feeling their duplicity like a dagger to her side. There was no preparing herself for his name, however: Christos Panagos. She had checked and double-checked. She had allowed herself to fantasise wild explanations: perhaps he had been framed? Perhaps his personal email account had been hacked? Surely no one could be so callous. Surely, she would have seen such tendencies in her partner, her friend, her lover. Her breath quickened with the memory and she stepped away from him, her chest growing hot. 'Yes, I was betrayed.'

'I committed no crime.'

'We do not align ourselves with extremist groups,' she said, casting her mind back over the unidentified bodies from years ago. 'And you were *accused* of no crime.'

He studied her, taking his time to drink in her face, her lips. Her heart pumped through the thin fabric of her dress; her cheeks grew red. 'Still so beautiful when you're angry,' he whispered.

'Goodbye, Christos,' she said, handing her glass to him.

As she walked away, infuriated that she had been taken in, he called after her, 'Be careful on your way home, Sofia, you never know what the night conceals. Difficult to tell the snakes from the men between the shadows.'

She stopped in her tracks and spun around. 'What do you know?' Her voice rang loud, cutting through the string players. Interested murmurs simmered through the guests. She marched up to him and grabbed his arm tightly. 'Tell me what you know, Christos.' His bodyguards appeared behind him from nowhere. 'You work for me,' Sofia snarled at them.

'Stay where you are,' Christos ordered them quietly. They nodded in obedience. Sofia felt her mouth sag a little.

'You are defying the orders of the Hellenic police?' she asked Christos.

He shrugged. 'It's not like I have ever paid them proper heed, as you say.'

Sofia pulled him close to her, so that she could whisper into his ear. She hoped her words would strike him like poison. 'If you hinder another one of my investigations and cost another's life, I promise that I will see you dead. I will not say when, nor how, but trust me when I say, I will see you dead, whether you bring me down with it or not.' Her eyes stinging with hot moisture, she stepped away, shaking.

Basil pushed past her, chuckling maniacally. 'Everything all right, Sampson? I see there's a bit of a scene being staged here... now, does anyone need reminding of their duties?'

'No, I was just leaving.' Sofia did not take her eyes off Christos.

'You are too late,' he said, bowing his head as if in prayer.

'What?' Sofia barked. The room seemed to descend in a whirlpool around her, multicoloured and garish.

'You are late,' Christos said. She staggered backwards. 'I mean, it is late, that is all. Like I said, watch out for the snakes.'

Sofia did not waste another second. She hauled herself towards the entrance hall, hitting the stairs at full speed, reaching into her bag to send out the alert.

Erichthonius

The box was placed in the centre of the inner room of the Parthenon, framed by the building's gigantic fluted columns. It looked as if it had been put there as an offering to Athena. Perhaps, Katerina mused grimly, that was not so far from the truth. Michail had explained in detail that an ivory and gold statue of Athena would once have towered above the box, at the back end of the room. According to ancient descriptions of the now lost sculpture, her son, the snake-man Erichthonius, would have been depicted with her.

Katerina listened to a near-hysterical Sofia shouting at Yiorgos. 'How can I know who to trust?' she barked, her voice shrill and broken through the marble walls. Her ball gown was tied in a knot above her knees, making her seem deranged. '*He* has followed me here, you know, Yiorgos? Hot on my heels as I left. Gathered his cronies from that godforsaken party. I bet he has had this planned for weeks!' Katerina thought someone ought to calm her down: she was not doing herself any favours by behaving publicly like this. She was certainly not going to volunteer herself for the job, however.

Swathes of press gathered at the foot of the hill in response to the fourth #MythMurder. On the way up, Katerina had seen that television channels had their anchors lit, made-up and ready to go. She was surprised to see Christos Panagos, also in formal attire, holding some sort of a rally amidst the media crews. That's who Sofia must have been talking about. Indeed, a particularly large crowd – some also in dresses and suits – regarded him patiently as he shouted into his microphone from a podium. Katerina had heard him ask, 'And whose place is it to question whether acts are human or divine? Certainly not mine! If the goddess claims to have reawakened, then who am I, a mere mortal to deny her? It is not for us to disagree with Athena. She is our city's patron, as we know!' To Katerina's disbelief the crowd had erupted into applause at this proclamation. It was amazing what people would believe.

'We must open the box,' said Michail abruptly. Katerina nodded, hoping that Sofia would regather her senses soon.

'Do you think it will be Mani?' she asked, conscious that her voice was shaking. She did not want Michail to think she was afraid, although she supposed she would rather him think that than know how mortified she was really feeling. She did not know what had come over her earlier that night; Michail probably thought she was a sex-crazed lunatic. All her hard work to impress him had, no doubt, been wasted. He would never take her seriously now! She could have kicked herself. Katerina cringed as she remembered how quick he had been to get away from her. What an embarrassment.

'I am certain,' replied Michail. 'Especially if I am correct in deciphering – between Ms Sampson's indecipherable outbursts – the hints Christos dropped her at the *Hellenakratia* newspaper party.'

'Let me guess, something about snakes but nothing solid enough to bring him in?'

'Correct. But what have Laurence-Sinclair and Christos got to do with each other?'

Katerina shrugged. 'It's frustrating. He is down there, on the street, inflaming all sorts of fanatical propaganda.' Michail rubbed his temples and tapped his legs on either side; an indication that he was nervous or thinking something through in intense detail. Katerina continued to stare at the box as Sofia's irate allegations bounced from the walls on the temple.

'Who are they *really* working for, Yiorgos, can you tell me? Am I to assume I am no longer in charge?'

Eventually, Yiorgos held his hand up to Sofia and said, 'Enough. You will believe what you want. Shall we get on?'

Sofia looked like he had slapped her firm in the face. However, turning to observe her team, her lips unusually pale, she nodded grimly, apparently remembering why she had called them to the Parthenon so late at night. She seemed to hold her breath for a few seconds, and then shut her eyes. When she opened them, her demeanour was more like her usual self. 'Mikras,' Sofia said. 'Do the... honours, please.'

Michail nodded, his chin jutted forward, and he approached the box. Katerina held her breath as he knelt stiffly, pulled on his gloves, and fiddled with the lid.

'It is unfastened,' he shouted. He leaned over and sniffed the box. 'Olive wood, of course.' The forensic team stood behind him, ready to do their work. 'One,' Michail began. Katerina concealed a small smile at his earnest countdown. 'Two. Three.'

He pushed the lid up with ease. The thin golden chains that were wrapped loosely around the wood chimed melodically. The team watched in silence as Michail inspected the contents. Although his body remained perfectly still, Katerina noticed his lips moving quickly, as if he was talking to someone. Unable to hear what he was saying, she crept closer. 'I am sorry, I am sorry, I am sorry, I am sorry,' he repeated in a monotonous chant.

'Sergeant!' cried Sofia, striding towards him, pushing Katerina out of the way. Michail did not look up.

'As expected, Ms Sampson,' he said in a small voice. 'I can confirm that this is Mani. His tattoo is a distinguishing feature...'

'Oh God!' Sofia sprang back from the box, batting at her arms. Michail turned towards her, frowning. 'It's filled with snakes!' she screamed. 'Why didn't you say?'

'Was this not what we expected?' Michail seemed angry; he gripped the sides of the box tightly, despite the now audible hisses of agitated snakes. 'We knew this was coming! The clues were all there and yet we did not prevent it.'

Katerina hurried towards Michail, who had begun to rock gently backwards and forwards. She wished she had not looked, as the contents of the box were a horrible mess. Sure enough, it held Mani's corpse, curled in a foetal position, the tattoo on his scalp dark and obvious. He lay ensconced in a cradle of snakes. They were alive, writhing around his limbs; a thin black one coiling about his neck, its head writhing across Mani's peaceful face. A sharp, confident tongue darted in and out, like it was tasting his flesh. Looking at Mani's body from above, it seemed as if his tattoo had been animated as his skin melded into the living scales that slithered over him. Michail shook the sides of the box, crying out, 'We could have saved him!'

The snakes reared up at the sound of his voice and rose to the challenge, needling their diamond-shaped heads towards Michail.

'Hush,' said Katerina, pulling him away from the box carefully. 'Hush.' She led him from the temple, nodding at Yiorgos on the way out. The forensic team bustled behind them, opening the containers ready for the snakes. Seating Michail on the temple steps, Katerina attempted to calm him down.

'He was here,' Michail said, his head hung low. 'Laurence-Sinclair was here.'

'We couldn't have known it would be tonight...' Katerina began, looking up at the sky. 'There were no clues this time.'

'I saw a light from my apartment earlier. It was him. I know it. I could have stopped...' He let out a frustrated, animalistic cry.

'Stop it.' Katerina made sure her voice was sharp and firm. 'No. You couldn't have guessed this. This was a part of the plan. He leads us to the bodies, entices us with clues, but never enough to intervene, to save them. We could not have stopped this, Michail. He has been dancing ahead of us from the very beginning.'

The press raised a loud cheer that carried up the slopes and into the skies. Despite the warm night air, Katerina shivered. She patted Michail on the back. 'Come on, we must keep trying. You can't give up.'

'How?' Michail asked, his lips quivering. 'How, Katerina? When they,' he thrust a finger at the crowds below, 'disgrace the city by submitting to utter madness? To chaos? The very people we are trying to protect! They believe Athena is doing this? That the gods walk once again? Well good luck to them!' He turned towards the Parthenon, which towered above them. 'What if they are correct?' he whispered, falling to his knees. 'What if this *is* a monument of hate and intolerance? All my life I have treasured it; it has been my stability, and now... they twist it. They pollute it and my city.' His hands tapped angrily on the marble steps.

'You know the golden ratio?' he continued. 'I think of it often, it is a comfort to me. The Parthenon was built according to it.'

'Yes, I know it. You say it aloud sometimes: one point six one eight?'

Michail nodded. 'It's rounded up. You see, it is an infinite ratio really. The human mind cannot conceive it fully. So, we make it simpler.'

'Well...'

'I cannot know, can I, Katerina? I cannot *know* that this temple is good. Its very numerical order is hidden from me. My mind literally cannot know it. Perhaps goodness is a lie we tell ourselves.'

Katerina, thinking carefully about what to say, finally placed an arm around his shoulders and turned him so that he was viewing the temple.

'They cannot be right,' she said, her eyes following the straight marble lines. 'It is just stone.' He opened his mouth in protest, but she stopped him. 'Listen, Michail, it is stone, that is all. It is what we bring to it. That is why we must keep fighting for what is right, what is just. It is *people* that celebrate tolerance, Michail. Not stone. This monument – the ratio – is only good if the city it stands in is good.' She looked across at him, smiling. 'And I think, with you in it, we stand half a chance of reminding this city of how to behave.'

Michail wiped a tear from his eye on his sleeve. 'Thank you, Katerina.'

'No need to thank me. Now stand tall, Sofia looks like she has another job for us.'

Sofia marched down the temple steps; the knot in her dress had come untied and her skirt billowed dramatically behind her in the warm breeze. She lit a cigarette and placed the back of her hand onto her forehead.

'I need you two to try and break up whatever media circus is happening down there. Christos knows we have nothing on him, but that doesn't mean we can't disrupt his one-man show.'

'No clues as to where Laurence-Sinclair might be?' Katerina asked.

Sofia rolled her eyes. 'No, as usual he manages to be everywhere and nowhere at the same time.'

Breaking up the press circus was more difficult in practice than in theory. Most of the other news channels had called it a night, but Christos and his fans remained tireless. The more Christos spoke, the more fans seemed to arrive, and the more hysterical the cheers became. Michail could not understand how these people fooled themselves into thinking this was a man worth celebrating. As far as he could tell, Christos had a few headline phrases on a constant conveyor belt, occasionally mixing up certain words or rambling nonsense in between.

'He has them in the palm of his hands,' said Katerina, watching the crowd, who were now raising their palms to the sky and shouting, 'She arises! Athena the Protector! Here she rises! Purge, purge, purge!'

'Surely Sofia can give the word to arrest them?' Michail asked, taking a step back. 'They are inciting hate.'

'No, apparently they are reciting poetry. Athena is not considered an official goddess nor an organised system of belief, so this doesn't count as a celebration of terrorism.'

'But Athena isn't real! They are celebrating Laurence-Sinclair, a human!' A few unfriendly glances were shot their way.

Katerina nodded. 'Keep your voice down, Michail. I'm not agreeing with it, but that's the genius of all this, isn't it? They're not celebrating anything illegal at all, because they are celebrating a fantasy. It would be ridiculous in the eyes of the law – as you say – to acknowledge them celebrating a murderous ancient goddess. Christos can encourage this all he likes: he's untouchable.'

'You can't kill an idea,' said Michail quietly. 'It's written all over Exarcheia.'

'Well, it would be nice to kill this one,' Katerina said. 'But it's the same sentiment.'

Christos's voice pealed out once again. 'How long have you been feeling like this? Be honest, please! This is a place of safety! Who has money troubles? Raise your hands. You, you, you... all of us! And what has anyone done to help you? What changes have been made to support you and your hard-working Greek families? There has been no help! There have been no changes! Instead, we open the floodgates to outsiders. Shout with me: she will hear us tonight! We are her citizens! We are her children! Athena! Athena! Athena!'

The crowd roared in agreement.

'Half of them will be immigrants or children of immigrants themselves,' Katerina said. 'How can they be so stupid?'

'There is another body on the hill, I hear! In Athena's ancient temple. I hear it crawls with snakes. I hear it is a dedication. I hear there arrives a second Erichthonius! Athena's own son! This is a call to all of *you*.' Christos lowered his voice, his eyes twinkling. 'Perhaps in death, we find hope. Greece was golden once and it will be golden again! Take action! Ready yourself for the great awakening!'

Michail scanned the area behind Christos's platform, trying to work out if he could disrupt the sound system without being seen. He jumped as he caught Theo staring back at him from the shadows behind the podium. Theo's eyes burned into his like black cuts of coal. Michail nudged Katerina. When she saw Theo, the colour drained from her face.

'What is he doing?' Her breath seemed to quicken.

'Should we go over...?' Michail began, sure that there would be a rational explanation. Theo had been so helpful recently.

'No!' Katerina hissed. 'Look, he's with the other constables.

They're applauding Christos! It looks like they're supporting him.'

'If that is true, it is outrageous,' Michail said, glancing at her. 'He has been so helpful, too! This is highly irregular. Katerina? Are you all right?'

She steadied herself, her hands resting on the front of her thighs. 'Sorry,' she replied, without taking her eyes off Theo. 'He... he just spooked me.'

Michail was sure that such a dramatic reaction required further examination but calculated now was neither an optimum time nor location. 'Ignore him,' he said, conceding that he had been hasty in welcoming Theo's help. 'We need to think of a way to silence Christos. It looks like he's planning to go on all night.'

'I am here to protect you,' Christos continued. 'It is all I have ever wanted to do. The citizens of Athens are my life. I want to hear your woes, I want to hear what impurity, what dilution of our people has done to your family...'

'It's worth a try,' Katerina said. Michail watched, amazed, as Katerina raised a bold hand and pushed herself to the front of the crowd. He followed her, folding his arms tightly around his front. 'Christos!' Katerina shouted. 'Christos, it's me, Katerina Galanis! We met at your office!'

Christos scrutinised the crowd, searching for the source of the voice, until eventually he rested his eyes on Katerina. Michail was compelled to stand in front of her, due to the festering excitement he noticed in Christos's eyes. 'You came to your senses, Katerina. I remember you.' He raised an eyebrow at Michail. 'And your friend?'

'This is Sergeant Michail Mikras. We have been investigating the... return of Athena.' She took a deep breath as Michail frowned at her. 'You are right, Christos. I have found my senses. Everything you are saying rings... true.'

Michail noticed Theo take a step forward, his hand hovering over his gun. He hoped that Katerina knew what she was doing. They were very exposed in the crowd of supporters.

'Well, please,' Christos stepped to one side, inviting Katerina to the stage, 'come and share.' He spoke into his microphone. 'The Hellenic Police Force support Athena's cause! Again, who am I to deny what is undeniable?'

A quieter cheer bristled throughout the crowd as Katerina climbed onto the podium. Christos pulled her into a tight embrace and whispered something into her ear. Michail noticed Katerina tense a little. He pushed her forward, not taking his eyes off the stage for a second. The cheers bled into hushed whispers. The sound reminded Michail of scuttling rats. Katerina looked out into the full and wide street and took a quick breath. Then she began, speaking in rapid, urgent spurts, as if she intended her words to sprinkle the crowd from above and dampen their fires.

'Like I say, we have been investigating the case. Let me tell you...' She checked behind her shoulder. 'This is not magic! This is *murder*, brutal murder! This man,' she pointed at Christos, 'is...' Theo took a step forward, ready to intervene on Christos's behalf. However, Christos did not seem perturbed. He held a hand to Theo and the other constables and began to laugh. His fans conversed excitedly in response. Perhaps this would work? Michail nodded at her to continue. Katerina spoke faster still. 'He is lying to you! Athena is not arising! Think about it, please! How can this be true?'

Christos's laughter reverberated along the street; his microphone held close to his mouth. Around him, Michail saw that people had started to film the scene on their phones. Katerina paused, her chest rising and falling heavily.

'Please,' said Christos, dipping his head towards her. 'Please, do not let me interrupt you.'

'You are lying to them!' Katerina shouted, her frustration spilling over in trembling words. The crowd made an 'ooh' sound. Someone shouted, 'Hysterical woman!' Laughter ensued. Katerina looked at the crowd in disbelief. Christos leant close to her and tried to take her hand; she pulled away and Christos obstructed her movement, making it seem that Katerina was flailing about, as if she was attempting to attack Christos, who managed to radiate a sense of serene calm and control.

'You cannot be serious!' Katerina screamed at the crowd, batting Christos's arm away. They met her with more jeers, laughter. *Get down! Take the woman away! She's crazy! Did you see her attack him? She cannot handle the truth! Non-believer! Non-believer! Non-believer!*

Katerina faced the crowd, and Michail saw in her expression what he was thinking himself: these people were too far gone. They had been brainwashed. They would not listen to reason because they did not want it. They wanted change, brought about by any way that they could seize it. She jumped down from the platform and the crowd cheered.

Christos raised his arms for silence. 'Friends,' he said. 'As we know, it takes bravery to conceive the unbelievable. You will meet adversity; I have told you that before. There are those who will call us stupid. There are those who will deny our truth for their own gain! What do I say to that? Why, I expose these non-believers for the liars they really are!' He pointed at Katerina, who stood close to Michail, huddling in the centre of the crowd.

'This is the scorned ex-lover of my loyal bodyguard, Theo.' Theo waved as more cheers erupted. 'She is nothing but a madwoman trying to get back at an ex-boyfriend. You know, a similar theme runs through the entire handling of these so-called murders. Sofia Sampson, you have heard of her, the *foreign* woman in charge? I did not want to share this with you, friends, as I believe in keeping our personal lives personal, but since I have been driven to it: she is an old flame of mine. You know what she did when I broke up with her? She sacked me! This is all verifiable, open for all to see. How can you trust a team who are led by the whims of scorned women? How can we trust anything they say? Are we content to leave the city – our citizens – in their hands? They are biased! There is a reason why they don't want you to see Athena's sacrificial bodies. They want to keep her a secret!'

The response was thunderous. Michail covered his ears and peered up the slopes at the Acropolis, from where Mani's body would have now been carried. The stars did not shine brightly in the sky tonight. He thought of his apartment, only minutes away, and wanted only to shut himself inside. He grabbed Katerina's arm. 'I think we must leave.'

But Christos had not finished. 'And if you need any more proof as to the unreliability of these people, Theo has just informed me that the officer with the hysterical woman is an imbecile!' A hundred or more heads turned to peer at Michail. 'He has psychological problems! He is not fit to work, let alone protect you!'

Michail recited his numbers, quickly, willing himself not to rock back and forth. The attention turned to him was like a thousand rats' whiskers bristling over his bare skin. 'One point six one eight,' he said, closing his eyes. 'One point six one eight. One point six one eight.' The laughter was painful. There was the sensation of being dragged, prodded. He kept his eyes closed, his fists down by his thighs. 'One point six one eight,' he repeated, allowing himself to be guided through the night, lifting his thoughts out of his body. Eventually, the voices sounded further away. The air was thinner.

He opened his eyes and realised he was walking past the open-air cinema, which meant he was almost outside his apartment building. The pink fingers of dawn had begun to unfurl, as if paving his way home to safety.

Katerina walked next to him, holding his arm, checking behind them periodically. 'Michail? Michail, do you hear me? Are you all right?'

He nodded, allowing the tension to ebb from his bones. 'Yes, Katerina. And you?'

She yawned, checking her watch. 'My goodness, it's morning. We're due at headquarters in a few hours. Sofia is on the warpath.'

'It is understandable. There have been three deaths, one suspect is untraceable, the other is hiding in plain sight; it is far from ideal.'

Katerina laughed, a desperate sound, and nodded to his door. 'Right, I will see you shortly. Mama will be wondering where I am...'

'Stay.' He said the word very quickly, so that his brain did not fidget its way out of it. 'Stay, Katerina. It is the rational decision; it will optimise your resting time, therefore rendering you more efficient for the day ahead.'

Katerina looked like she would certainly refuse, but, as she turned towards the direction of the sunrise, the rosy rays bathing her face, she shook her head and smiled. 'All right. I'll take the sofa?'

'Of course,' Michail said, wondering why on earth she thought it a possibility that he would offer her his bed, as they ascended his stairs and reached refuge at last.

———

The door was opened in a violent smack. The metallic hinges rattled in alarm. Michail paused, about to get into his fold-out bed. He had forgotten to secure the locks. A tired and catastrophic error. Katerina sat upright on the sofa, clutching her sheets, disorientated. A large figure stood in the doorway, his arms pushing on each side, as if trying to break the walls down.

'Theo!' Katerina rolled from the sofa.

Theo snarled at her. 'His bed too small for you, Kat?'

'What? No...' Katerina was slow to react. Theo slapped her with the back of his hand and she collapsed onto the tiles with a soft thud. The sound that escaped her lips caused Michail to let out a wordless shout. Seeing Theo place Katerina's gun under his belt, as well as her phone, Michail reached for his own gun, but Theo's fist met his jaw with brutal precision before he could get there. Michail felt the force in slow motion, his eyes rolling into their sockets, his mouth flailing loosely as his head swivelled to the side, spraying blood across his sheets.

'Michail.' Katerina sounded faraway as she stirred.

Another blow shattered Michail's train of thought, this time across the top of his head. Michail exhaled painfully, thrown into an excruciating confusion. He rolled onto his back and held his arms in front of him, shielding his face. Theo loomed over him, a beating, angry mass. Michail saw him draw back his leg before the assault to his stomach arrived. He doubled over, straining to call out to Katerina. Then, the feeling of panicked breathlessness. The feeling of quiet, momentary death. Michail's breath returned in ragged gasps in enough time for him to hear Katerina shout, 'Theo, please! You'll kill him!'

'I want to feel you squirm between my bare hands,' said Theo. Michail could not think how to respond.

He was dragged across the floor, his hands clambering against the smooth tiles. He was no match for a man of this size, not without a weapon. Theo threw him against the wall so hard that the bookshelves rattled. As he recovered, Michail was aware of a struggle happening by the sofa. He hoisted himself to a seated position and propped himself up. Theo had Katerina in both hands. He was shaking her, so her hair fell over her face in tousled jolts. She was sobbing, screaming. Michail leaned against the wall to push himself up but a sharp pain in his side caused him to slump back onto the floor. He was helpless. He felt his eyes haze over; Katerina's screams became distant. 'No,' he spat, tasting blood. 'Theo.' Michail grunted the word, his chest tightening. 'Theo, it's me you want. You... you bully. Why don't you finish the job?'

Theo began to laugh, but he released Katerina. She fell to the floor, sobbing. Theo stepped over her and approached Michail with slow, confident steps. 'I'll enjoy this,' he said. Michail scrunched his eyes closed, readying himself for the onslaught. He arranged his body in the optimal position, pulling his knees to his chest and folding his neck over so that it was protected by his arms.

Michail was vaguely aware of screams for help. Katerina's voice, high and shrill, echoed down from the floor above. 'Help!' she screamed. 'I need some help! Let me use your phone!' There was a hammering sound, and then a door being opened. Michail opened his eyes, waiting for the blow, and saw that Theo had stopped mid-motion. For a second, Theo seemed to consider his options, clearly expecting Katerina to be calling for backup. Michail noticed that Theo, although wearing his standard constable uniform, had replaced his insignia with a new badge: the symbol of an axe and two snakes. Theo grinned, following Michail's line of sight. 'It's just beginning, idiot. You're on the wrong side.' He left, his footsteps thundering down the stairway.

'Michail!' Katerina called him from upstairs.

'It's all right, Katerina, he's gone.' Michail pulled himself up, glad that the pain in his side was abating.

'Michail, can you come up here? Are you able to?' Katerina's voice was fragmented, alarmed. It sounded like Moira was speaking rapidly, he could hear her throaty voice through the ceiling. 'Michail!' Katerina shouted again.

Pushing himself from the floor, allowing himself a low groan, Michail lurched towards the door. He hoisted himself up the stairs using the railing, swinging himself around the corner. Moira's door was open. He slumped against it and lowered himself to the floor. His eyes were watery and swollen. Nevertheless, through the bulging slits, he saw why Katerina stood in the centre of the room, holding Moira by the wrists, her mouth agape. The older woman's eyes were downcast. Pinned to the walls of her small apartment were print after print of Marius Zamfir, Oscar Mathers, Iman Samaan and Mani. In the centre of all of them was a large photograph of Laurence-Sinclair.

Moira raised her head slowly as Michail's eyes widened. 'I told you that you could not fight it,' she said. 'She is back.'

Moira

Sofia stared at the woman, who appeared to be in her seventies and had allowed her grey hair to grow past her shoulders. She fiddled with her fingers nervously, her head tilted forward, snatching short glances now and again at both her and Yiorgos, who sat to the left. Her glasses were too big for her face and kept slipping down her nose before a trembling finger was raised to push them back up. A translator was present, for Yiorgos's benefit, although the woman persisted in attempting to speak Greek. Sofia persevered in English. 'You realise this is a murder investigation?'

'Yes,' Moira replied in a small, yet gravelly, voice. 'Yes, I realise that is how you see things.'

Yiorgos shuffled impatiently on his chair. Sofia sympathised as she took a long sip of tea. She opened the file containing the photographs found in Moira's apartment. Images of Marius Zamfir's corpse were easy enough to find online, however, the press had not had access to the other three bodies. It was a mystery as to why this woman, a friend of Michail's, as he had seen fit to disclose with vigorous protocol, had them pinned to her wall.

'Tell me again, from where did you get these images?' Sofia splayed the photographs on the interview table. Against the black matted surface, they were bright and garish, which was the point.

Moira peered over at them, making a show of moving her head from one to the other. She then looked back up at Sofia and said, 'He gave them to me, I told you.'

'Laurence-Sinclair? The man in this photograph from your apartment?' Sofia placed the photograph on the table.

'Yes.' She shook her head, confused again. 'I have already said, dear.'

Sofia ignored the comment. 'You know him?'

'Yes,' the woman said. 'No. I used to, once, a long time ago. I suppose you might say that we were recently reunited. I only moved to Athens last year. Your colleague Michail can confirm that.'

'How did you *used* to know him?' Sofia leaned forward, trying to scrutinise the interviewee's face. This woman was one of the most unreadable people she had ever met. She had an expression that seemed to harbour tens of emotions all at once. Her eyes shone with whatever she said, even when asking for a cup of water, suggesting that her brain was dancing with hidden scenarios and outcomes. It was disarming. Alarming. Moira raised her eyebrows and her glasses fell even further down her nose. She pushed them back up, wrinkling her nose with thought.

Yiorgos checked his watch impatiently. 'Go on,' he commanded. Sofia had the feeling that this Moira Fordman would not be rushed.

'I work at the British School, in research. I didn't know he worked there too, at the museum. I knew him from university, you see. Simon is his first name. He... was very dear to me, for a short but significant time.'

'In what capacity did you know him?'

Moira's eyes glowed from behind her spectacles. 'I was one of his Bright Eyes.'

Sofia frowned. 'His club? Laurence-Sinclair – *Simon* – called the members his Bright Eyes?'

Moira folded her arms at that. 'Simon's club? He shouldn't take all the credit. Yes, he started it. He advertised the meetings on the faculty noticeboard. It was just an academic discussion group; they were common. He had some interesting ideas about modern interpretations of myth; it's all old hat now, of course, but his thoughts were cutting edge then. I found him... intriguing. This was before I met my husband.' She looked down at her hands for a short while and then resumed. 'We were students. It wasn't unusual to experiment with substances, Simon was no different. The meetings quickly developed into secret parties. I thought he lacked imagination, however. I had always been interested in Athena. Even as an undergraduate, I had begun researching the ancient cults that surrounded her, how she had managed to survive in various forms throughout the millennia: she is indomitable, you know. I thought the drugs could help us get closer to her. I wanted the Bright Eyes to feel her, really feel her presence. So, the parties became a time of worship. Simon and I led the celebrations together. We were inseparable, connected by a larger, ancient force.'

'But he was sacked?' Sofia interjected. 'For eliciting drug use in his undergraduates?'

Moira's face fell. 'Yes,' she replied. 'That's how it ended for us.'

'You didn't hear from him until you arrived in Athens?'

Moira nodded. 'It was quite out of the blue. I did not... I did not have much else going on.'

'You are a recently retired lecturer?' This from Yiorgos, sifting through his notes. The translator echoed his question.

'Professor,' replied Moira. 'Of classical art and myth, specifically Greek sculpture.' She looked at her hands again. 'I recently lost my husband. That is why I moved here; it was time for a change. I found it easier to concentrate away from home, away from the memories. Somehow, the memories make him feel all the more distant.' Sofia and Yiorgos waited in silence as Moira gathered herself. She eventually slid a thin hand along the table and touched the edges of Sofia's photographs.

'Simon sent me these, yes. Is there a problem?' Her eyes bored into Sofia's. 'Like I told my young neighbour, Michail, we are wonderfully powerless against the goddess. These pictures are upsetting at first, I see that. But you must learn to embrace them. I made them a shrine in my apartment. The gods never treat deniers with mercy. They are vindictive, brutal. We know this.'

'Do you know why?' Sofia leant forward, noticing that Moira's eyes had become cloudy, as if remembering something long dead. 'Moira?'

'Why?' She shook her head. 'What do you mean, why?'

Sofia placed both her palms on the table so that she did not strike it out of frustration. Yiorgos groaned beside her. 'Why did Laurence-Sinclair – *Simon* – send you these photos?'

Moira shrugged, and rolled her head back so that she looked at the ceiling, hands laced behind her head. Sofia averted her eyes as she noticed the two dark patches of sweat under her armpits. 'I suppose he thought I would be interested,' mused Moira.

'Why would he think that?' It was not his turn to speak, but Sofia let Yiorgos take this one. She would not give this woman the satisfaction of losing her composure.

Moira turned to Yiorgos with a vacant smile, as if she did not fully understand him. 'Who would not be interested in the reawakening of an ancient goddess?'

Sofia cleared her throat before Yiorgos said any more; it was important to allow the interviewee to explain events exactly as they saw them. This was not the time to reason, to change minds. 'But you would have a special interest, no?' Sofia pressed. 'Given your specialism? The club you ran together, the Bright Eyes?'

'Yes, of course.' Moira nodded enthusiastically. 'That is why Simon sought me out. I have venerated Athena for most of my career. I have proof: my books. I have written at length about her effect on the world, how her images have guided, shaped our very ways of being. She is familiar to me and I am loyal. As is Simon, as he has shown in his work for the museums here in Athens. She will show me special consideration, I am sure of it.'

Sofia scribbled in her notebook, shaking her head. The connection should have been clear. They should have investigated the members of Laurence-Sinclair's university club; Michail should have joined the dots. 'I'm not following. Consideration? For what? What do you want from her? From the goddess?'

'I am not Greek.' Moira faced Sofia, with a more serious expression. 'When she returns, permanently returns – and it will happen soon – she will cast out the impure and non-believers. But I have made myself pure. I have proven myself pure. She will want me here, in Athens, in the Golden City. I will shine brightly forever.'

Sofia was at a loss as to how to reply to that; obviously, this woman had allowed her mind to soften. It was a shame; she would have been intelligent once. Yiorgos leaned forward, ready to tear her words to shreds, but Sofia stopped him. 'Where is Simon, your friend, now?'

Moira leaned forward, her mouth poised in an open position. 'I have no idea, specifically.'

'Unspecifically?'

'He will be worshipping Athena. He will be preparing.'

'For what?' Sofia gripped the edge of the table.

'You will see. She will reveal herself as she sees fit.'

Yiorgos could contain himself no longer. 'Unfortunate she sees fit to support the butchering of innocent people, isn't it, Mrs Fordman? Can I remind you that this is a serial murder investigation? You realise that your friend, Laurence-Sinclair, sorry, *Simon*, is a lead suspect?'

Moira sat back in her chair. 'As I have said, I realise that is what you–'

'It is not just what we think, it is facts, brutal facts!' Yiorgos swore loudly and beat his fist on the table. Moira jumped. He swung about the table and knelt in front of her, pointed a finger in the old woman's face. 'You will answer these questions with the seriousness they deserve, you mad old bat.'

'Yiorgos...' Sofia felt she ought to warn him, but, despite her professional judgement, she was interested to see where his aggressive tactic would get them.

'Have you seen Laurence-Sinclair recently? How did he deliver these photographs?' Yiorgos picked up the images in one hand and waggled them in her face.

Moira held herself impressively, retaining an air of dignity. Sofia had never seen anyone sustain such righteousness in the face of Yiorgos's rage. 'He slid them under my door. I have not seen him in weeks.'

'Weeks?' Yiorgos barked. 'Can you be any more specific? The morning of the first murder, Marius Zamfir, for example?'

'You cannot convict an immortal for murder–'

'Will you shut up!' Yiorgos stood, scattering the photographs onto the floor. Then, in an enraged whisper, 'You are a lying, manipulative, stupid woman.'

'Well,' replied Moira. 'If that is what you must believe.'

'Oh, I must,' said Yiorgos in a low tone, walking back around the table to his chair. 'The morning of Marius Zamfir's murder: did you see Laurence-Sinclair then?'

She shook her head. 'Why do you ask?'

Yiorgos tapped the spacebar on his laptop. A small figure emerged from the left side of the screen, filmed from the angle of a security camera. She wore thick-rimmed glasses and hobbled confidently, as though on a practised morning walk, around the long street of Adrianou. The diagonal shadows cast by the early sun next to the Stoa of Attalos flickered upon her face like an old film reel. Arriving at a café, she helped herself to a plastic chair and sat back on it, before removing a laptop from a square wicker bag. She placed it on her knees and opened it. Staring ahead for precisely three and a half minutes, the woman then began to type. She typed quickly and without needing to watch her hands. Her gaze was focused on the mutilated body of Marius Zamfir, but also upon the figure approaching her from whence she had come. She waved at her friend, Laurence-Sinclair. Yiorgos paused the footage, Moira's hand caught mid-motion.

'Forgive my curiosity,' Sofia interjected. 'But I would hardly call this a normal meeting between friends.'

Sofia would have described it as Moira freezing, but it was not that. She did not so much freeze, paralysed by the truth, as was often the case. It was more like she was hardened, turned to an impossible substance that hung between animate and inert, almost stone-like, yet each tiny breath, each twitch at the corner of her eye was magnified and purposeful.

'The footage of the murder itself is missing, so we thought this security footage was useless. However, a junior engineer accidentally left the tape running last night. Look at what turned up. Almost fate,' Yiorgos spat. 'Otherwise, we would have found you immediately.'

The silence was like no silence Sofia had experienced

before. Usually, in moments like these, the interviewee was dumbfounded, their expression blank or strained, depending on how determined they were. Moira, however, worked the silence in a most calculated manner. There was the tangible impression this was a silence of her design and that, though they had caught her, she would sit there for as long as she intended. Still, stony.

Finally, she said, 'It would not have mattered. I am a mere mortal, an observer. Her work would have continued without me. Yes, as you can see, I could not help myself. When Simon told me of Athena's first act, I was powerless to her call. I had to see it with my own eyes. The beauty...'

'The murder of an innocent?' Sofia whispered. 'Is that beautiful?'

'The sacrificial message of a goddess,' replied Moira, squarely. 'Yes, that is beautiful.'

'We have enough to hold you here,' Yiorgos barked. His patience had run out; it was fair enough. Sofia judged that they had got all they would from this wretched, deluded woman.

'As you wish.' Moira bowed her head. Submitting, Sofia thought.

Michail sat in the Myth-Buster Unit office with Moira's laptop. Cyber had taken all they needed and now he was able to dig through her files. He had refused hospital treatment after conducting a thorough self-assessment. Theo's attack had left him worse for wear. However, nothing could be more important than the case at hand. He would manage the pain with appropriate medication and keep himself well-hydrated.

The whereabouts of Theo remained a mystery, as did the whereabouts of much of the department. In fact, the whole headquarters showed a depleted turnout today; clearly, not everyone possessed the determination and sense of justice that Michail Mikras did. Katerina worked on her own laptop, scanning the files Michail sent her.

'Are you sure that you're okay?'

'Katerina, please. I am fine. But time is of the essence, so please concentrate on Moira's documents.'

'She seems so...'

'Harmless,' Michail finished. 'Correct. I allowed myself to be taken in by her friendly countenance. It is clear now, however, that she is a monstrous threat to the safety of our society.'

'I wouldn't beat yourself up,' Katerina said. 'I know all about misjudging people.' Her eyes lingered upon Michail's face, which was now sprouting a colourful memorial of Theo's handiwork.

Michail sighed. 'People are impossible,' he said. He clicked to open a new file, entitled '*Reading Athena*'. The documents here were labelled curiously. Being a professor of mythology, Michail would have assumed that Moira need not take notes on the more obvious aspects of the goddess, yet here they were, neat reminders of Athena's trivia:

1. *Worshipped as protector of the city, Athena Polias (see Xenophon, Hellenika, 1.6. and Herodotus 5.77)*

2. *Birth from the head of Zeus (see various sources; Iliad V, Hesiod, Theogony.)*

3. *Virginal goddess, Athena Parthenos, for whom the Parthenon is dedicated. Worshipped by the ancients by the Great Panathenaia on August 13th...*

'It's odd,' Michail said. 'These look like teaching notes, as if she is explaining the facts to someone.'

Katerina got up and stood behind him, studying the screen.

'Yes,' she said. 'Almost like she is giving somebody the headlines. Have a look at her emails. See if she was messaging someone.'

Michail searched her Sent box with the term '*Athena*' and was met with hundreds of results. He scanned the notes again and tried a more specific term '*Parthenos*'. A long thread appeared. Clicking on it, he blinked a few times at the screen.

'Oh my,' Katerina gasped.

The email attached to the '*Reading Athena*' documents read as follows:

```
Dear All,
    You are correct about the signs: a
snake and an axe are completely
consistent with the goddess's imagery
and are undoubtedly attributed to her. I
must admit, at first, I thought that
your esteemed selves were playing some
sort of joke, though the more I meditate
on it, the more it is revealed to me.
Why not Athena, that Bright-Eyed
goddess? Why not the Greek pantheon? Do
we laugh at Christianity? At Islam?
Hinduism? We do not. It is not a stretch
to believe that a Greek goddess would
return to her homeplace, then or now:
the Olympians did not require blind
faith of their followers, unlike so many
modern religions. They showed themselves
to mortals regularly, in their various
forms. This is why they punished non-
believers so unflinchingly.
    I am humbled that you look to me as
your expert and urge you to read my
```

books, both about Athena exclusively and other Hellenic matters in antiquity. I look forward to guiding you through any more signs Athena sees fit to leave us.

Until then,

Moira Fordman

The recipient list was expansive. 'It's sent to... to over one hundred people,' whispered Katerina.

Michail nodded, searching for a specific name. 'There! Christos Panagos, he is a recipient. Basil Arvanitis...'

'The police director!' Katerina grabbed her chair to sit beside Michail. 'It's a list of the who's who in Athens.'

'Correct.' Michail nodded, copying and pasting all the names on the screen. 'The prime minister's name is here,' he noted grimly.

'What does her next email say?' Katerina asked. Michail clicked on the next instalment.

Dear All,

I saw it with my own eyes this morning. The message is clear to me: this is Athena's birth (you will remember I sent you the full extent of this myth, with references, in my last correspondence). I was amazed and terrified as I looked upon the work of an immortal. I am reminded now of a most moving Ancient Greek word: δεινος (deinos). A lazy translation would be simply 'terrible', but this would not do the word justice. That boy's body filled me with awe. This is δεινος. It is

terrible in the sense of things
transcendent, godly. It is
inconceivable, as the gods are. I
watched the body for some time and felt
the hands of the goddess as she would
have touched him, laying him to rest. It
was golden, that feeling, breathtaking.
I sat in the wake of an immortal. The
boy no longer feels the pain of being a
half citizen here. He no longer feels
the pain of polluting the city. Athena
has helped him, as she will help us.

Perhaps she will remember my life's
dedication to her? But such hope is
hubris, and I will be happy with my lot.
Of course, you may notice (and now it
seems so prophetic as I help you usher
in the birth of a goddess!) that my
name, Moira, means Fate.

You have my complete notes on Athena
so that you can take in the signs. I
feel that she will thunder on, like her
father, with quick and raged
decisiveness.

Athena's true disciple. She has
arisen!

Moira Fordman

'She believes,' said Michail. 'She believes that the goddess Athena committed these murders.'

'She's insane!'

Michail began to agree, but then shook his head grimly. 'She is lonely, vulnerable. She told me she had just lost her husband;

it sounds like he was all she had. Perhaps… perhaps she needed something more to believe in. Illogical, but understandable.'

'Well, she's not the only one,' said Katerina, walking to the window. 'Have you seen outside?'

Michail joined her at the window. The wide road below was gridlocked with parked cars. People stood on the bonnets, weaved between the cars, holding banners. 'What are they doing?'

'The banners say the usual.' Katerina sighed. '#awakening. But they haven't been this… obvious before. They're holding up the whole road!'

A jolt shot through Michail's spine. He ran back to the laptop and scrolled up the email thread.

'Michail? Michail? What is it?'

'The 13th of August,' he shouted, pointing to the street, then looking back at Moira's notes. 'The Great Panathenaia, Athena's festival, happens on the 13th of August. It is today, Katerina! This is what everything has been leading up to. The #awakening has been talking about some great event for some time… remember Christos told the crowds to prepare for a great awakening? But there has been no specific date mentioned.'

'Probably so we didn't get involved and stop it. They must have organised this through word of mouth.'

Michail nodded grimly. 'We need to get to the Acropolis. We need everyone we have!'

He ran to the door, gasping lightly as he remembered his injuries. But there was no time to lose. 'Ms Sampson! Yiorgos!' he shouted, limping towards the interview room. 'We need to attend the Panathenaia immediately!'

Peripatos

It was early afternoon and very, very hot. Michail was also very, very tired. He took a sip of water from his bottle and stepped to one side as a group of young people carrying rucksacks and banners pushed past him. Even at the height of tourist season, he had never seen the streets so busy. Groups of people, both young and old, huddled in packs, sporadically bursting into chants, swigging beers, laughing, celebrating. A woman with her face elaborately painted in gold and white, an owl's head emerging from the top of her nose across her forehead, approached him. 'The facilities?'

'Excuse me?'

'The facilities. Where are they? I've been here all afternoon. Bursting!' She slurred her words, evidently already drunk. Michail shook his head and turned away from her. 'The facilities!' she insisted. 'I need to go.'

'You can try the toilets at the museum.' Michail pointed to the large white building. 'The queues are long, though.'

'A public event like this and no toilets?' The woman swayed, stamping her feet. 'Outrageous! Oh, don't tell me. Public funding cuts, is it? Hardly a surprise...'

'This is not a public event,' Michail said, for what seemed like the hundredth time. 'I – the Hellenic Police Force – are paying due diligence by being present at a privately organised parade. This is not state funded. We are crowd control.'

'What?' She hiccoughed loudly and giggled, almost stumbling backwards. Michail grabbed her, wincing.

'Careful,' he warned. 'It is hot. Drink some water.'

'To Athena!' The woman lifted a plastic cup to the sky. 'She walks again. Bringing peace to our city. Athena!'

As she shouted, the people in their vicinity reciprocated her cry. They raised their own drinks and cheered. Michail frowned, taking a step back to observe the scene. It was astonishing. The whole city was filled with the 'revellers', the new term coined by #awakening. Michail skirted past a large piece of cloth spread on the floor, with about half a dozen people on their knees surrounding it, painting it carefully. Michail squinted to look at what they were drawing. '*The Awakening*' it read, written in serpentine, scaled letters. In dark silhouettes were representations of the four deaths: an axe, an olive tree, a spider and a snake. A subheading was scrawled: '*The goddess arises to purify our city!*'

'It's not a crime!' a man shouted at him, paintbrush in hand, seeing Michail looking over his shoulder.

Michail shook his head and sighed. 'Correct. Painting is not a crime.'

'Panagos! Panagos! Panagos!' shouted a small group of what looked like teenage girls. They posed in front of a selfie-stick, jutting their hips to one side, squeezing their lips together and hollowing their cheek muscles. Fiddling with their phones, one cried, 'Make sure you tag me! Tag him too, it's @PanagosHellenakratia.'

Most of the people here seemed like normal, intelligent, humble Athenians. Did they realise what this parade stood for?

Did they understand the damage they were causing? They could not; Michail refused to believe it.

'Freedom to Athens!' A large group, dressed in blue and white, marched down the centre of the road, banging drums and blowing party horns. 'Freedom to our citizens! Freedom to Athens! March, march, march!' Most of the men in this group had shaved heads and overtly muscular arms. They were existing members of some far-right organisation. This parade would, of course, suit their agenda perfectly. Michail watched as they pushed through the crowds. 'The little spider starts from the beginning! The little spider starts from the beginning!'

Michail was pleased to hear a chorus of angry shouts in response to the group. Clearly, the #awakening supporters were not quite a united front yet. His hand hovered over his gun as a small crowd surged to meet the blue and white parade in the centre of the road. 'Fascists!' someone called out. 'Fascists!'

The word only seemed to encourage the men, who cheered in response. 'Purify Athens!'

'We'll listen to Athena! Not you Neanderthals!' replied one woman.

Michail shook his head and reached for his radio. 'Sergeant Mikras here. Looks like a fight might be emerging. My location is Apostolou Pavlou, just down from the cinema.'

He was pleased to hear Sofia's crackled reply. 'We're sending backup. Is Katerina with you?'

Michail stared at his radio. 'No, she went to find us some water.'

'Good. Let me know when she returns. Anything else?'

Even over the radio, Michail heard the desperation in her voice. This impromptu parade had caught them all off-guard. He was still none the wiser as to what they should be looking for. If this was going to mimic the events of the ancient

Panathenaia, then that could mean a number of worrying things. On top of this, as well as half of the Special Violent Crime Squad going AWOL, the local stations reported that hardly any of the Hellenic Police Force had shown up for work. 'Unfortunately not, Ms Sampson,' he replied into his radio. 'I will continue to be vigilant.'

'Please do.' Her line went dead. Michail watched as the skin-headed men began to unfurl from their tight-knit formation. Thankfully, they did not show any signs of bearing weapons. They held themselves like tightly wound coils, though. Most of the people who had called them fascists had backed down. A small, muscular man with a shaved head was pointing up at the Parthenon, his face drawn close to a man holding a plastic spear and shield.

'They had the right idea! We've had enough! It's time to stand up to the barbarians! We are not afraid to say it! We are on the same side as you! Free Athens! Free Athens! Purify! Purify! Athena arises!' The words undulated through the masses. 'Athena arises! Athena arises!'

Michail walked towards the pair, both hands on his hips. 'That is enough. Please move on,' he said to the man with the shaven head.

The man turned to him, revealing a straight set of yellowed teeth. He bowed his head, smiling as if sharing a private joke. 'All right, officer, we're all in it together,' he said, winking. He punched Michail's chest in a gesture of solidarity.

Michail stepped back. 'This way if you please.'

The man laughed and sauntered close, pushing his bony chest out. 'A non-believer, eh? You need to follow the example of your colleagues, son. I'd watch yourself. Everything changes tonight.' Michail reached for his radio, but the man grabbed his arm. Michail met his eyes. They were sharp and bright. Michail remained silent as the thug whispered, 'No need to call your friends. We're off anyway. Think about what I said.'

With that, he blew into his fingers, making a loud whistle sound. The blue and white men drew themselves up into their formation and continued to march down the road. Michail watched the back of them, baffled and overwhelmed. There had not yet been an official count, but it was estimated that three-quarters of the city's population was gathered around the Acropolis hill, or as close to it as they could get, in preparation for the event that evening. As he had told Sofia, he assumed that the plan was to follow the Panathenaic Way, beginning at the entrance to the ancient agora, and that it would end at the Parthenon. Michail gazed up at the familiar sight and, yet again, those meticulous columns filled him with a sense of unease. This was not order. This was chaos. In the name of his favourite temple, according to the latest social media posts.

Gunshots sounded from the slopes of the Acropolis. The thousands lounging on the hillside became agitated, some tumbling down the steep hill, using the trees as stabilisers. Michail looked to his right and saw the Reinstatement Unit, in their black and heavy armour, running towards the sound. Looking back to the slopes, Michail's mouth dropped open as he watched an avalanche of bodies bundle down the hill. The shots grew closer. All about him, people began to dart in different directions. Chants erupted, ragged and enraged. 'Freedom! Freedom! Freedom!' The word lost its meaning, became senseless. Michail was hit in his bruised ribs by a man running past carrying a large machete of some kind. It was grotesque. A perverted fancy-dress party. Michail blew out through his mouth. Three times. Then in. Three times. He knew he should remove himself from the danger, but he was unable to move. His hands tapped the sides of his legs in their usual rhythm, invoking calm, invoking strength.

Sofia's voice bellowed over his radio. 'Michail! Michail? Will you reply? Get yourself out of there, now. That is an order. You and Katerina, out!'

Sofia's voice reverberated on his radio again. 'Are you and Katerina safe? There are reports of gunfire.'

Before he could reply, a crowd of men trampled past him, knocking the radio from his hand. 'Watch it!' one shouted. Michail tried to catch it, the voice of Sofia still crackling from its speaker, but it smashed onto the ground and Sofia was silenced. Michail peered down at the broken equipment. He had failed. Ms Sampson had failed. The city was dying.

Michail backed into a shady corner, his legs unsteady. The world moved about him relentlessly. The pounding footsteps, the screams, the celebrations, the shots, the chants. A time passed. Nobody paid him much attention; they were swept away with the selfish buzz. Michail wiped his face with his sleeve, steadying himself, and began to look for Katerina. She should not have been taking so long.

He swallowed firmly, attempting to regain some moisture in his dry throat, and frowned, scanning the crowds. This was certainly not the moment for her to become distracted. He understood that the Theo episode had been highly unnerving – for them both – but they had a job to do. He thought she had been coping very well. As soon as he thought it, a dread crept into the pit of Michail's belly. She had been coping well indeed. Furthermore, this case had seen Katerina's time-keeping and organisational skills improve exponentially. It was, therefore, highly irregular that she should be missing.

Missing.

Just as the thought occurred to him, a voice sang to him through the crowds. 'Michail! Over here! Quick!' Where? Where? He looked up, shaking the wetness from his eyes, urging them to focus. A primal feeling invigorated him. Once, as a young child, like most children, he had lost his mother in the market. He had been too afraid to shout her name aloud. 'Mama,' he had whispered to himself, hoping, with a child's propensity to believe in magic, that his desperation would speak to her, one way or another. But she did not hear him. 'Mama,' he had whispered again. He had forced himself to move, twitching his tiny feet forwards, one step after another, surrounded by unfamiliar legs. The legs of strangers are like trees to a child. He had been lost in a forest, blocked from the one he needed the most. 'Mama,' he had whispered again and again as he pushed on. Then, the utter and pure relief of clasping his mother's leg. Of looking up and seeing that warm and comforting glow.

He would find her. He must find her. 'Katerina,' he whispered. Then more loudly, 'Katerina!'

'Michail!' Her voice cascaded through the commotion. He wiped his face and propelled himself from his hiding space. He scanned the crowds, forcing himself forward, searching the manic faces within his vicinity. She was calling to him. His partner needed him. Their partnership was vital; this he knew. One square metre after another. Scan and move on; scan and move on. There! Her hair pulled back into a swinging ponytail, being dragged by someone in the opposite direction.

'Katerina!' he called out. He thrust forward through the centre of the wide road, holding his hands out before him to clear a path. 'Katerina!'

She twisted her face towards his, her eyes darting about. She was afraid. Michail broke into a run, ignoring the pain from his injured ribs. The back of Katerina's head disappeared into the multicoloured crowd. His chest tightened, limiting his breath. He stopped, placing a hand on a bench, panting. His eyes watered as he steadied his lungs. The sharp edges of panic needled their way through his gut. He could not lose her. He would not lose her. He hauled himself up and stood on top of the bench, shielding his eyes from the sun. As he straightened up, he coughed throatily, almost losing his balance. There she was, being pulled in a resolute line towards the right-hand side of the road. Michail squinted. Her figure was slight, silhouetted in the afternoon sun. Her legs worked quickly, and her arm was held straight out before her. As his eyes swam into focus, Michail saw that it was Theo's tremendous figure that pulled her away.

Michail scrambled down from the bench and launched himself into the commotion. His throat convulsed as he struggled to breathe. He wondered whether he should call her name again; he did not want Theo to know he was tracking them. Michail made a diagonal line across the crowds to the right side of the road and skirted the short green railings. He saw them ahead, Katerina's feet scraping along the pavement, struggling against Theo's determined strides.

Michail held his head low, keeping his eyes steady and alert. He forced his mind to forget the pain in his chest. He stepped behind a group of people and watched Theo force Katerina's head through a small gap in the railings. She struggled, her hands clinging to the iron spokes, but he tackled her through with violent ease. Michail ran towards the opening, shielding himself behind revellers. He fumbled for his radio, forgetting for a moment that he had dropped it. Peering over the fence, Michail watched as Theo pushed Katerina down the sandy surface. She tumbled frantically, her arms reaching in vain to brace her fall. Theo grabbed her roughly and dragged her through the trees towards three wide steps leading to a cave. He stopped to observe the location: they were in the cave sanctuary of Pan. Michail slipped through the opening in the railings and crouched behind a wide cedar tree. Through the branches he saw Theo push Katerina down the large steps.

The cave itself was guarded with old rusty gates. Michail

had never visited the cave sanctuaries before. Interesting as he found the concept, he had always found them to be primordial, murkier than the cool organisation of the monuments on top of the Acropolis. Theo checked behind his shoulder, and then glared at Katerina, as they entered the narrower cave opening on the right. Michail pressed himself closer against the bark of the tree.

The gate screeched as Theo kicked it, and the hinges swung, broken and loose. Michail watched Katerina disappear into the darkness, out of the light, and felt a distinctive pang of icy fear. A ridiculous sensation, he calculated. It was imperative, for Katerina's sake, that he remain calm. He waited a few long minutes and slid down the steps himself, keeping as low and as fluid as possible. Once in the base of the sandy sanctuary, beneath the street-level chaos above, he kept close to the wall, forcing his breathing to keep quiet.

When he reached the opening of the cave, he sank close to the ground and retrieved his gun from his holster. Straining to interpret their precise location within the cave, he crawled through the gate, which Theo had left swinging open. Voices echoed from the darkness within. 'Theo! Please, it must be kept a secret. They cannot know.' Katerina's voice was shrill, yet wispy; almost undetectable, like an odourless gas.

'Are you stupid? Are you a completely stupid bitch?'

'Let me go!'

'Kat, you worked *with* us. You can't turn back the clock now; you are bonded to me, joined with us.'

Michail thought he heard the shuffle of an additional person within the cave.

Katerina's voice broke into sobs. 'Stop it!'

Theo's laughter danced with the sound of her cries. 'What will he say when he finds out, Kat? Poor little Michail. What will he do when he discovers his precious partner is working for The Awakening?'

'Please,' Katerina whispered. 'You cannot tell him.'

A strange and horrible fog engulfed Michail. He heard the words, strong and visceral, yet could not quite grasp the meaning. Katerina? He almost said her name aloud. It could not be. He clenched his eyes closed and counted silently. She was not denying it. He waited for her to laugh, perhaps to tell Theo that he was imagining things, that he was mad. But she did not. She continued to beg Theo to keep her secret. *Their* secret. It was his partner, his friend who had infected the city. She was the pollutant. The mole. The thought skittered in Michail's mind. He could not bear it. It made his stomach churn. Greasy memories slid before his eyes: her jitteriness as evidence had been discussed, her shiftiness as Sofia touted her theory of a mole. Her strange behaviour around Theo. How could he have missed it? How could she have lied so well, so convincingly? His mind could not accept this revelation. A low, animalistic moan escaped his lips.

He felt as if the world around him was peeling away. Only the entrance to the cave existed. He entered, his body moving independently of his mind. He was aware of the glee in Theo's eyes. He was aware of Laurence-Sinclair hovering in a dark corner. But he only saw Katerina, her trembling mouth spattered with blood. Her eyes were wide, her red mouth moving, soundless. He was pulled to her, he needed to understand. He needed her to explain, to soothe him.

'No!' Her voice was a shard of glass to Michail's heart. A blunt force exploded at the back of his head. He fell to the floor, not once taking his eyes off Katerina, a thick hum ruminating in his ears. Another blow, this time from Theo's foot, hit the side of his face, throwing him onto his back. Michail hoped there was more; there was sense in pain. There was truth in Theo's violence.

'Theo, stop it, please!' Her siren voice sang sweetly as Michail gave way to his eyelids, letting the darkness engulf him.

One Point Six One Eight

The change in light enveloped his senses; a torch shone in his face. Michail opened his eyes, squinting into the brightness, calling upon his ears to make up for the lost sense. He turned towards a scuffling noise behind him. Theo was tying Katerina up, her mouth already gagged with a dirty rag. 'If you won't join us, you stay here,' Theo hissed. Her hair fell across her face, framing her reddened eyes. She was screaming something, but Michail could not understand her. The shadow behind the torchlight moved into view: Laurence-Sinclair. Michail groaned, as a deep ache ebbed through his skull.

Katerina let out another muffled noise, her cheeks expanding against the taut material that covered her mouth. Michail felt Laurence-Sinclair's hands press down on his neck; he struggled beneath the weight of the old man, feeling his windpipe begin to collapse. As he tried to reach for his gun, Laurence-Sinclair batted it away, sending it flying into the shadows.

'Make it quick,' Theo shouted. 'But painful. I want him to hurt.'

Katerina's cries were ragged now, cutting through the air.

There was a moment in which Michail thought this would be the last sound he heard. He prepared himself to slip away, silently, and envisaged his limbs growing limp, their lifeblood growing colder. But then something comforting emerged from Katerina's wordless screams. Was he imagining it? He thought he heard an element of structure: pauses between breaths; faint vowels; attempted consonants. Numbers. It sounded like she was saying numbers. He observed the dark roof of the cave. Laurence-Sinclair's hands still pressing onto his neck, he watched the dancing lights projected from the back of his eyes line themselves up into a pleasing pattern. They echoed Katerina's shouts. *One point six one eight. One point six one eight. One point six one eight.* She was a traitor, a liar, yet he could hear it now, clearer than ever, through her muffled lips. *One point six one eight.* Katerina was giving him strength. She was trying to help him.

Michail held Laurence-Sinclair's gaze for a second, before utilising the last modicum of life he had left to drive the older man's body away. Laurence-Sinclair cried out in surprise as Michail heard him stumble to the floor. Without stopping to look behind him, Michail rolled himself to all fours, pushed himself up and escaped into the shadows.

He hoped he was correct in remembering the geological structure of the cave that he had once read about. If he recalled accurately – and it was no small task amidst the raging pulse thumping between his ears – the cave led to a labyrinth of low passages. He pressed his hands into the thick black before him and, crouching, felt the cold, damp ground beneath his palms.

'Get him!' Theo's voice roared from behind.

Michail pressed on, methodically moving his hands in an outwards pattern, finding the passage walls, and moving deeper into the recesses. Footsteps echoed behind. A circle of torchlight grazed the tip of Michail's head. He lowered himself down further to the floor and pulled himself around a corner, curling his body up into a tight ball so that he would not be seen.

'It is futile!' Laurence-Sinclair shouted into the darkness, his torchlight dancing in circles across the jagged rock. 'There is no point hiding. Show yourself. Join us! It is too late to stop it. The Awakening is happening, a bright new dawn! Only a fool will hide in the darkness!'

'Stop making poetry, old man, and bring him here!' Theo shouted from the main cave.

Michail kept himself very still, keeping his breathing shallow and silent. The torchlight edged closer. He kept his eye on it, listening carefully to Laurence-Sinclair's footsteps. There would only be a split-second chance for this to succeed.

'Come now, Mikras.' Laurence-Sinclair's voice grew closer. 'Choose your allegiance. You are not a stupid man, I know. Join the enlightenment.'

Michail moved silently and swiftly. Pushing his weight onto his left side, he swung his legs into the narrow passage so that his shins connected with pleasing force against the ankles of Laurence-Sinclair. Michail followed the motion through, keeping his body tense and felt the man's body hurl forwards, a cry of surprise echoing through the stone.

'Laurence-Sinclair? What's going on?' Theo's voice again. He sounded irate.

Michail grasped Laurence-Sinclair's torch and shone it straight into his face. 'I apologise for this, but it is quite necessary,' he said quickly, before bringing the torch down with considerable force against the crown of Laurence-Sinclair's head. Michail breathed out in three successive blows: violence was a final resort, yet the objective was to save Athens, and that was more important than anything.

'Laurence-Sinclair!' Theo bellowed through the darkness.

Michail kept low. 'He is incapacitated, Theo,' he said,

wishing that he could find his gun. His hands scrambled along the floor in front of him, but there was not enough time to conduct a thorough search. He would have to attempt to escape the cave without a weapon. Michail emerged from the shadowy tunnels, forcing himself to remain calm.

Theo now cradled Katerina in his arms, stroking her hair. It took all Michail's energy not to run straight at him, but he forced himself to remain stationary; he needed time to assess the situation. He did not want any sudden motions to cause Theo to do something unthinkable.

Theo's lips spread into a wide grin. In the torchlight, his teeth shone like white boulders. 'You heard us earlier?' He laughed. The sound was clamorous, causing Michail to flinch. 'Ha!' shouted Theo. 'I gave her a chance, Michail! I let her in. She is nothing with you!' His hands slid to Katerina's face as he pulled her head towards his, kissing her forehead. 'Accept it, Kat. Be proud of your part in the cause. I will protect you.'

Michail could see Katerina shaking from where he stood. He stepped forwards. 'Let me speak to her.'

'Why?' Theo mocked. 'Final goodbyes? She has nothing else to say to you.'

'I want to know what... what part she played in...' Michail looked about the cave desperately. 'All of this. It is clear I am defeated, Theo. Please allow me the truth, at least.'

Theo smiled, bringing Katerina closer to him. 'She can tell you herself.' He ripped the gag from her mouth and she fell forward, saliva and blood spewing onto the floor.

'Michail.' She reached out a hand to him. Michail stayed put. 'It is not what you think, Michail, please trust me.'

'Get to the point!' Theo roared, shoving a gun to her head.

Katerina closed her eyes, tears falling down her face. She nodded frantically. 'I planted the snake ring, Laurence-

Sinclair's snake ring, Michail. Please look at me! I had good reason–'

Michail's breathing grew heavy as he thought of all the signs he had willingly ignored. She had helped Laurence-Sinclair up on the slopes of the Acropolis. Had he given her the ring? Had she slipped it from his finger? She had been the one to spot the ring on the slopes, even though the chances of finding such a small item were inconceivable. She lied to him. Lied to Sofia. 'You are working with Laurence-Sinclair?' Michail spat the words at her. 'He gave you his ring?'

'No!' Katerina's neck bent with the pressure of Theo's gun. 'Well, yes. He gave me his ring, but I had no idea, Michail, no idea until tonight that... all I was told on that night was to find the ring on the slopes and draw attention to the snakes. I think Laurence-Sinclair was meant to do it but...'

'He panicked.' Theo rolled his eyes. 'As usual, he makes a useless partner.'

'You.' Michail glowered at Theo. 'You orchestrated this?'

'He said it would save Sofia! Michail, I had no idea that Theo– ' Katerina screamed as Theo kicked her over. 'Michail, please!' Theo placed the gag around her mouth again as Katerina squirmed violently.

'She lied to you,' Theo said flatly. 'She has no loyalty to you, nor the Hellenic Police Force.'

Michail agreed. Katerina could not be trusted. He should have relied upon his own good instincts throughout the case, as he always had done. He had allowed himself to become too close to her, and she had dazzled him, softened his senses. Well, no longer. He would find out every detail possible tonight, through rigorous and brave enquiry. Athens depended on it. He looked straight at Theo. 'Why is Laurence-Sinclair here with you? What is your relationship?'

Theo secured Katerina against the cave wall and faced

Michail. 'You didn't think that creaky old man was capable of it all on his own, did you? Sure, he's good at the talking, well-practised at that, but he can hardly lift a body into a box on his own, let alone attach an axe to the top of a temple!'

Michail's head was spinning. This could not be. 'You and Laurence-Sinclair? You are responsible for the murders? The Awakening? Together?' Katerina writhed in her ropes; her eyes locked on Michail. He ignored her.

This sent Theo into rapturous laughter. 'Responsible for The Awakening! Oh, sorry, sorry, Michail, but you are hilarious. Think about it, over half the force have not turned up for work today. The same is true all over Greece. You are the minority. We are all The Awakening! We have controlled you, Michail, from the very beginning.'

'No,' Michail said. 'That cannot be true.'

'Yes!' cried Theo triumphantly. 'I have outwitted *you*, Michail Mikras! God, it was fun, watching you pore over your stupid little myths. Thinking that you were getting somewhere, that you had any control over what was happening. You even thought I was helping you when I told you when the next murder would happen! So easy to mould, the lot of you. It was so satisfying to watch you all lag behind.'

Michail heard a groan from the tunnel behind him. Laurence-Sinclair was stirring. 'It was you who stole the security footage? You tampered with evidence? Thwarted our inquiry? You and Laurence-Sinclair preyed on the Exarcheia immigrants?'

'They were willing sacrifices.' Laurence-Sinclair's voice rang with a cold clarity from behind him. Michail jumped to one side, ready to defend himself. Laurence-Sinclair chuckled, his eyes gleaming, raising his hands. 'Don't shoot,' he said, waving his hands in the air; his tone was sarcastic, considering Michail was clearly unarmed.

Michail looked from Theo to Laurence-Sinclair. They were certainly an unlikely pairing.

'Willing?' Michail said to Laurence-Sinclair. 'Why would they want to die?'

'Because I told them to want it.' Laurence-Sinclair twiddled his fingers. 'That is what young Theo here doesn't understand: the delicacy of my role. He is impatient. He prefers brute force. Christos, however, appreciates me. He appreciates my prowess, my potential, unlike so many others.'

'Christos Panagos?' Michail was thrown off-guard by Laurence-Sinclair's conversational stance.

'He values me! He sees my worth. It is powerful to have someone see you in the way you should be seen, how I *should* have been seen, after all this time.'

'Your worth?' Michail persisted. It was not right that Laurence-Sinclair be allowed to delude himself. He had brought mayhem to the city. He was deranged, dangerous. 'You drugged innocent people and killed them. Marius, Iman, Mani... I am right in thinking Oscar was an accident?'

Laurence-Sinclair nodded. 'I thought that was a mistake. The Awakening leaders heard about the boy's accident through their sources and decided they might as well throw it into the pile. They called me last minute and the only thing I could think of was to plant my ring; it matched our imagery. I hoped you would connect the snakes to Athena, and you did, especially with her help.' He nodded to Katerina. 'The rain and dark disorientated me, my legs don't work like they used to. So, Theo contacted her. It's a shame: I have worn that ring since university. It was not planned, I was rushed.' He shrugged. 'Though I suppose it worked. It fitted the narrative; the olive tree could not have been more perfect. So what if you saw me? You didn't detain me. It hindered nothing.'

'The sources? What do you mean sources?' Michail already knew the answer but thought it would be useful to confirm.

'It cannot be news to you that your organisation is corrupt.' Sinclair laughed, tossing a nod at Theo. 'The leaders were alerted to Oscar's fall as soon as it was reported to the police. It could have been any one of your lot. The list of supporters grows constantly.'

Michail frowned. 'The leaders are...?'

Laurence-Sinclair chuckled. 'Christos, the prime minister, the police director, the chief of police... need I go on? There are more. It is over, sergeant. You have lost. They have utilised their power.'

'But I don't understand,' Michail said. 'You drugged your students when you were a postgraduate, the university sacked you for it; but you didn't kill them. Why kill the Exarcheia immigrants here, in Athens?'

For a moment, Laurence-Sinclair looked deep into Michail's eyes. Michail thought he saw a sliver of regret creep across his face. Then, Laurence-Sinclair gave way to an unexpected fit of anger. 'Did you not hear? Christos appreciated me! I was a man ruined when I left London. Decades, *decades*, I spent here, working behind the scenes of the museum, pandering to tourists' needs and wants. It was excruciating for an academic of my calibre. Finally, I made it to management. I thought that would be it, that I would be able to fly! But no! Because *she* arrived with her books and her expertise and her professorship, ripping the attention away from me–'

'Who?'

'Moira,' Laurence-Sinclair whispered. 'You are acquainted, I gather?'

Michail nodded, his head beginning to spin again. He needed to think of a way to escape. At least if he could keep Laurence-Sinclair talking it bought some time. 'She is my neighbour. We know about the photographs you sent her. And that she was a Bright Eye.'

'She lapped those photos up,' Laurence-Sinclair mused. 'You know, she wanted to believe in the gods so deeply, that she barely took any persuading.'

'Why did her arrival in Athens upset you?'

'The Acropolis Museum wanted to hire her, the star professor, the world expert! They wanted to replace me with her! Do you have any idea how that felt? I had finally managed to build a life here, and now – Moira Fordman – my ex-student, a former Bright Eye, threatened my career all over again.'

'You were jealous?' Michail asked, wondering silently how much more patience Theo would sustain. In the corner of his eye, he saw that he had not lowered his gun from Katerina's head, although he had his phone out and was attempting to catch a signal, scrolling incessantly with his free hand.

'Jealous? I was furious! It was her, you know, who testified against me to the board of directors. I remember her, a silly, simpering little thing, mooning about the campus, following people around, trying desperately to engage them in conversation.'

'What was the problem?' Michail asked. 'As I understand, you ran the Bright Eyes together?'

'You must realise that I was the faculty's golden boy. I was poised for greatness: they said as much. They loved that I pushed the boundaries of academic enquiry; my commitment to the subject was unparalleled. Promotion was around the corner: I was to be the next big thing. But it was her idea, wasn't it?' Laurence-Sinclair said. Even in the darkness, Michail could see his thick cheeks growing dark with anger.

'Her idea?'

'The cult for Athena. I don't know, she didn't have any friends, she wanted to feel a part of something, I suppose.' He sighed, making a sound somewhere between a laugh and a groan. 'She was the one who gave me that ring, with the snakes. I think she thought we were... close.'

'You weren't?'

'For a while, perhaps. But then... I began to tolerate her. I liked the idea of it: any excuse for a party. It was supposed to be harmless fun. I supplied the nectar...'

'The hallucinogenic drugs?'

Laurence-Sinclair rolled his eyes. 'Indeed. Yes, and she dressed the scenes. She was pretty marvellous at it, actually. She brought in candles and robes, went to great lengths to create numinous atmospheres. Once, she managed to source an original marble bust: the head of Athena. I have no idea how she did it. She treated it as the focal point of the meeting, got us to stare at it intensely, move around it, chant and chant and chant until the flames licking the marble seemed to be the living skin of Athena herself. Moira said she saw the goddess move; she heard Athena speak to her.'

'You are referring to the effects of hallucinogens,' explained Michail, helpfully.

'Moira did not think so, or at least, she did not want to think so. I did not pay her enough attention, I suppose. I was responsible for the recruitment process. I persuaded undergraduates to join, to lose their inhibitions. I approached them after lectures, engaged them in conversation, left them wanting more. It was... a fun project. I realised how exceptional I was at enticing people, manipulating their behaviours. They hung on my every word. Most of them believed that something mystical was happening. The chanting, the... rituals, coupled with the nectar, the food of the gods, it was easy to believe. But I was *too* talented; and Moira became intense, untenable. She became obsessed with the drugs, with Athena. She began to worship her outside of Bright Eye meetings. It got to the point where she would turn up at my flat in the middle of the night demanding more, another meeting, another opportunity to meet the goddess.'

'What did you do?'

'I am not completely morally inept,' Laurence-Sinclair replied. Michail struggled not to balk. Laurence-Sinclair offered him a grim smile. 'I wasn't then. I told her she should pursue a new interest. The Bright Eyes had gone too far and that she was distracted from her studies.'

'How did she take that?'

'She howled. I remember, she beat her fists against my chest and howled like a Bacchant. She thought I was breaking up with her, that is what she said. That I had used her, implored her to open herself up, only to dispose of her.'

'Had you?'

Laurence-Sinclair's eyes shone with the memory. 'It was a different time, sergeant. For me, it was a game, a fun dalliance. I barely remember it. Perhaps I should have been more careful with her, she was eager, too eager...'

Michail heard Theo shift in the corner of the cave; he was growing bored, his gun now lowered and resting by his thigh.

'Let me guess,' Michail said. 'She reported you as an act of revenge?'

'Bingo,' mumbled Laurence-Sinclair, looking at the floor. 'And so that was the end of life as I knew it.'

'You continued to wear her ring though?'

Laurence-Sinclair smiled again, though this time, he seemed sad. '*My* ring, and yes. I don't know, I thought of it as a relic. I did not want to allow myself to forget, sergeant, in case I should ever have the chance... to balance the justice scales. Over the years, it became a part of me. A burning symbol of regret, a focus for the fantasy of revenge. I knew it would come in useful one day, I just did not predict how.'

'But it doesn't explain why you murdered all those people,' Michail pressed, edging slowly towards the entrance of the cave. Laurence-Sinclair was so enraptured by his own story, that he did not notice. Theo was fiddling with his phone, bored the attention was not on him. A steady flow of tears erupted from Katerina's eyes, but she seemed to be wriggling her ankles against the ropes in minute, almost indetectable movements.

'I followed Moira's career closely. I was bitter, more bitter each year. Her success was a constant source of humiliation. Book after book... When I heard she would be replacing me at the museum as a mere retirement hobby, I... I could not bear it. I was transported back to those heady nights, the guttural whisperings, the animal desires. I hadn't thought about that part of my life for so long! I yearned for it. I realised that in leaving London, I had left behind that excitement – that exciting part of me! It was stupid, an old man's cliché some would say, but I overheard a conversation between two of the young museum interns about Exarcheia. They were talking about some party they had been at and I thought, well why not? It was easier than I expected. The streets around that square are joyous at night! The people just wanted to talk, hear my stories, and I listened too – there was anger, creativity, the juice of youth. Then one night, I met a man who saw the colours of my very soul. It was like an invisible hand reached out from across the table and touched me on the chest. He seemed to know exactly how I felt, he made me feel... wanted.'

'Who was it?' Michail continued to edge, millimetre by millimetre, towards the cave entrance. Theo now sat back against the stone wall with his arms folded sulkily, still looking at his phone. Michail caught Katerina's eye and froze. She blinked slowly at him, her eyes big and wet, then looked away.

'Christos Panagos.' Laurence-Sinclair smiled as he said the name, his head cocked to one side, residing in balmy memory.

'He made me feel like I could tell him everything. I didn't hold back, my whole life, the light and the dark, poured from my mouth that night, and he embraced it all. We started messaging, and then meeting more. I realised who he was, learned of the success he had made of his newspaper. He told me about how he had been sacked from the police force unfairly. Oh how I related! After a while, he asked whether he could trust me with something. I was honoured; to be trusted by anyone, especially Christos, was a thrill. He needed me. He said that a seismic shift was about to occur. He wanted me as an associate, a partner. A man like him! Not only that, he wanted me as a senior colleague, used for the most delicate and important of tasks. You will not understand, sergeant, I do not expect you to, but he gave me power. I was offered the apple and I took it. I deserve it.' Laurence-Sinclair seemed to consider something for a second and then shook his head.

His voice wobbled, growing louder as he asked, 'What is good, anyway? Is this world not a collection of random debris! Moira got her wish in the end. How serendipitous, that the woman who ruined my life by believing that gods could walk the earth, now helped mine and Christos's cause only *because* she believed. She was all too happy to hear from me. I apologised for good measure, said that I should never have taken advantage of her, blah, blah, blah. It was perfect: Christos plans to use her as a sacrifice tonight. My revenge will be sublime. She will die, forgotten and stupid, and I will live. Her expertise was also invaluable. The death is in the detail. Even I, a classicist, do not match her level of knowledge. She is obsessed, always has been. It had to be authentic. The deaths had to look divine, you see?'

'You drugged them?'

Laurence-Sinclair laughed. 'A little sharpener, of course.

They all believed, when the time was right, that they would be better off dead. They submitted to Athena. To me...'

'Will you shut up!'

Michail froze. Theo pounced to his feet, his arms tense by his sides, glowering at Laurence-Sinclair.

Laurence-Sinclair turned to Theo, emboldened. 'I will be a god,' he said, his voice rising to meet the cheers from the crowds outside. 'You will not speak to me that way. Christos has given me the highest authority. I...' Theo began to snigger. Laurence-Sinclair continued, though Michail noticed that his chin dropped slightly, the skin around his eyes tightening. 'You will listen, henchman! I am chosen! You are merely the legwork. Christos knows my mind is precious. He wants to elevate me. I am important, he looks up to me...'

Theo played with his gun between his fingers and slinked towards Laurence-Sinclair, trapping him with triumphant eyes. 'The highest authority!' he mocked, imitating Laurence-Sinclair's voice. 'A god!' He stamped his foot, laughing. 'Ha!'

'What are you doing?' asked Laurence-Sinclair.

Theo was encircling him, a restless lion. 'You are pathetic.' Theo said each word as if spitting bile. 'You think you're clever? Better than me? You are muck on the bottom of my shoe.' In a fluid motion, Theo raised his leg and kicked the old man in the stomach, sending him crumpling to the ground.

Michail hovered in the centre of the cave: no matter what he thought of Laurence-Sinclair, he could not leave him to Theo. It went against every teaching, every moral code. Intervening unarmed did not seem a sensible alternative, however.

Theo placed a foot on Laurence-Sinclair's chest and positioned his gun. 'Christos doesn't care about you,' he said. Dark blood dribbled from Laurence-Sinclair's mouth onto the ground. He moved his lips silently, as if trying to work out the meaning of Theo's words. 'He doesn't care about you! Do you hear me, old man?' Theo's words thundered with confidence.

'He... yes he does. He said that he would lead with me... the forefront of the dawn of a civilisation. He needs me...'

'He used you.' Theo knelt next to the old man, whose head had begun to shake, his lips moving incessantly, tearing through barren conversations, promises. 'He used you and now he has no need for you.'

'No, I helped...' Laurence-Sinclair whined in reply. He was a wounded animal, clinging to a last thread of hope.

'You helped, yes. I am sure he is grateful. You helped us. But that is all.' Theo steadied his gun and aimed for the space between Laurence-Sinclair's eyes.

'You cannot mean this,' Laurence-Sinclair whimpered.

'You are foreign!' roared Theo. 'You are not Greek! Be a man! You will end up the same way as your victims...' Theo snarled. 'A willing sacrifice.'

'Christos!' The echo of Laurence-Sinclair's final word rang out in brutal dissonance against the gunshot. It was too late.

But there was no point waiting. Each second ticked with excruciating delay. Theo stood over Laurence-Sinclair's body, chuckling. The cave's entrance smiled open and free. Michail dived towards it, pushing his tired body through the dark space, willing himself to move faster.

He found himself suspended in the air, a sharp pain impacting his shins. He opened his mouth as an anguished cry escaped him. 'No!'

He saw Katerina's shape, her arms still tied behind her back, lunge between himself and Theo's gun. He had moved too slowly. He would have been shot in the back had Katerina not tripped him. She had saved him. And placed herself in harm's way.

Katerina, letting out a ragged cry, drove Theo to the ground, pushing her elbows into his ribs. He did not shoot her – which was illogical, but useful, Michail thought, forcing his shaking legs to push him from the ground.

'Kat!' Theo roared, as she rolled over him, the bindings on her hands breaking with the force, and attacked him like a demented banshee.

Michail lunged over to help and secured Theo's weapon by kicking it from his hand as Katerina held him in place. She maintained her position, weighing Theo down, her face scrunched and determined, as Michail patted him down for further weaponry. 'If you remain still then this process will be more efficient,' he reminded Theo, joining Katerina by taking his own seat on Theo's back. Theo roared senselessly at them.

When he was satisfied, Michail observed Katerina, whose face was red and blotchy. Her cheeks were bloated, still restricted by the muzzle. It was fair, Michail considered, for him to remove her gag. He reached out and tugged it from her lips. Before letting her speak, he said, 'Good work. We must contact Ms Sampson. And then, we must place you under arrest, Katerina.'

By now, the cries from the revellers outside were a constant roar. Katerina hung her head, her hands still tied behind her back.

'I am sorry, Michail,' she said.

Proper Practice

In the cave sanctuary of Pan, Michail stood next to Sofia Sampson and worked through a list in his mind. He knew he was humming as he worked, but he did not care. The forensic team were busy. The riot continued to rage outside on the streets. The sun was setting. Michail would find some sense. Theo was handcuffed in the corner of the cave, guarded by two officers, who refused to look at him. Katerina sobbed intermittently, also in cuffs. Laurence-Sinclair's body had been taken away. A large pool of sticky blood stained the ground.

Sofia placed an arm around his shoulders. 'Michail, it will be all right.'

'Yes, thank you, Ms Sampson. I am attempting to decipher the information received tonight. When information is presented in a tangle, it is sometimes easy to miss the obvious thread.'

Sofia shrugged, looking around the cave. 'It seems clear to me. Laurence-Sinclair and Theo are our murderers, working under the orders of Christos. And Katerina... well, we must speak about that. What is terrifying,' she pointed to the cave opening, 'is that Christos seems to have mobilised all of Athens into believing that a goddess will greet them on the Acropolis tonight.'

'Correct,' said Michail. 'All a guise for a right-wing social ideology.'

'Yes,' said Sofia. 'And he has countless officials throughout the country on his side, by the looks of those emails you recovered from Moira. I think we must assume that those officers who did not turn up for duty today are also part of The Awakening.'

'Theo said the same has happened throughout the country, is that true?' Michail could not help but look at Katerina, who continued to cry.

'Unfortunately, yes,' replied Sofia. 'Which means we cannot call for backup. We have who we have.'

Yiorgos walked over to them, casting Theo a filthy look. 'If I had my way, he would be killed.'

'But...' Sofia raised her eyebrows.

'Being the two-faced, spineless thug he is, he has agreed to a settlement.'

'Oh? So, his loyalty is as thick as water.' Sofia smiled, her red lips glowing in the dim light. 'What's the exchange?'

'He reckons he has access to the original footage of all three murders. It was Theo and Basil's thugs who shut the power down outside the cotton mill by the way,' Yiorgos said. 'I suppose that's why Basil had them transferred.'

'He is a disgrace,' muttered Sofia.

'Well, there will be plenty more of those,' replied Yiorgos. 'The security videos will be useful. If the names on that list tell us anything, then our case needs to be irrefutable. We cannot afford to leave anything to chance.'

'What does he want in return?'

'*If* he faces prison time, and the lunatic doesn't think he will, given *what's about to happen* – his words – then he wants a pardon.' Yiorgos snatched another furious look at Theo.

'He thinks he can avoid a life sentence?' Sofia's laugh sounded more like a bark. 'Is he out of his mind?'

'Clearly,' said Yiorgos. 'But he's slippery enough to hedge his bets. If this Awakening succeeds tonight and our world changes forever, then this deal means nothing, whether we have the footage or not. On the other hand, if he faces trial, and an inevitable life sentence, then he thinks the deal will save him.'

'Let him think it,' said Sofia. 'I have no qualms about lying to a murderer, especially as all protocol seems to have been thrown to the breezes. Take him to the station and hold him there.'

Yiorgos commanded two officers to remove Theo. As they watched him leave, he crossed his arms. 'At least we can trust each other. The other side have revealed themselves by now. Anyone wearing a police badge today marks themselves a non-believer. Thank God we're both here.'

'Yes,' Sofia replied, removing her arm from Michail's shoulders. There was a very detectable tone of apology in her voice.

Yiorgos heard it too. 'You didn't think...'

'Of course not,' Sofia snapped. 'Don't be ridiculous, Yiorgos, I have always trusted you.'

Yiorgos chuckled. 'You were concerned with my texting...?'

'It is unprofessional to text on duty, as you well know.' Sofia's cheeks were flushed.

Yiorgos held up his hands, surrendering. 'I know, I know! It's just been busy at home; Thalia wants to know–'

'Thalia?'

Yiorgos frowned. 'My wife, Sofia.'

'Ah.'

'She is always keen to know when I'll be home because of our newborn.'

'Newborn? You mean a baby?'

'Yes.' Yiorgos grinned.

'You didn't say!' Sofia, clearly flustered, rubbed the sides of her arms.

'You didn't ask,' replied Yiorgos.

Sofia looked as if she were about to say something further but Michail saw this as the perfect opportunity to interrupt. They could not afford to waste time speaking about Yiorgos's family matters, though it was clear that Sofia needed to pay better attention to her colleagues in the future.

'Is Moira still in the detention cell?' Michail demanded. He had experienced a glimmer of an idea, still flickering and dim, though he thought it worth pursuing.

'Of course, why, Sergeant Mikras?'

He could not be sure, but there was something that stuck in his mind, like a chip in a glass vase. 'Something Laurence-Sinclair said; that Moira would be used as a sacrifice tonight. I cannot work out what it means. I feel... she did not realise what she was doing...'

'She is an accessory to serial killings!'

'Yes, yes, that is true. But may I speak with her? She trusts me, I think. We have conversed together on a number of occasions.'

'I'm aware,' Sofia replied, in an excessively dry tone.

'I may have a plan,' said Michail, noticing that Katerina was looking at him hopefully, wishing she would not. 'But I will need to speak to Moira, as well as read the transcript of her interview, any evidence that is extracted from Theo and,' he knew it was an unorthodox request, but this was unprecedented, 'Sofia, I need your senior cyber clearance code.'

'What on earth for?'

Yiorgos gestured to the streets outside. 'We have run out of time. Whatever Christos is planning tonight is already underway. We need to be here. We have no idea about what twisted event he has in store.'

'But I think we can stop it!' Michail said. 'Please, I agree, there is not enough time to explain and I am the only one whom Moira might trust.'

Katerina, who had been unable to speak for the past hour, seemed to find her voice, her face shining with new tears. 'Listen to Michail. I trust him with my life, he's our only chance.'

'You've done enough,' growled Yiorgos. 'Can someone take her away too?'

'Ah.' Sofia raised a hand. 'Michail, you will want to listen to this, Yiorgos, you too, this is important. Now the situation is stabilised, and we have our killers, I think there is just about enough time to share the following. When half the force did not show up this morning, I requested clearance for access to all their communications: emails, text messages, etc. Theo's were particularly illuminating. It is true that Katerina planted the ring—'

'Traitor,' Yiorgos grumbled.

'*But* she did it for, well, what she thought was a good reason. From what I can gather, Theo led her to believe there was a plot against me: that the closer I got to finding the killer of Marius, the more danger I was in. She was easily persuaded, it seems. Katerina?' She looked up; her cheeks swollen. 'Theo and his constable friends had expressed a hatred of me before, had they not? Based on my "impure" heritage? Being half-Greek is apparently not good enough for them?'

Katerina nodded, slowly, her face turned plainly up to Sofia. 'They thought you had stolen the job. They hated that you had outed a lot of the right-wing extremist sympathisers, too. They drank with a lot of those men. I am ashamed I put up with their ideologies.' Katerina let out a ragged laugh. 'I thought it was all talk, harmless, at first. But it was why I left him, in the end. Then, when he came to me about you – asked me to plant the ring – I thought he was trying to make amends, distancing himself from that sort of crowd.'

'It was no stretch to believe that he had uncovered a conspiracy against me?'

'I... I am so stupid!' Katerina took a deep breath, swallowing tears. 'He said that if I could divert the attention from the actual murderer, blame it on someone else, then I could save you. He said that you were treading on dangerous ground and had to be kept away from the truth, for your own good. The ring would distract you. Obviously now I know it was all a lie. It wasn't a diversion at all – the ring brought the attention to #awakening they wanted! But I didn't have time to think it through. I was so tired; he messaged when we were leaving the canteen in headquarters. Do you remember, Michail? We were both shocked, exhausted. He told me exactly what to do. That's why I suggested going off the beaten path: I guessed Laurence-Sinclair would likely be lost there. I did it. I thought... Sofia, I thought I was protecting you. I was so shocked when Theo turned up at headquarters, then when Laurence-Sinclair became a suspect... I should have said something! I wanted to. I told myself it was nothing, that it was not as if Theo was...' Katerina's face grew stony. 'There is no excuse. You should arrest me.'

'Agreed,' Yiorgos said, moving towards her.

'There will be no need for that.' Sofia placed an arm over Yiorgos's chest. 'In my view, you have a great amount of making up to do.'

Katerina frowned, uncertain of Sofia's meaning.

Sofia nodded promptly. 'No better time than the present, is there? We're down on numbers and I don't need a competent officer thrown away for the night due to – an albeit grave – error of judgement. Show yourself to be useful tonight, Officer Galanis, and we might be able to forget this sorry mess.'

'Sofia,' Yiorgos began. 'She is a criminal...'

'This night is like nothing I nor anyone has ever seen before,' Sofia replied. 'We need all the help we can get. The laws of proper practice are... suspended.' Sofia turned to Michail, who had been waiting in perfect silence. 'Is this agreeable to you, Sergeant Mikras?'

Michail looked at his feet, knowing that his response must be succinct. 'Katerina was my most trusted partner,' he began. He looked his friend in the eye. 'And I think, like my favourite temple, trust can be rebuilt, if only to strengthen its ties. She saved me from Theo, at least.'

'Michail–' Katerina began.

'No time for that now, Katerina, obviously,' Michail cut in. 'Temples are not built in a day, as you well know. I must speak to Moira.'

Sliding Red Door

One year ago

C hristos watched the man enter the warehouse through the sliding red door. He sat in ripped jeans on a step on the opposite side of the narrow street, his hair messily arranged in deep waves, a cigarette hung between his fingers. The camouflage was possibly unnecessary, though it was fun. How he enjoyed embodying them. It was too easy; they were all so replicable. Perhaps it began with the uniform, so self-conscious, so uniquely homogenous, then permeated through their paper-thin skin to the mind? Vague, gassy notions: they had to be angry about something; they had to be shouting, fighting; never minding the practicalities that most had to consider.

Houses like this were the rats' nests. They believed it was arty, he supposed, anti-establishment, to live in such shared spaces. It was surely obvious to anyone who thought about it seriously enough? Without proper responsibilities, the mind grows bored.

He had never allowed it to happen to himself. In the brief time he had spent out of work, what had he done? He had

written, he had convalesced by robust planning and thought. He
had built a media phenomenon. The opportunity was open to
anyone who had the gumption to take it. Instead of
complaining, he had acted in an effective manner. The
individuals living in these houses could not say the same.
Instead, they wrote songs, staged random protests, argued that
the floodgates of the country should be opened to all, to anyone
who wanted to take advantage of their rich and ancient land.
They claimed they were treated unfairly, without ever
considering their barefaced irony. Unfair? What about the hard-
working citizens of this country? Torn to financial ruin to allow
for a group of foreigners to paint insipid slogans. Christos
laughed; he could not help himself. See? Even now it was
important to self-assess. Hard-working citizens? That was a
stretch. The Greek public had been allowed to grow flaccid,
reliant. It was why they were so responsive to his ideas, to him.
They were powerless without him. They had been waiting for
someone to say the things they were thinking but dared not put
into words. He was what they wanted to be: brave, clever. It was
why they would follow him to greatness, he was sure of it. All
they needed was a little magic. They were stupid enough to
believe in that, certainly.

His eyes traced some graffiti on the wall opposite him. He
recognised the oversized boot, kicking in the face of a cowering
policeman. It was well done. The artist had gone to the effort of
painting the tiny droplets of blood that sprayed from the man's
mouth. The teeth were pointed; the policeman seemed
demonic. They wanted to create a villain, assign blame for their
poverty, their aimlessness. Fascist? Such a lazy word. Purist,
realist, were more accurate terms. But these people did not
bother to think about things carefully. They were happy
spewing out the half-formed contents of their liberal brains.

He took a long, languid drag from his cigarette. When he

had been in the force, they had raided a building further along the street to deport its residents. He had volunteered to co-ordinate it, wanting the experience, an opportunity to show his skill. That had been a step too far; he was sure Sofia had begun to suspect something after that. *Why target them? They have done nothing wrong. There is no need for such violence; it worsens tensions. We should strive for peace, Christos.* Her tone was always so sanctimonious, as if she had nothing to do with the raids, as if she could not stop them – an official of her seniority – had she wanted to. No, she was happy to criticise from a distance. Happy to keep her hands clean.

The pro-Islamic journalist in the south, whose death was reported in a sombre tone by the newsreader, was an opportunity to test her true inclinations. 'It is not entirely undeserved,' he had said, slowly enough to scrutinise Sofia's face as the event unfolded on the television screen. She had said nothing, her face like a sealed mausoleum. She enjoyed wearing that reverent English expression, as if her lack of emotion elevated her above the mere Greek mortals she worked with. She had not argued with him, and instead waited for him to leave her apartment in a thick silence. She would have been a strong ally, if she could only have let go of that female pride.

When some anarchists – scum – as they had been widely known within the department, had been mowed down in a hit and run, he had tried it again, this time in her office. 'Do they really deserve justice, Sofia? Nobody wanted them on the streets, causing havoc,' he had said, keeping his voice tentative, studying her face for any sign of agreement. But he had only detected a quiet disappointment. She had simply replied that they must continue to do their job, whatever their personal views. That was when she had stopped visiting his apartment. That was when she had started, he was sure, to gather her evidence.

The first unidentified bodies around Exarcheia injected fire into her veins. She had never believed they were a result of drug crimes. She had a notion that someone inside was thwarting her investigations. *Look at the victims' profiles, Christos, they are all immigrants. That cannot be a coincidence. We should be following up extremist groups.* But she was weak. She could not allow herself to believe that he, Christos, could be disloyal. It reflected on her judgement, which she held, as she applied that lipstick so artfully every morning, in great esteem. So, she manoeuvred opportunities for him. Chances to escape her Great Shakedown. A document here, lying surreptitiously within reaching distance on her desk as she turned away and admired the view, a mistakenly sent email there, intimating her darkest suspicions of corruption within her team. She had even cornered him, her desperate eyes reddened, and pretended that she had discovered a lead. She could not have, he knew. He had humoured her, let her finish her rehearsed speech. Then he had said, 'Let it go, Sofia. It will be in your best interests to leave this be.'

That had spurred her on, as he had intended. She could no longer ignore the truth staring her in the face. Christos made things easy for her, knowing he was destined for greater things. Calculating that, to make a real change, he would have to devise far greater plans: a strategy that reached the heavens. A few junkie deaths were not enough; they were child's play. He left his personal email account open on his desk. There was nothing that tied him directly to the bodies; he had not committed those crimes, however much he supported the sentiment of those who had. All Sofia found were messages of support between him and like-minded colleagues. He could not even be charged for radicalisation: he had merely been expressing a view. But he allowed himself to be let go without too much of a fight. Basil had called him unprofessional and explained how extremist views had no place within the force. Christos had noted the complacent tension in the man's cheeks, the puffy exhalation after each sentence. This was a man who needed to be liked, *wanted* to be liked. He could turn him, add him to his list of loyal devotees.

The red door remained unopened. For a while, when he was building the *Hellenakratia,* he questioned himself. He was strong enough to admit this. He had no money, was driven by ambition alone, so it was natural that he gazed into the proverbial mirror. What did he see? On the one hand, a broken, raving individual, with only a tarty receptionist to seduce. On the other, the leader of a new order, a brighter world. 'Choices,' he had whispered to his reflection. 'All it takes is a choice. The greatest of men carve out their own way; they know better than the masses, their insight is golden and shines above all else.' It had been a defining moment, a private oath.

He smiled at the wall opposite him, thinking of all the *Hellenakratia* had already accomplished, how he was only a few small steps away from the beautiful ending, the commitment of all citizens, the purification of first Athens, then the country. The snakes rattled in his belly. There was an ease with which he tilted his tongue to the roof of his mouth, curled his lips and clenched his cheeks. It was such a convincing mask, one that had won him many friends. He stood, stretching himself. It would not be long now. The red door would slide open at any second and the events would be put into motion.

From inside the warehouse, the bolts on the red door rattled. There was laughter; the old man had ingratiated himself already. If Christos did not know better, he would have called their first meeting in the square's corner bar an act of divine intervention. He was perfect! Skilled in deception and mind games; bitter, seeking redemption, attention. Fiddling with that snake ring over and over. The idea had engulfed Christos's schemes before the end of the night. A symbol of belief, a symbol of the immortal. That is what people needed to make the final push. They needed to see something greater than themselves, they needed to be guided by an unquestionable power. Athena was obvious: the city's patron goddess, a symbol of a time when purity was celebrated. They even had a deranged world-expert at hand who worshipped the goddess herself!

He lit another cigarette and sank back, relaxed. The threads had already begun to spin. The tapestry was almost complete. And there he was, emerging through the door; Christos bowed his head into the shade. Dr Simon Laurence-Sinclair: overweight, rich-looking, sort of. A man who drank too much wine. A man who did not iron his trousers. An easy man to trust, yet respect. He stood idly in the doorway talking to a young man. The conversation was cheery. Christos shifted to get a better view. The younger man was undeniably stunning. His blue eyes were noticeable from here, his straight nose cut down the centre of his face with striking symmetry. They embraced; the touch lingered just a second too long before Laurence-Sinclair pulled away, wearing an expression of slight surprise, awe and embarrassment. He was good, thought Christos. He was very good.

Christos waited for a few moments, stubbing out the cigarette, to follow Laurence-Sinclair. They had more to talk about, now that he had confirmed Laurence-Sinclair was obedient. As he pushed himself from the wall, some primal urge called Christos to look up again at the doorway to the warehouse. The beautiful man remained, looking straight back at him. His smile was strange and mournful; it almost brought a tear to his eye. The man was perfect where he stood, between the bright light of the sun and the darkness behind him. Christos allowed himself to smile back. 'Nice day,' he said.

'Yes,' said the man.

Christos looked up at the sky and shrugged, throwing the man a wave before he caught up with Laurence-Sinclair.

'Goodbye,' the man called behind him, and again, his voice carried a mournful note. Christos did not turn around to see if he re-entered the building, but instead made for the square, where he sat down at the corner café.

Panathenaia

The sky darkened and the revellers were filled with ecstasy. Although Sofia did her best to station her depleted team strategically, the floods of crowds easily overpowered any pretence of order. Short of shooting members of the public for partying, there was not a lot to be done but wait. Sofia was located among the ruins of the ancient agora, along with Katerina and Yiorgos. She checked her watch impatiently, Michail was due back from headquarters. He was cutting it too fine. He had at least radioed through some useful information about this ancient festival, presumably gathered from Moira. Apparently the original Panathenaic procession had ended with the presentation of some sort of dress, a *peplos*, to the goddess Athena. This did not sound too sinister. He had added that it also ended with countless bloody animal sacrifices and there was a strict rule regarding entry to the Acropolis sanctuary: only 'pure' citizens of Athens were allowed. This sounded more sinister. Short of that, Sofia had no more information, and they were left inconceivably outnumbered, treading water in uncharted territory.

Sofia made sure that Katerina remained by her side. She

wore a hollow expression; one that suited a face much older than hers. Hopefully, Theo's betrayal would not do permanent damage. She would blame herself, of course, wonder how on earth she had not noticed what was right beneath her nose, perhaps question whether she had known all along. Sofia hoped this would not shatter the girl's sense of trust; time, of course, would tell.

'Ms Sampson,' her radio buzzed.

'Here,' she said.

'Movement towards you. Looks like the procession is beginning. No stampedes yet. Just movement your way.' Sofia looked over the fence that sectioned off the ancient agora from the street. A wall of bodies stood surprisingly still as though they were waiting for a signal. She took a step back from the middle of the ruins, onto the platform of the arched monument behind her, beckoning her team to do the same.

'We're prepared,' she responded into the radio. 'As much as we can be.'

She held Katerina's arm in a gesture of comfort and turned to Yiorgos. 'It's beginning.'

Yiorgos lit a cigarette and looked up at the sky. 'Madness,' he said. Sofia nodded, her eyes scanning over the thousands of people moving with slow, assured direction.

A loud voice erupted into the agora. Sofia froze, her grip tightening around Katerina's arm. 'Revellers!' it said. It was quite unlike any voice Sofia had ever heard before. It had a rasping quality to it, high-pitched, yet ethereal. It was not unpleasant. Its timbre felt as if it wanted to massage the inner passages of the brain; the words vibrated long after they had finished.

Sofia motioned for her team to locate the source of the voice. Six men scattered amongst the ancient rocks, their black, padded bodies like obedient insects in the night. 'Revellers!'

The sound of hundreds of thousands of voices cheering was deafening. Sofia looked at her feet.

'She is here!' one excited man screamed. 'She is really here! Athena! Athena! Athena!' Others joined him with their own prayers, all shouting the goddess's name. All thanking her for her guidance, her help.

How quickly belief could shift. Sofia thought of the respect being a police officer used to command. She had wielded power; she had exerted it. She had been able to do this because of a collective belief in her authority. How had she never seen how precarious this was? She removed her hand from Katerina's arm and rested it on the hilt of her gun.

'Your goddess is here! You, who have come to celebrate, you will be rewarded! Raise up your voices in honour of something spectacular. Our city has been downtrodden! Left to rot! Forgotten! Its riches pillaged! You are discarded as if entrails in a bucket!' The crowds responded with a deafening booing noise.

'Help us, Athena!'

'You understand our needs!'

'Lift your spirits! Abandon your senses, disciples! Because tonight, you may allow yourself to believe in this city once again. Tonight, we enter another Golden Age! Tonight, we celebrate what it is to be Greek! What it is to be pure! I invoke the ancient call for greatness and prosperity!'

Yiorgos leaned over to Sofia. 'This is crazy.'

She looked over at him, her eyes wide. 'It is crazy, but it is working. They all believe.'

The formless voice continued, rising to an even higher pitch. 'You may believe in yourselves once more! Yourselves! Praise me! Athena! Athena! Praise the city of Athena!'

The crowds rumbled in excitement, repeating the chant. Sofia's heels reverberated against the hard ground; the sheer magnitude of the crowd caused the earth to tremble. She leaned down, barely believing it, and touched the marble floor. Sure enough, she felt small vibrations. She looked up at Yiorgos. 'They're coming.'

A fleet of lanterns, torches, and luminous screens drifted into the agora. 'Athena! Athena! Praise the city of Athena!'

Sofia spoke into her radio, her throat closing with panic. 'Team, they are in the agora, heading up towards the Acropolis gate.'

'Affirmative,' the voice on the other end replied.

'Be... be careful,' Sofia said, wondering if she ought to tell them to stand down.

Yiorgos pushed the radio down. 'They are on the right side,' he said.

Sofia could not find the appropriate reaction. She had an urge to sink to her knees. She was witness to an unbelievable sight. Half the city mobilised to celebrate an ancient goddess. Young and old marched towards the Acropolis, their faces set in a rhapsodic glee. Snake banners weaved between the bodies. Axes and snakes were painted onto T-shirts, faces, flags.

Katerina finally spoke quietly, not taking her eyes off the scene. Her face reflected the orange lanterns, flickering dark and light. 'They are brainwashed.'

Sofia breathed, unable to look away. 'They are unhappy. The Awakening, Christos, has given them hope.'

'Hope?' Yiorgos spat the word.

'Hope that it's not their fault. Hope in a higher being, and why not Athena? If they worship hard enough, she will save them. Not everything they say is untrue. This city has been struggling for years, Greece has been struggling. We have ignored the signs. That is why Christos is so persuasive, he muddles lies with the truth. Same old story, different country.'

'You were right to sack him,' Yiorgos grumbled.

'I was thinking the opposite,' Sofia replied, her voice soft. 'I gave him the platform he wanted.'

No one replied, and Sofia shifted from side to side, unable to find comfort. Hordes of revellers swamped past them, each new group shouting with more conviction than the last. There was a shuffling movement from the end of the stoa. Yiorgos swung around, his gun pointed.

'Sergeant Mikras here!' Michail shouted, emerging from the shadows. 'Apologies for causing alarm.'

Yiorgos narrowed his eyes. 'The long-awaited hero returns.'

Michail hurried down the long passageway, his energetic frame enveloped by the marble peristyles. 'My task took a little longer than anticipated.' His eyes flicked to a lump of marble behind Sofia. 'Ms Sampson, you have chosen a pertinent location.' He pointed to the oblong block of marble. 'The stele of the birth of democracy. There she is, crowning the symbolic people of Athens. In fact, the monuments in this building are all connected by themes: fairness, equality and reason.'

Noticing Yiorgos roll his eyes, Sofia did her best to humour this strange new recruit. 'I am glad you noticed, sergeant. As Yiorgos said earlier, we are on the right side.' Michail nodded sagely, whilst Yiorgos gave her a knowing stare. She was about to ask Michail to explain his plan when a loud cheer interrupted her.

'Jesus.' Yiorgos pointed to the revellers who stood yards away from them.

Sofia strained her eyes to see through the dark. 'What is it?'

'Police.' Yiorgos stepped forward, his fists clenched. Sofia dragged him back; this was no time to start a fight. Sure enough, a group of constables, identifiable by the odd bits of ravaged uniform, danced, wearing masks and banners, shouting 'Athena!' in between sips of beer and bursts of laughter. Sofia watched them, a burning anger simmering in her chest.

'Theo's mates?' Yiorgos asked, blowing smoke into the colonnade.

'I don't know,' replied Sofia, grabbing her radio. 'How many more will turn up? It feels like most of Greece has come to join the fun.'

'The roads are still full, Ms Sampson. There are plenty more.'

Sofia studied the hill. The burning snake of people had reached the top and was dispersing at the Propylaia, the grand gate to the Acropolis.

'What's going on up there?' she said into her radio. 'Anyone at all? Can you hear me?' The channel crackled and then went dead. She swore under her breath, looking behind her. 'What's your plan, Sergeant Mikras?' she asked, walking under the colonnade towards Michail. 'Please tell me it is a good one.'

Yiorgos swore too, squinting up at the hill. 'Looks like something's kicking off.' Indeed, a larger fire had been lit and it looked as if spotlights had been turned on. 'Is that a stage?'

Sofia nodded. 'We need to get up there.' She shouted into her radio again. 'Officers on the Acropolis, can you hear me?'

'Leave them,' said Yiorgos, already making for the hill. 'We need to go, look.'

A circle was forming outside the entrance to the Acropolis. Down in the agora, ripples of excitement spread through the crowd. Sofia detected a horrible imminence in the air. 'Right,' she said, motioning for Katerina and Michail to follow. 'If we are separated, get up there as quickly as possible. I've lost comms with the officers,' she shook her silent radio, 'which means we do not know what to expect.'

In a moment that she was unable to explain, she took Michail's face into her hands. 'Sergeant Mikras, listen to me. You have proven yourself a most impressive officer today. You have exceeded all expectations of dedication and resilience.

Whatever you have planned for tonight, know that I have every faith in you.'

She let go of his face and he jumped back, his fists clenched. However, after taking three quick breaths, he replied, 'Ms Sampson, it has been a pleasure to serve you in this investigation and lead the Myth-Buster Unit.'

Sofia, despite the impending sense of unmitigated doom, smiled broadly and took the man's hand. 'The pleasure is all mine, Sergeant Mikras.'

'Come on then!' shouted Katerina, already running towards the Acropolis.

———

At the top of the hill, the revellers spoke in hushed and reverent voices. Sofia balanced herself on the far side of the Propylaia steps with Michail, Katerina and Yiorgos, rammed against the warm marble columns. There was no impression at all that the masses respected them as law enforcers. In fact, they were ignored completely, disregarded as fellow celebrants. Michail seemed more alert since climbing the hill. He scanned the crowds fastidiously, metre by steady metre, and kept stealing furtive glances to the top of the Propylaia structure. Yiorgos smoked intently, frowning darkly at anyone who happened to catch his eye.

Attached to the columns of the Propylaia, at the entrance to the Acropolis sanctuary, were two large speakers, poised above a makeshift stage, onto where the lights they had seen from below shone. From the speakers, Athena's voice boomed again, this time louder and more urgent.

'Revellers!' Cheers erupted down the hill, through the trees, past the marble. 'You have done well so far in your duties of celebration. For that, I thank you. How does it feel to be a part of the new dawn? Part of a movement so potent, so momentous?' Whistles blew and horns sounded in lurid appreciation. The voice paused for a few moments and then spoke in low tones. 'You have come to purify the city, have you not?' The question was asked with a quiet intensity. There were a few cries of agreement from the people by the gate, but most nodded silently, enraptured.

'Then come, tell me, who will volunteer?'

Sofia frowned, confused by the question. 'What does that mean?' she wondered aloud. Yiorgos shook his head, his bottom lip puckered with confusion. Intuition prompted her to speak quietly into her radio. 'Get everyone here. I repeat, leave your posts and get to the hill. Now.' She glanced at Michail.

He nodded patiently. 'We must wait, Ms Sampson.' Sofia tried her best to believe in him.

Yiorgos shifted from side to side. He was nervous too. Sofia thought about what Michail had said about sacrificial victims. She forced her breathing to remain slow. A drunk voice from the crowd called, 'Go on then, I'll volunteer!' Laughter followed, as well as a round of applause. From the sanctuary, two masked men appeared from the Propylaia's entrance hall. 'I'll volunteer!' The masked men found him in the crowd, a young man, unsteady on his legs, laughing along with his friends. 'See you on the other side!' he joked.

'It's just for show, right?' said Yiorgos under his breath. 'They wouldn't do anything... illegal? In front of all these people?' From the tone of his voice, it was clear that Yiorgos was trying to convince himself.

Sofia did not reply, silently hoping Michail knew what he was doing. He had removed a rucksack from his back and was crouched over, fiddling with a mobile phone. 'Sergeant Mikras...' She could not risk more lives.

The chanting resurfaced. 'Athena! Athena! Praise her city! Athena!'

Michail looked up at her, his face completely calm and without worry. 'You said that you trusted me. Therefore, I must ask for no further distractions.'

Sofia opened her mouth to answer back but Katerina, who was standing behind Michail, silently raised a finger to her lips. Sofia backed down, allowing Michail to continue.

Within a few minutes, the volunteer resurfaced out of the dark columns, wearing a black cloak and carrying a long dagger. Behind him, the two masked men dragged a pig onto the stage. The animal squealed terribly, its eyes darting at the crowd before it. Its trotters scratched against the marble pathetically. Sofia felt Yiorgos reach for his gun. 'No.' She held an arm over him. 'It's just a pig. Wait for Michail.' Yiorgos mumbled something beneath his breath. A cooling breeze flustered through the columns. The pig lowered its head, petrified.

'Can we really do nothing?' Yiorgos asked. Sofia scanned the crowd. A few of the revellers had removed their costumes and were staring at the scene before them with wide eyes. The rest jostled as before, cheering the volunteer on.

'If this is the worst that happens tonight, then I can live with it,' replied Sofia firmly.

A chant began to emerge from the slope. It was melancholy, resonating from the bottom of people's throats. The effect was a wall of thick sound. Sofia's neck craned under the weight of it. 'Blood is life. Blood is life. Blood is life.' The vibrations of hundreds of thousands of vocal cords incited the pig to panic again. It convulsed against its ropes, kicking forwards and back, wailing in response.

'Oh my God.' Yiorgos leaned back against the column in disbelief.

'It's just a pig, Yiorgos,' Sofia whispered, watching the colour drain from his face. 'You've seen worse.'

He hung his head, wiping his brow. 'I'm a vegetarian,' he said, indignant. She was learning all sorts tonight.

The volunteer, baptised with bravery through the unanimous chant, plunged the knife into the back of the pig's neck. It was an inexperienced blow. Blood spurted from the puncture; the animal's eyes grew red and small as it squealed horrendously. Mercifully, its mouth lolled open, reducing its squeals to a dying gurgle. Yiorgos groaned next to her.

The crowd did not cheer as Sofia expected, instead they fell upon their knees as the animal collapsed. They rocked backwards and forwards, mesmerised by the pig's final breaths. A few individuals needed to be encouraged to the floor by their friends, but they eventually submitted. From the throats of the kneeling revellers came a low and chthonic whirr. It was an engine of intent. Of prayer.

Like one organism, the sound stopped. Sofia spotted torches dotted about the dark foliage of the site. The silence was a wonder, that was for sure. How could so many people gathered in one place achieve such a perfect absence of noise?

'Is that it?' Yiorgos asked. Sofia nodded, more out of hope than anything else. She reached for her radio, ready to instruct her team to supervise the revellers safely down the hill, when the voice from the speakers resumed.

'Athenians! What a start to reclaiming our city, to reclaiming yourselves! Sacrifice breeds life, citizens! Blood breeds life! We should not be ashamed of this, this most ancient tradition. We must build upon the past, surpass our ancestors' dedication. I must witness the ultimate mortal sacrifice. It is only through a pure, selfless act of submission that I can accept you as humble followers. You have seen my sacrifices! You have seen how they gave themselves to me fully: by celebrating my birth, my punishments, my immaculate offspring. We will all bear witness, and by our testimony we shall share the responsibility.'

'If they all participate and play witness to a human sacrifice...' Yiorgos began.

'Then they are all implicated,' Sofia whispered. 'It's a way of tying them to The Awakening cause.'

Michail shuffled forward to whisper into Sofia's ear, holding his mobile phone gently in his hands. 'It is nearly time, Ms Sampson. Please, you and Yiorgos, stand behind me, and Katerina.'

Sofia held his gaze, pleadingly, and ushered Yiorgos behind the columns. As they hid behind the marble stones, a group of people were paraded onto the stage. They were bound with chains around their ankles. Some were weeping. Others shook with inconsolable anger.

'Jesus,' choked Yiorgos.

'Blood is life, citizens! Blood is life!' As Athena spoke, four more masked men carried a great, purple cloth into the darkness of the sanctuary. They paraded it across the stage, pulling it across the prisoners' faces. 'The peplos! You invoke an ancient tradition. You please me, citizens. You do yourself honour in honouring me. Blood is life.'

The crowd began to chant along with the voice, following a purple cloth through the gate. 'The robe,' Sofia said. 'For the goddess Athena.'

As the robe moved past the prisoners towards the entrance to the Acropolis, the revellers followed. 'Athena, Athena, Athena,' they repeated, fixated on the purple fabric, drawn by some invisible force to the sanctuary entrance. A commotion broke out at the threshold of the gate. 'I came all this way, let me in! I swear, I belong.' Sofia craned her head out of the shadows to see a woman demanding entry.

A masked individual shook his expressionless face at the woman. 'Proof of identity is needed. Only Greek citizens can enter.'

'But that doesn't make any sense! I've lived here for over fifteen years!'

Similar conversations sprung up across the threshold, which was guarded by the masked keepers. Sofia's eyes turned from those who had been rejected to the prisoners, who began to appeal to the people still waiting outside the gate. 'Help us!' a man shouted in a thick accent. 'Help us! They are animals! Please!' In a swift motion, the masked guards batted him down with heavy clubs. 'Please!' The man's voice abated; he fell to his knees, relenting, pulling the prisoners down around him too.

'Michail, hurry up!' Yiorgos hissed from behind the column. Michail turned, his face set in determination. He responded with a short nod; his finger hovered over the mobile phone.

Athena sounded again. 'A sacrifice then! And who better than a resident foreigner?' Cheers sounded from within the sanctuary as fireworks were released over the ancient temples. 'A volunteer! Another pure volunteer to make a greater sacrifice! One that will bind you all to me.'

The mood shifted with the flicker of a flame. A panicked murmur caught flight through the remaining crowd. The prisoners pressed against one another closely, visibly shaking. Sofia watched in horror as more masked guards surrounded them, forcing them to form a tight circle, guns pointed at their heads.

Yiorgos swore quietly. 'Sofia, we have to do something.'

She grabbed her radio. 'Is anybody out there? Can anyone hear me? Sofia Sampson, requiring urgent response...'

Sofia held out her own gun, knowing it was insufficient against so many. She searched the darkness for her lost men. Then her limbs grew weak. Emerging from the dark trees were more gorgon masks, holding rifles. They moved steadily, the deadly masks hovering almost bodiless under the night sky; their guns pointed proudly at her small team.

'It's the army,' Katerina whispered shakily. 'They have the army on their side.'

Sofia realised there was nowhere to run. 'We're alone,' Sofia said, lowering her weapon. She would do no good dead. 'Raise your hands. Do as they say,' instructed Sofia. She was aware of Michail behind her, who was still standing with his phone held out in front of him. 'Sergeant Mikras, that is an order, do as they say!'

'A volunteer to make the next great sacrifice!' the voice bellowed. Their guards kicked the prisoners roughly, jeered at them. 'Prove yourself worthy to me, people! Show that you fully understand Athena's cause! Or will you prove yourselves weak? I offer you an opportunity: sacrifice one of the impure in my honour! Cleanse the city of their pollution! Human blood must be spilled for our city to truly awaken.'

More masked guards moved in precise amalgamation, marching from the gate. An excited chatter came from within the Acropolis. 'My God,' Sofia whispered. 'They are considering it. Someone's going to volunteer.'

The people who had been rejected at the gate realised too late. They were also encircled by guns. 'No!' one of them shouted. 'I am here to celebrate Athena! I am loyal!'

'You are foreign,' a guard replied, shoving the woman to her knees roughly. 'You are not welcome.'

The prisoners on the stage screamed as their own guards also readied their weapons. Athena's voice rang high and mighty. 'If no one will do the sacrifice, then let me be clear: all of the foreigners die. Do it for Athena's society! Blood breeds life! Blood breeds life! Blood breeds life! Sacrifice to me! Show me your loyalty!'

Sofia allowed herself to close her eyes as the sound of a hundred metallic clicks signalled the weapons making ready. Indignity. That was the overriding taste in her mouth. It was the pumping between her ears. Utter indignity. The situation had escaped her. She had allowed it to escape her. Opening her eyes, she mouthed an apology to Yiorgos, to Katerina, who grabbed her hand. Their faces were blank, uncomprehending. Yiorgos held his gun outward still, his arm shaking, determined. Sofia understood. She prepared her body for the final onslaught of bullets.

As Sofia breathed in, a papery figure danced in her peripheral vision. Sofia's eyes swam; she was sure she was imagining it. She blinked, confused, her senses overwhelmed. Sofia turned her head, away from the guns, and towards Michail. 'Look,' he said, confirming that what she saw was real. Standing metres up, reaching her hands towards the sky, above the gate to the sanctuary, caught in moonlight, was Moira.

It was as if time stood still. The gorgon masks looked up at her, expectant. The prisoners on the stage strained their heads from their crouched positions, cowering under the weapons, struggling to see what everyone else watched. Athena's voice rang out through the stillness, 'Praise the priestess! The pinnacle of the procession! She understands the meaning of sacrifice!' The old woman held up the purple robe that had been paraded past the stage earlier. 'The priestess brings the peplos, signifying her, your, dedication to me.' Moira knelt; her arms still stretched up to the night's sky. Her eyes were closed; she was praying. Then, she stood, allowing the peplos to stream to the ground. 'She will inspire us, followers. As priestess, she will be our first sacrifice. She is devoted, though she understands her limitations: she is not Greek. As her final act, she will submit herself to me in the most immortal of ways. Let her self-sacrifice spur you on to do my will. She will purify herself in sacrifice.

And in return, Athena will grant her a place in the sky, with the gods in Olympus. She will be a part of the stars.'

'Shine in the Golden City,' Sofia whispered. 'That is what she meant.'

In the moment when a decision like this is made, a grateful hand is extended through time and generations. This was something Moira came to find. Her body hauled itself up the smooth stones, concealed by kindest darkness and she thought, *This will not be easy*. She chuckled at the response she awarded herself, the diamond of a tear in her eye. She found the strength in those limbs. She slid onto the top of the tall gate and looked down upon the world. Here was her life's work betrayed. Here was art used for death. They stole her being, these people. They stole her love.

She stood, and raised her hand to Michail, the polite policeman, who nodded, the mobile phone ready in his hand. He was clever, this young man. He would give to these citizens what she was not given: the truth. They would not be tricked, unlike her. They would not be responsible for the death of innocents. Unlike her. She whipped up a ragged wail over their heads. It hit her hard when Michail revealed the truth, as is often the way. The deaths were the hand of man. They were atrocities. They were not divine acts. How she had wanted to believe! The kind policeman had seen that in her. He had listened to her. Heard the hurt in her stories, her loss, her husband, so sorely missed. Michail had understood that if the immortals walked the earth, then the afterlife was certain. And there he would be with her. Andrew. Her husband, their love made immortal. But it was a lie. A selfish lie. And now guns surrounded innocent people.

'Is it time?' she asked the sacred air, and it breathed ancient breezes in reply.

There was no certainty that this would work. But there was hope in the action. She volunteered for goodness; she subverted The Awakening's request, stole it and made it her own. Christos expected her to fall, that was his requirement of her, but he did not expect her to speak. Her dry mouth opened and she was prepared.

'This is not a sacrifice for you, fascists, frauds.' Faces turned to her. Michail's microphone system worked, that skilful man. He nodded encouragingly.

'This is an apology to the city, Athena's city, and the damage I have done it. May my blood make it right. Do not kill for lies! They are innocent. Your commander is not. *No pasarán!*'

The fall did not last for long. She heard Michail's cry of surprise. This was not his instruction. But it was necessary, she knew. Her mind unravelled in a colourful story as she slipped through the air. She kept her eyes closed, wrapped herself in the gasps of humanity, held on to the image of his face as flesh met stone.

For a while, on the ground, she was sculpted. She was still and heavenly. She would become myth and the space in between.

The crowd began to teeter, they stared at the body before a song of ringtones and vibrations alerted them to the message. They did not want to drag their eyes from her, the old lady exuding dark fluid on the marble, but the alerts continued, stubborn buzz after buzz, ring after ring. Masks were removed. Guns were lowered. The prisoners sensed a hopeful shift in the mood. A thousand lights appeared in the palms of the crowd. They reflected the stars in the heavens. Michail forced them to see the truth. They looked down at a livestream of Christos Panagos, in a cheap-looking sound booth, speaking Athena's words defiantly, unaware that he was being watched. 'Celebrate!' he shouted; and wondered why he only heard a confused stutter in return. There was a silence as this first part of Michail's message illuminated the revellers' faces. The realisation spread, fast and breathless. The spell began to disintegrate.

Then the revellers were shown the missing footage: Theo and Laurence-Sinclair butchering Marius, Iman, and Mani. They manoeuvred the bodies into decadent positions. They were so ungodly. They were brutal. The crowds hollered in anger. They wept as they realised their gullibility.

And there was Risto, standing at the head of the Exarcheia army as he led them up the Panathenaic Way. He held a banner above his head: *No Pasarán*! it said. *No Pasarán*.

The screams arose. The gunshots sounded. The hill trembled with excitement. The clouds moved across the moon, and the city of Athens waited for the certainty of dawn.

Healing

Michail sat upright in his hospital bed as the nurse brought in his guest. Sofia smiled as she entered, her lips as immaculate as ever. 'Michail,' she said in greeting, flagrantly ignoring any sense of professional formality. He supposed, given the circumstances, an exception could be made.

'Ms Sampson.' He nodded.

'You are well?' Sofia glanced at his midriff, concern surfacing in her face.

He patted his stomach proudly. 'I am told that I am healing exceptionally, Ms Sampson.'

She grinned. 'Well, I would expect no less.'

She placed some flowers, already very thoughtfully cut and in a vase of water, on his bedside table. They looked lovely. Then she pulled up a chair and sat down beside his bed. They remained in a comfortable silence for a long while; Michail saw no immediate need for chatter. Eventually, Sofia nodded towards the small television across the room. 'You have been watching the news?'

'Yes.'

'The Awakening, it seems, stretched deeper than anyone

could have imagined. The night of the procession, at least, revealed the main players.'

'They are all on trial?' Michail struggled to picture how so many of the police force, the military, most high-ranking politicians, as well as Christos Panagos, would be dealt with efficiently.

Sofia clasped her hands, nodding. 'Yes. As best as the state can manage. Most of them will serve a life sentence.'

'And the rest?' Michail winced as he overexerted himself.

Sofia leaned forward, softening her face. 'The cause is dead. They have lost mainstream public support...' Her voice trailed off. 'We remain vigilant, of course.'

'The correct response,' replied Michail, attempting to sit up straighter. 'I hope the Exarcheia residents will be honoured. They fought with bravery and they owed us nothing. Risto did himself proud.'

'*No pasarán.*' Sofia nodded. 'They only requested that their graffiti be preserved and properly venerated. It is an odd request...'

'But art is important,' Michail said.

'Correct,' Sofia said, smiling. 'Risto left us a message at headquarters, by the way. He said that if ever the police needed real heroes again, then to drop him a line.'

'Ha!' Michail yelped, unable to control his delight. 'He is humorous.'

'You have gone some way to healing the relationship between the police and a large group of citizens. I am grateful, Michail.'

He nodded; he was quietly pleased too. 'And how is Yiorgos?' Michail felt the familiar knot tighten in his belly.

'Still in an induced coma. Thalia visits daily with the baby.' Sofia looked towards the corridor, smiling. 'We are hopeful, of course.' Michail frowned. Sofia took his hand and said, 'He is strong, and we were lucky. We must remain thankful.'

'People were hurt. Some irreparably.' Michail wriggled his toes, right foot first, then the left, then the right again. 'I just wish I had... I did not know what she was planning.'

Sofia observed him with an unusually serene look about her, before saying, 'Moira is a hero, Michail. The mobile message would not have been as effective by itself. I think she knew that. She showed everyone what a true and selfless sacrifice is, as opposed to what The Awakening was demanding. She redeemed herself.' There was a long pause before she added, 'Katerina asked after you.'

Michail's chin tightened. He looked out of the window, pretending to be interested in a flock of birds flying in the distance.

Sofia continued to speak. 'She will be treated to the proper processes. As you might imagine, we have a lot of conspirators to investigate...'

Michail remained silent, grinding his teeth.

'She believed what she was doing was right,' Sofia finished.

Michail nodded, patting his bandages once more. 'Things take time to heal.'

At a particular hour in the morning, when the sun has begun to stretch its rosy fingers over the Acropolis hill, a small and new monument by the ancient Propylaia is hit by effervescent light. In centuries to come, students and academics alike will visit it. Its photograph will be printed in journals and books. University lecturers will analyse it, finding its inscription irresistible. The technological revolution brought with it a wealth documentation and catalogue: the problem for historians of this period is deciphering the truth from the chatter. This monument rises above the chatter. A sculpture of an axe, entwined with two snakes, reads: *In commemoration of the residents who fought with bravery to preserve the freedom of our Great City. May that night never be repeated and may we learn the lessons well. Here is a symbol of Athena reclaimed, as it is meant to be seen: a symbol of equality, a symbol of fortitude, a symbol of humanity.*

THE END

Acknowledgements

Writing this book was tremendous fun. Athens is a city I love from the depths of my heart and I hope this book inspires many to experience its unrelenting richness. Please, take time to wander the streets. Soak up the people, the food, the constant sway between hush and bustle. I recommend visiting the Agora (where you find the Temple of Hephaestus) as early as possible (I believe it opens at 8am) — you will have the site to yourself, save the cats, which is a real treat.

I am extremely lucky to have the world's most supportive and clever 'Chief Editor' — thank you, Dad, for reading my first drafts, for managing to encourage me whilst giving an honest opinion, and for having a sense of narrative logic far stronger than mine. I could not have written this without you. Mum, thanks for always thinking everything I write is superb and for reading the manuscript even though it wasn't on paper... you can read it on paper now!

Thank you to my husband, Will, for being a constant source of calm and a pillar of support... as well as lending Michail a line or two.

To my fellow writer and brilliant friend Estella Shardlow, thank you for always being a champion and having a contagious 'go get it' disposition. You're a huge reason I keep writing.

Huge thanks to Nick Baker for reading an earlier draft and appreciating the cats. Joking aside, you and Amy are two of the most intelligent people I know, so your approval means a lot.

Thank you to Abbie Rutherford, Associate Editor at Bloodhound, for so thoroughly, enthusiastically, and carefully working on this manuscript. I am in awe of your eye for detail.

To Betsy, Tara and Katia at Bloodhound — thank you for believing in The Athenian Murders.

About the Author

V.J. Randle read Classics at King's College, University of Cambridge before teaching Latin and Greek for over a decade. She has given many a tour of Hellenic sites over the years, both in a capacity of educator and (to her husband's unwavering delight) holiday-maker. If you spot an excitable woman in a maxi skirt waving her arms about on top of The Acropolis, chances are it's her. Do say hello!

She now lives and writes in the North-East of Scotland (with a brief interlude in Canada) with her husband and cat, Athena (who is every bit goddess of stratagem as her namesake).

A note from the publisher

Thank you for reading this book. If you enjoyed it please do consider leaving a review on Amazon to help others find it too.

We hate typos. All of our books have been rigorously edited and proofread, but sometimes mistakes do slip through. If you have spotted a typo, please do let us know and we can get it amended within hours.

info@bloodhoundbooks.com

Printed in Great Britain
by Amazon